The Alien Who Looked Like Kang Ji Soo

Kathryn Welch

IMPRINTS

Dedication

Dedicated to my mother Mary and my late father Sidney. And to Michael, Alyssa and Mikey.

Prologue

Malaga Island, Florida – 1994

Grandpa Morrow was weeping again in front of the television set. Seven-year-old Jasmine sat down on the carpet next to his chair. The tears didn't disturb her. She had seen them before. As he did every day at 1:00 P.M., he was watching *Tomorrow's Dream*. "Time for my story," he would say, and Jasmine would come to sit beside him.

The proximate cause of today's tears was the current predicament of Lionel and Vanessa Tremaine, the drama's supercouple of the day. Vanessa had carried on an affair with Lionel's best friend, resulting in a pregnancy which she promptly miscarried. Lionel was understandably dismayed, but his steadfast understanding and forgiveness were so touching that Grandpa Morrow, along with millions of other fans no doubt, was unable to contain his emotions. Out of the corner of her eye, Jasmine saw him furtively whisk a tear from his cheek.

The aroma of his pipe tobacco hung pleasantly in the air. Clinking noises emanated from the kitchen where Grandma was cleaning up the lunch dishes. Everything was perfectly normal—reassuring, comforting.

Grandpa Morrow did not read soap opera magazines or even know such a thing existed. He probably had no idea that, including its run on the radio before the advent of television, *Tomorrow's Dream* had been on the air for more than fifty years. Back then, he'd been too busy to pay much attention to television shows.

Little did Jasmine know that twenty years hence she would still be following the adventures of the Tremaine family and obsessing over various descendants of Lionel and Vanessa. Each time she tuned in the broadcast or selected her DVR recording of the day's show, part of her heart was right back there next to Grandpa Morrow's easy chair with the aroma of tobacco in the air and the sound of Grandma puttering about the kitchen.

In his later years, Grandpa Morrow suffered from dementia. He would forget to turn on the television. He didn't know what time it was or even what day it was. If Jasmine happened to be at her grandparents' house on a holiday from work, she would pick up the remote and sit cross-legged on the floor by Grandpa's chair. "Time for our story," she would say as she turned on the TV. She would smile up at her grandfather and believe she saw a flicker of recognition in his cloudy blue eyes.

Cody City, California – 2010

When Tracy Malone was twenty-three years old, her father died. He had a massive heart attack just after mowing the lawn. He walked into the kitchen where his wife Lydia was baking an apple pie for that evening's dinner and collapsed. Lydia adored and depended on her husband more than most—more than she should have.

The sight of the strong and indestructible Paul Malone lying helpless on the floor, threw her into a state of hysteria. Anything she had ever known about CPR, which was not much, flew right out of her head. The only thing she could do was kneel next to him calling his name and sobbing.

Later, the doctors would reassure her that it had probably been too late anyway, but she would always be haunted by the thought that she should have done more. The feelings of guilt combined with the loss of her husband—her love, her rock—were unbearable.

Of the seven Malone children, Tracy was expected to be the responsible one. No one was quite sure how this had come about (she was not the eldest), but somehow the entire family, including Tracy herself, had tacitly agreed to the arrangement.

It was early afternoon the day after Paul's death. All the paperwork done, relatives notified, Lydia lying sedated in her room, Tracy finally had a moment to breathe before an appointment scheduled for later in the day with the funeral home. She had barely slept the night before. Exhausted, she fell onto the sofa in the living room.

Everyone knew how much Lydia loved her husband. Tracy was well aware that not even the children—not even herself—were quite so dear to Lydia's heart.

Tracy had been so concentrated on being strong for her mother that she hadn't a moment to think about grieving herself. She loved her father. Out of all the children, two of them had been exceptionally close to Paul—Tracy and Ethan. Ethan because he was the ne'er-do-well who seemed to need Paul more than the others. Tracy—well, nobody knew exactly why except that they had always seemed to share a special bond. Perhaps it was because she was most like her father with her sense of responsibility and loyalty. And now she wasn't even able to grieve. She had to take care of everyone else.

Now, sitting here in the dimly-lit living room with its shabby furniture, faded carpet and nicked woodwork, she had a sinking feeling that this was to be her life indefinitely. She had dreamed of moving away someday, after she had saved up some money. That seemed impossible now. How could she leave her mother? And worst of all, Dad was gone. She would gladly trade all her dreams to have her father back.

The Malone house was the sort where the television was always on except in the middle of the night. Reflexively, Tracy's hand fumbled for the remote and found it between the sofa cushions. She flicked it on.

At once, the room was filled with the mellifluous tones of the late actor Jackson Carter, who had created the role of Lionel Tremaine, patriarch of the Tremaine family. Although Carter had died a few years earlier, his recorded voice still provided the daily introduction to the show. "Let us seize today, for tomorrow is but a dream."

Once again, Tracy heard the time-honored words intoned in that iconic, honeyed voice. She had been an on-and-off viewer for most of her life. During her college years, the show had achieved cult status and she had watched loyally along with her roommates. Nowadays she kept track on her days off. Today Carter's words were inexplicably comforting.

Jackson Carter's voice faded away, and the show began. All the familiar, beloved faces were there—even the villainous Charles Marchand, who appeared in the very first scene today.

Tracy settled back on the sofa and pulled the afghan over her. She even loved Charles Marchand today. When the world was turned upside down, at least some things never changed.

Chapter 1
The Chat Room

Tracy   Remember when we used to have more than a dozen people in here on a Friday night? Sigh. ***looks around deserted chat room***

Jaz   Those were the days. When they canceled all the soaps, that was pretty much the death knell for our little chat group.

Tracy   A lot of the girls followed Brice Harlowe over to The Reckless Heart.

Jaz   Sorry, just can't stomach that show. I don't care if it is practically the only soap left on the air. It still sucks. Besides, Brice without Arianna just doesn't do it for me.

Tracy	Most magical acting couple ever. Sigh again.
Jaz	I don't know why we keep the old chat room open anymore. We're the only two left since Lynn disappeared.
Tracy	Stubbornness?
Jaz	Tradition?
Tracy	Whatever.
Jaz	So… what do you think of the prez's new proposal on Wall Street reform?
Tracy	Sounds good. DOA in the House tho.
Jaz	As usual.
	Oh, my phone. BRB

Jasmine Morrow picked up her cell phone despite noting the caller ID.

"Hi, Mom. What's up?" she asked in a tone meant to convey the appropriate degree of annoyance.

"What? Can't I even call my own daughter? What are you doing that's so important?"

"Chatting with Tracy. You know very well that we always chat on Friday night."

"And that's the problem."

"What problem? I don't have a problem."

"You do have a problem."

"Enlighten me. I know you're dying to."

"Why are you talking to some girl you hardly know all the way on the other side of the country?"

"But I do know Tracy. We've been chatting for like six years. And what about all those soap events we went to together?"

"That soap opera thing is so silly. I don't know how you got into that."

"Yes, you do. Grandpa Morrow, remember?"

"Oh, yeah. Your father's side of the family. They were always the sentimentalists. Even so, I'm sure your grandfather would take it all back if he had known you would come to this end."

"Isn't that a bit over-dramatic, not to mention insulting?"

"Oh, hon, you know I love you. I just want you to stop living in a fantasy world and..."

"And what? Get married and have a bunch of kids?"

"I would like to have some grandchildren at some point."

"I don't see that happening. And you were never much of a kid person anyway."

"I would be if they were my own grandkids. And since you don't have any siblings, you're my only hope."

"Oh, for God's sake."

"Look, this is all beside the point. The point is on a Friday night you should be out there having fun... meeting people."

"And by people, you mean men."

"Of course, I do. You're not getting any younger you know."

"Mom! I'm so bored with this topic. Gotta go. Tracy's waiting for me. We'll talk later, okay?"

"Wait! Don't you dare hang up. I wasn't finished."

"Of course, you weren't," Jasmine groaned. "What is it?"

"Somebody's got a birthday next week," Jenna Morrow trilled.

Jasmine quickly ran through a mental list of all the family birthdays she could think of. "Sorry, I have no idea what you're talking about."

"Benjy, of course."

"Benjy Bryant?"

Jenna sighed. "How many Benjys do we know?"

"Ah. That's nice. Tell his mom I said happy birthday."

"Tell him yourself. We're all meeting Wednesday night at Maison Pierre to celebrate."

"What do you mean by all?" Jasmine asked warily.

"Your father and I, the Bryants, you and, naturally, Benjy."

"Maaaaa," Jasmine wailed. "You know I hate these occasions."

"And I can't see why. The Bryants are our oldest friends. You've known them all your life. Honestly. Pretending you don't know who I was talking about. It's quite ridiculous."

"It was a joke, Mom. You never get my jokes. The Bryants are nice enough I suppose."

"Nice enough? They're lovely, and you know it."

"It's just that I resent you and Dad constantly trying to push Benjy and me together."

"What could possibly be your objection to Benjy? He's good-looking, he's a nice guy, he's always adored you—and he's an orthodontist for God's sake. I have to believe the only reason he's still single is because he's holding out for you. There's no other explanation for why he's still on the market."

"Maybe he's gay."

Jenna snorted. "If he were gay, he would have been snapped up by some other gorgeous gay guy."

"Joking, Mom. I know Benjy is not gay. But don't you think, since I've known him pretty much since birth, that if there were any chemistry there, it would have happened by now?"

"He obviously feels the chemistry."

"Chemistry can't be one-sided. It's an oxymoron—or something."

"Pfft! Chemistry is overrated. Do you think your dad and I have chemistry?"

"My point exactly."

"Dad and I are very happy—in our own way."

"Don't you see, Mom? I don't want that way. I want more than that."

"Jasmine Louise Morrow." Jenna's voice had taken on the hard, icy tone that Jasmine hated. "You are twenty-nine years old. That's almost thirty. You're old enough to stop living in a fantasy world. Any girl would be crazy to pass up Benjy Bryant. Look, I'm tired of arguing with you. Be at Maison Pierre at seven o'clock Wednesday night. Don't be late—and *bring a gift.*"

"Aw, Ma!"

"Be there."

14

Jasmine repeated "Ma" into the phone several more times before realizing her mother was no longer there. She slammed the phone down on her desk and turned back to the computer screen.

Jaz   I'm back.

Tracy   Anything important?

Jaz   Just Mom.

Tracy   Ah. Gotcha. LOL

Jaz   Still trying to fix me up with Benjy Bryant.

Tracy   Isn't he the one you've known all your life? Wouldn't something have happened by now if it was going to?

Jaz   One would think.

Tracy   Uh...Just what is your problem with this guy? Not to take your mom's side, but from what I recall, he sounds like a pretty good catch.

Jaz   He is. For someone else. Maybe I've just known him too long, but I don't feel any sparks between us—at all.

Tracy   But he does?

Jaz	Apparently.
Tracy	Describe him again. I'll be the judge.
Jaz	Good-looking, very smart, kind—like he'd give you the shirt off his back. Successful orthodontia practice. But...
Tracy	But what?
Jaz	I don't know what the word is. Priggish maybe? Yeah. There's something slightly priggish about him that's a turn-off.
Tracy	Only slightly? Are we being perhaps a bit too picky?
Jaz	You really are on Mom's side, aren't you?
Tracy	No!
Jaz	Don't you believe in chemistry? Brice and Arianna-type chem?
Tracy	In all fairness, that is not reality.
Jaz	I know, I know.
Tracy	You might want to give Benjy another chance. It couldn't hurt.

Copy/Paste   jhp wqlomxi

Tracy   I didn't do that.

Jaz   Weird. Remember when Lynn used to be here—every once in a while her post would show up as a paste even tho she had not copied and pasted anything. Just something that happens now and then.

Tracy   No. I mean not only did I not paste anything, I didn't even type that. It never happened that way with Lynn, did it? It was always at least something she had actually typed.

Jaz   I think so. Really strange. I thought your cat got on the keyboard again.

Tracy   Nope. Not this time.

Jaz   Maybe we've been hacked by aliens. That gibberish probably means something in their language. LOL

Tracy   LMAO

Jaz   Oh well. Probably time to sign off anyway. I have an early mani/pedi in the morning.

Tracy   Yeah, I should go too. Have a great weekend—

and don't forget what I said about Benjy.

Jaz   I won't. By next Friday, I'll be able to report
          back to you. Mom has arranged an "occasion"
          for us.

Tracy   Can't wait to hear. Have a good one. Nite.

Jaz   Nite

Chapter 2
Benjy Has a Birthday

Jasmine blew into Maison Pierre twenty minutes late. Her party was already assembled at a round table near the terrace doors. Her mother glowered at her. Her father checked his watch conspicuously. Benjy beamed.

"Sorry," Jasmine mumbled, flinging herself ungracefully into the vacant chair between Benjy's and her mother's. "I got hung up at work."

"At seven o'clock at night?" asked Jenna with equal parts of skepticism and sarcasm.

"It doesn't matter," Benjy piped up. "She's here. That's the important thing."

Jasmine picked up her napkin and spread it across her lap. "I need a drink. I see you've all started already."

"We weren't going to sit here for half an hour doing nothing," said her father.

Benjy beckoned to the waiter. "We'll all have another round and a martini, extra dirty with two olives for the lady." He winked at Jasmine. "That's still it, isn't it, Jaz?"

Of course, it was.

"So…" said Mrs. Bryant once the waiter had taken their order, "shall we do presents while we're waiting or during dessert?"

"Um…I'm not sure." Jenna threw a wary glance at her daughter, who definitely had not been carrying anything resembling a gift when she arrived.

"I say now," said Benjy with all the exuberance of an eight-year-old birthday boy.

Jasmine smiled in spite of herself. You had to love that about Benjy—that unfailing optimism, that cheerfulness—and after peering into teenagers' mouths all day. It was really quite admirable. She envied it a little and understood it not at all.

One by one, everybody passed their gifts to Benjy. From the Morrows, a set of fancy monogrammed handkerchiefs; from his parents, a very expensive Movado watch. Before her mother got a chance to nudge her, Jasmine pulled a lavender Hallmark envelope from her bag and handed it to Benjy, who, with his usual impeccable manners, read the card aloud before even looking for any further contents. Jasmine knew that if there had been nothing in the envelope but the card, it would have been fine with Benjy.

The card was funny. Everyone laughed—even Jenna. Jasmine may not have been perfect, but no one, other than Jenna on occasion, could deny she had a sense of humor. Benjy smiled appreciatively as he took the actual gift from the lavender envelope.

"Really, Jaz?" Jenna hissed into her daughter's ear. "A Barnes and Noble gift card?"

"It's for fifty dollars!" Jenna hissed back. "Besides, Benjy loves to read."

"How nice!" Jenna lied out loud. "Not exactly personal but…"

"Nonsense," Benjy protested. "I love it. Jaz knows how much I love to read." With that, he leaned over and kissed Jasmine on the cheek. "Thank you, Jaz."

"See!" Jasmine mouthed the word in her mother's direction.

Eventually, there were desserts all round including the miniature complimentary birthday cake with one tall candle in the center. There was not one person at the table who did not know what Benjy wished as he closed his eyes and blew it out.

Leaving the restaurant, Jasmine felt gratified. The conversation, after those initial snide comments from her mother, had been amusing and comfortable, the food excellent, the wine expensive and mellow—and Benjy had liked her fifty-dollar gift card even more than the $1,000 watch from his folks. Best of all, the evening was over. She had made it through—almost enjoyably—and no harm done.

Feeling unburdened and certain she had paid her Benjy dues for at least another year, she started to pull her car door open. But she was stopped mid-motion when a masculine hand attached to a French-cuffed wrist reached around her and grabbed the door-frame. "Benjy!" she cried, for no one else in these parts wore onyx cufflinks—or French cuffs for that matter. "You scared the crap out of me!" She turned to face him and his disarming smile.

"Sorry. Didn't mean to."

"Did you want something? Uh…don't answer that."

"You know me too well."

"Seriously. What is it?"

"This." Reaching into his breast pocket, he pulled out two small rectangles of cardstock—tickets obviously.

"What is that?"

"Two tickets—fourth row center—to American Ballet Theatre, which just happens to be appearing downtown a week from Saturday." He quickly placed his index finger against her lips. "Don't even think about saying no. Do you have any idea what I went through to get these? Besides, you love ballet."

"You don't."

"I don't *love* it," he admitted, "but it's okay."

She narrowed her eyes and studied his open, vulnerable face with its bright blue eyes and smooth skin that turned mottled red when he was excited or embarrassed. He was so…*wholesome.* Yes, that was the word—not priggish. She made a mental note to clarify that point to Tracy next time. "This isn't a date, is it?"

"Not if you don't want it to be." He allowed just a touch of excitement to color his tone as he sensed her weakening.

"Look here," said Jasmine. At the risk of giving him a terribly wrong impression, she took his hand in hers. "Benjy, it's not that I want to be difficult or ungrateful. It's just that I know you and I view our relationship quite differently. If I do go with you, I don't want you to think it's something it's not."

Benjy gave her hand an almost imperceptible squeeze and raised his other hand in a gesture of surrender

"I won't. I promise. Just friends. Okay?"

Jasmine smiled and gently disengaged her hand from his.

"Okay then. Honestly, I was dying to see that performance. It's a date…uh, I mean not a date…oh, hell, you know what I mean."

Benjy grinned. "Dinner first—even though it's not technically a date?"

"Not technically nor any other way."

"Got it. I'll text you the details."

Jasmine climbed into her car. "Happy birthday, friend." She glanced at the tickets he still held. "And thank you. I mean that." She pulled the door shut and drove away, leaving Benjy smiling in the parking lot.

Chapter 3
Selected Scenes from a Chat Room

An Intruder

Tracy	Hi. How was your week?
Jaz	Okay I guess. You?
Tracy	Oh! I almost forgot. How was the "occasion" with Benjy?
Jaz	Don't ask.
Tracy	Spill.
Jaz	The upshot is I'm stuck going to the ballet with Benjy!

Tracy	You love the ballet.
Jaz	But it's with Benjy.
Tracy	It's not as if you dislike the guy. Can't you just go and enjoy it for what it is?
Jaz	It's just that he'll take it as encouragement.
Tracy	Then you should have turned him down.
Jaz	He doesn't make it easy. Never mind. Long story.
Copy/Paste	Hello. Correct.
Tracy	WTF was that?
Jaz	Hee. Our alien is back.
Copy/Paste	Hello. Can you see me."
Jaz	Yes. I can see you.
Tracy	WTH are you doing? Conversing with a hacker/stalker/possible psychopath?
Jaz	I guess I am. LOL
Tracy	Remind me to close out this chat room tomorrow

Jaz	No! This could be fun.
Tracy	Groan.
Copy/Paste	Hello. Correct.
Tracy	Why does he keep saying correct?
Jaz	Because he's an alien and doesn't know English well. He's checking to see if he has the right word. He probably hasn't gotten to punctuation yet.
Tracy	Are you putting me on or being serious? You're starting to scare me.
Jaz	Hold on. I'm gonna try responding. Where's the harm?
Jaz	Hello, Mr. Hacker. Who are you?
Copy/Paste	Contact made. Good. I am friend.
Jaz	Where are you from?
Copy/Paste	Galaxy
Jaz	Yikes! He really is an alien. Which galaxy? LMAO

Copy/Paste	Contact. Good.
Jaz	Yeah. You already said that.
Copy/Paste	I will find more words. I will come back.
Tracy	Geesh! GMFB
Copy/Paste	I will come back. Good bye.
Tracy	Don't bother and don't let the cyber door hit you on the way out.
Jaz	Hello? Mr. Hacker, are you still here?
Jaz	I guess he's gone.
Tracy	I'm closing the chat room tomorrow. It was silly keeping it open anyway. We can chat on Facebook. Or, hey, here's an idea—we can talk on the PHONE! Remember that device?
Jaz	No, don't! If he comes back, he won't be able to find us.
Tracy	Exactly.
Jaz	Besides you don't even belong to Facebook.
Tracy	I'll join.

Jaz	Please. **kneels in supplicant position** I just want to see if he'll come back and what he'll say next. It's like a little adventure.
Tracy	You do realize what that says about the current state of your life?
Jaz	Duh!
Tracy	I think we should sign off for tonight. I'm not in the mood anymore.
Jaz	Are you mad?
Tracy	No, not mad. Just a little concerned
Jaz	You think I've lost it?
Tracy	You're getting there.
Jaz	Oh, pish! It's just a lark. Besides, he probably won't be back anyway.
Tracy	We can only hope.
Jaz	Still...promise you won't close the chat room?
Tracy	Promise. For now. See you next Friday?
Jaz	Of course. Have a good week.

Tracy   You too. Nite

Jaz   Nite.

Getting to Know You

Copy/Paste   I am here waiting for you Tracy and Jaz. I have studied your language. I absorb information very quickly. I am not perfect yet but I will be. I look forward to communicating with you.

Tracy   Oh dear God. He's back.

Jaz   Yay! Welcome.

Copy/Paste   Thank you. I have learned the answer to your last question. Last time I did not have the vocabulary.

Jaz   What question?

Copy/Paste   My galaxy. On your planet it is known as Aletheia.

Jaz   Hold on while I google that.

Copy/Paste   No need. It is basically two galaxies away from your galaxy.

Jaz   Wow!

Tracy   Horseshit.

Jaz   You must be very brilliant to have found your

way into this little chat room and learned a whole language in a week.

Tracy   Groan.

Jaz   Just play along, Tracy. It's fun.

Copy/Paste   You know that I can see what you are saying about me.

Jaz   Sorry.

Copy/Paste   It took me a very long time to find this chat room by random hacking. Longer than you can conceive of. Your chat room led me to your internet where I learned the first few words with which I approached you. I should have studied more before I spoke but I was anxious to make contact. I understand this is difficult for your rudimentary intelligence to understand. Do not play along. I am not playing.

Tracy   That sounds rather ominous.

Copy/Paste   You have nothing to fear from me.

Jaz   I hope we haven't said anything hurtful.

Copy/Paste   That means nothing to me. We do not have

31

what you call emotions here.

Tracy	Geez. It's getting pretty thick in here.
Jaz	Just ignore her. Why do you always appear as "Copy/Paste?"
Copy/Paste	I do not know. Perhaps a glitch in the program.
Tracy	A glitch? Really? Is that the best your brilliant mind can come up with?
Copy/Paste	I did not say I know everything.
T*racy*	Why did you type gibberish as your first post? You should have acquired a few words already through your research. Unless you were just an average geek trying to look believable.
Copy/Paste	It was a test to see if I could.
Jaz	That makes sense.
Tracy	I don't think it makes sense.
Jaz	Do you have a name?
Copy /Paste	We do not have names here.

Tracy	No emotions and no names! Bwahaha!
Jaz	We must give him a name, Tracy. It'll make communication so much easier.
Tracy	Hey, we don't even know if he is a him, do we?
Jaz	Oh dear! I never thought of that. How about it, Mr. or Ms. Hacker? Are you a guy?
Jaz	Mr. Hacker??? Did you see the question I asked five minutes ago? Are you a male?
Copy/Paste	Yes.
Jaz	Oh good! I don't know why I say oh good but… oh good!
Tracy	Geesh.
Jaz	So—for a name, how about Alex?
Tracy	How about we just call him Copy Paste? We can call him C.P. for short.
Jaz	Very funny. What about Alex?
Tracy	Why Alex?
Jaz	I've just always liked it. I always thought if I

ever had a son, I'd name him that. At this rate, it looks like I'll never have kids so…

Tracy   Nonsense. I refuse to participate in this madness.

Jaz   Is Alex okay with you, Mr. Hacker?

Copy/Paste   I have no preference.

Jaz   Good. Alex it is.

Tracy   If you and the con man/hacker don't mind, can we talk about something normal? Would that be all right with you, Mr. Hacker?

Copy/Paste   Call me Alex.

Jaz   Hah! He even has a sense of humor. That was meant to be humorous, right?

Copy/Paste   Is humorous good?

Jaz   Yes.

Copy/Paste   Then yes. It was meant to be humorous.

Tracy   You two are making me nauseous.

Copy/Paste   Please, carry on as usual. I have no desire to disrupt. I am here to learn.

Tracy	Learn what? How to plan an alien invasion?
Copy/Paste	Now you are being humorous. Is that correct?
Tracy	Every joke contains a kernel of truth.
Copy/Paste	Please, converse as usual.
Jaz	Yeah, Tracy. What did you want to talk about?
Tracy	I was going to ask how was the date with Benjy?
Jaz	I told you it wasn't a date. The ballet was gorgeous. We had a great dinner at a Cuban/Asian fusion place in Tampa.
Copy/Paste	Ballet. Pavlova, Baryshnikov, Nureyev, Nijinsky, Fonteyn, Copeland.
Jaz	Wow! You have been studying.
Copy/Paste	It is necessary in order to converse with you. About your planet I have learned geography, geology, history, the English language, your version of science. I am currently working my way through popular culture. I hope to be finished by next week.

Jaz	You didn't mention math.
Copy/Paste	I already knew more about math than any human. Math is the same everywhere.
Tracy	You're good, Alex. Really good. That was sarcasm by the way—in case you didn't know.
Copy/Paste	I know the definition of the word. The concept is difficult for me to comprehend. It will become more clear to me in the future perhaps.
Tracy	Count on it, Bud.
Copy/Paste	Call me Alex.
Jaz	Bwahaha!

Getting to Know You Part II

Copy/Paste   You two are full of questions about me, but you never tell me about yourselves. Why should I be here if not to learn about you?

Tracy   You shouldn't be. That's why.

Jaz   Ignore her.

Copy/Paste   Okay, I will. Almost the only thing I have learned about you is that you are fans of the soap opera genre, especially this one couple.

Jaz   Yes, Brice Harlowe and Arianna Jones—or as we like to call them "Brianna." Or "Zeth" of course. Honestly, they were such a romantic couple.

Copy/Paste   Zeth?

Jaz   Their characters on the show. Seth and Zelda Tremaine, supercouple. That's how Tracy and I met—through an online fan group. This chat room was a subset of a group of 5,000. Then the show was canceled along with almost all other soaps.

Copy/Paste   Ah. I am sorry.

Jaz	It's okay. Whenever I lose one obsession, I replace it with another. First it was ballet, then the Detroit Red Wings, then Zeth, now Korean drama.
Tracy	And also now—apparently—you, Alex.
Jaz	Tracy! That's not true. I like Alex but I'm not obsessed.
Tracy	**rolls eyes**
Copy/Paste	Tell me more. There must be more than that.
Tracy	Nothing specific about me, please!
Jaz	I'll tell. My name is Jasmine Morrow. I was born and raised and still live in a little resort town, Malaga Island, just off Tampa, Florida. It's not a fancy resort area—a mom and pop motel kind of place. Although we are locals, none of my family is in the tourism business. My dad works for a big corporation in Tampa. My mom owns a small art gallery (I suppose that could be considered tourism-related but she sells a lot to locals), and I do mortgage loans at a local bank. I'm an only child. I graduated from Duke, so I should be doing something more impressive I

suppose.

Tracy   She's not ambitious.

Jaz   I'm not, but making it possible for people to
buy homes is satisfying to me. In addition
to Korean drama, which is my current
obsession, I like reading, movies (especially
old black and white ones and romantic
comedies), baseball, ice hockey, walking on
the beach and (unfortunately) eating. That's all
I can think of.

Copy/Paste   Thank you, Jaz. I appreciate your cooperation.
Now what about Tracy?

Tracy   I'm not participating.

Jaz   Then I'll tell.

Tracy   Nothing specific!

Jaz   Okay, I promise. She lives with her widowed
mother in California, but not in one of the
cool parts of CA. It's a small farming
community. She works in human resources at
a big regional hospital. She has a whole slew of
brothers and sisters—I've lost count. She's a
total techie. She's always doing stuff for other

39

people but never lets them pay her back. In her spare time, she volunteers for charities and makes websites for people and organizations who never pay her for her work. She loves the X-Files and Dr. Who.

Copy/Paste   She seems like an admirable person.

Tracy   Thank you…I guess.

Copy/Paste   X-Files and Dr. Who are of the science fiction genre, are they not?

Tracy   Yes.

Copy/Paste   Why is Tracy, the science fiction fan, more resistant to me than Jaz is?

Tracy   Perhaps my expertise makes me more discerning.

Copy/Paste   Logically, that seems to make sense. You are still wrong however.

Jaz   Let's change the subject.

Copy/Paste   All right. You both mention romance quite often in regard to television shows and movies, yet neither of you has a husband or boyfriend as far as I can tell.

Tracy	See! See how he brought us around to the subject of sex. He's fishing for something. He's hitting on us.
Jaz	Good grief, Tracy. He said romance not sex.
Copy/Paste	I am not hitting on you. How could I from two galaxies away?
Tracy	You are not two galaxies away. You are at a laptop in some dark basement somewhere in these United States.
Copy/Paste	That is incorrect, Tracy.
Jaz	You're right, Alex. Neither of us has a man in our life at the moment, but we appreciate the *concept* of romance. It's something we hope to experience in the future before we get old and dry up like a prune.
Tracy	Pul-eeze, Jaz. You're making it sound like we've never had bf's in our life. For the record, we have.
Copy/Paste	I do not understand this concept of romance.
Jaz	It would be difficult for a person without emotions.

41

Copy/Paste	The topic comes up frequently in my studies but I have not been able to internalize it.
Jaz	Okay, maybe this will help—because you are missing out on a lot. Here's an assignment. Watch these movies: Now, Voyager, Wuthering Heights and Laura (especially the scene where the hardened cop falls in love with a portrait). Listen to these songs: "I've Got You Under My Skin" and "More Than You Know"—preferably Sinatra versions of both.
Tracy	Or if you want to venture a tiny bit further into the **cough, cough** modern age, try You've Got Mail and "I Will Always Love You."
Jaz	Tracy! You're participating. Good girl.
Tracy	I just had to put in a word for things after 1950. Of course, it's hard to recommend anything from current times. Shows that feature one-night stands and diarrhea seem to be what passes for romantic comedy these days.
Jaz	LMAO
Copy/Paste	Thank you. I will study these items and report to you next week.

Jaz	Alex, do you think emotions are something you might be able to develop?
Copy/Paste	I will try. It is always my theory that I can do anything I apply my mind to.
Jaz	Even come to earth?
Copy/Paste	I have not thought about it but perhaps. I should come to earth. It would make stalking you so much easier.
Tracy	OMG!
Copy/Paste	It was a joke. Did I not do it right?
Jaz	You did it just right. Next time put "LOL" on the end of it.

Romance

Jaz   Alex? Are you here?

Copy/Paste   Yes

Jaz   Oh good. I'm dying to hear—did you complete your assignment?

Copy/Paste   Of course.

Jaz   Did you enjoy the movies?

Copy/Paste   Yes.

Jaz   Did you learn anything?

Copy/Paste   Yes. I learned that a good way to seduce a woman is to light two cigarettes in your mouth and give one to the woman. I learned that alcoholic beverages enhance romantic situations. I learned that a grandfather clock is a good place to hide a murder weapon.

Jaz   Um... I'm not sure those are the take-aways I had hoped for.

Copy/Paste   Do not worry. I believe I also understand the overall concept of romance.

Jaz	Good. Perhaps it's something you'll want to experience one day?
Copy/Paste	Perhaps.
Tracy	Hello. Sorry I'm late.
Copy/Paste	Hi, Tracy.
Jaz	Hi, Tracy.
Copy/Paste	The best one was You've Got Mail.
Jaz	Really! You liked that better than the old black and white ones? Why?
Copy/Paste	Because it was like us. Making relationships over the internet.
Tracy	Awww. That's kinda sweet.
Jaz	You're just saying that because YGM was your suggestion.
Tracy	I'm not!
Jaz	So can we assume that you are well on your way to developing a romantic nature?
Copy/Paste	No.

Jaz	Really? Damn!
Tracy	LMAO Jaz, you better go drown your sorrows in carbs.
Copy/Paste	I assume it is normal for earthlings to use food to soothe their emotions. I noticed this syndrome in multiple romantic comedies. Emotions are such inconvenient phenomena. Ice cream seems to be the most popular remedy.
Tracy	Yes. Preferably eaten directly from the carton. However, Jaz is a salty girl. Chips, cheese puffs, Doritos—that sort of thing.
Jaz	Yep. Tracy is the chocoholic.
Copy/Paste	Chocoholic?
Jaz	A person addicted to chocolate. I mean not an actual physical addiction like crack.
Tracy	Hmm… Or is it?
Jaz	LOL
Copy/Paste	LOL

Beauty

Tracy   I saw Arianna on a commercial today.

Jaz   Really? That's depressing.

Tracy   Not necessarily. Everyone does commercials these days. Jennifer Garner, Beyonce, JLo, JLaw, Nicole Kidman.

Jaz   But not Meryl Streep.

Tracy   No, not Meryl Streep. Not yet anyhow.

Jaz   What was it for?

Tracy   What was what for?

Jaz   The commercial.

Tracy   Dishwashing detergent.

Jaz   Ooh, housewife stuff. That's not good.

Tracy   Well, I don't care if she is playing housewives in commercials. I still say she's the most beautiful girl I ever saw.

Jaz   Totally.

Copy/Paste   Hello. Sorry I am late.

Tracy	No need to be sorry. I hadn't missed you.
Jaz	I missed you. We were just talking about Arianna, of the dear departed Tomorrow's Dream.
Copy/Paste	Your favorite canceled daytime drama.
Jaz	Your study of pop culture is continuing?
Copy/Paste	Yes. New data is added daily.
Tracy	Nothing your advanced brain power can't keep up with. Snerk.
Jaz	Well, we may be biased but we think Arianna is the epitome of beauty. Have you "seen" her in your studies?
Copy/Paste	Yes.
Jaz	And? Do you agree? What is your concept of beauty?
Copy/Paste	Marilyn Monroe, Grace Kelly, Audrey Hepburn, Elizabeth Taylor, Sophia Loren, Beyonce, Charlize Theron, Song Hye Kyo
Jaz	Aww. That last one was a nod to my Korean drama obsession, wasn't it?

Tracy	Pardon me but your list, while being perfectly valid, seems a bit unoriginal except for that shameless sucking up to Jaz at the end.
Copy/Paste	My concept of beauty comes solely from your internet.
Tracy	Oh-oh. I think we're about to find out that a concept of beauty is another one of the many things he doesn't have.
Copy/Paste	I would like to know what you two look like.
Tracy	I'll just bet you would.
Jaz	I think he was just trying to change the subject.
Tracy	You mean he hasn't checked us out on Facebook?
Jaz	You aren't even on Facebook and he doesn't know your last name.
Tracy	And we're keeping it that way.
Copy/Paste	I didn't check Facebook. I can't think of everything.
Jaz	I don't mind posting my picture.

Jaz	Okay. There it is.
Tracy	Don't you dare post mine.

Jaz	I never would without your permission. Alex, do you see the picture?
Copy/Paste	Yes. Long dark reddish hair with waves, appropriately proportioned nose, large

greenish eyes.

Jaz　　　　　Hazel.

Copy/Paste　　Yes, hazel.

Jaz　　　　　So what do you think?

Copy/Paste　　Tracy is correct in saying I never had a concept of beauty. All I can say is this image is pleasing to me.

Jaz　　　　　That's one of the weaker compliments I've ever received but I'll take it.

Copy/Paste　　Tracy, will you show your photograph?

Tracy　　　　Absolutely not.

Jaz　　　　　I'll describe her. That would be okay, wouldn't it?

Tracy　　　　I suppose. **rolls eyes**

Jaz　　　　　She has really short dark hair, sparkly blue eyes with long, thick lashes (I hate her for that). She's very tiny but has a good figure and cute freckles across her nose.

Tracy　　　　Thanks, Jaz. That was nice.

Copy/Paste	That seems agreeable. Perhaps Tracy will trust me enough one day to let me see her photograph.
Tracy	Don't hold your breath.
Jaz	Okay, Alex. Your turn. What do you look like? Is it possible to post a picture?
Copy/Paste	I cannot post a picture. It is difficult to explain. You may have guessed I am not in humanoid form.
Jaz	You're not like a lizard or something, are you?
Copy/Paste	No. Not like that. As I said, it is hard to explain. I do not think you will understand it.
Jaz	Try us.
Copy/Paste	I will try. If I had to put it into words in your language, I would say I am like a swirling mass of brain waves.
Tracy	Geesh.
Jaz	Wow. You mean more like a spirit?
Copy/Paste	Something like that I suppose.

Tracy	He keeps adding more things that he doesn't have—no emotions, no name, no concept of beauty, no body. What the hell do you have, Alex?
Copy/Paste	Intelligence.
Jaz	Bwahaha! Touche.
Copy/Paste	I am sorry that my form or lack of form is disappointing to you.
Jaz	So you do everything telepathically? Like even typing posts into this chat room? How do you do that without a body?
Copy/Paste	Your word—telepathically—is as good a way to explain it as any other. Brain power. I have very strong brain power.
Tracy	GMAFB He sounds like Donald Trump.
Copy/Paste	If I had emotions, I believe I would find that insulting.
Jaz	Hey, wait just a gosh darn minute here. You said you were a male. How can you have a gender without a body?
Tracy	Yeah, we asked you that point blank, and you

took a helluva long time to answer as I recall.

Jaz   Alex? You're taking a long time to answer.

Copy/Paste   From my studies, I gather that gender is more than just physical features. But to be honest, I didn't have that in mind at the time. I simply lied. I lied because I perceived that you preferred me to be a male. At least, I believe Jaz did. Also, to explain would have required me to describe myself as I have tonight. I was not yet ready to do that. I still do not want to. I think it is too hard to explain and too hard for you to accept.

Tracy   ROFLMAO. We—some of us anyway—have allegedly accepted that you are an alien from another galaxy with no name and no emotions, who hacked into our little chat room out of all the places in all the universe. Why not accept this latest load of bull?

Jaz   Of all the gin joints in all the towns in all the world, you walk into mine. LOL

Copy/Paste   Casablanca reference.

Jaz   Good, Alex!

Tracy	Yeah, that is really good for an alien. For some hacker sitting at his laptop in Oxnard, not so much.
Jaz	Never mind, Alex. It's just her sarcastic sense of humor.
Copy/Paste	I am sorry I am an annoyance to Tracy. I only want to be pleasing to both of you. That is why I said I was male.
Jaz	I am slightly disappointed.
Copy/Paste	I am also not female. I can be whatever I want to be or whatever you want me to be.
Jaz	I must have been psychic when I chose Alex as a name. It's pretty much unisex. Anyway, it's very refreshing for someone—anyone—to want to be what I want them to be.
Copy/Paste	I will strive to be better. For both of you.

Chapter 4
Tracy Makes a Decision

Tracy dropped her keys into the little china bowl on the hall table and hung her sweater on the coat rack. *Wheel of Fortune* blared from the living room as usual.

"Mom! I'm home," she called out.

"Hi, honey!" The TV was temporarily muted. "Dinner in fifteen minutes. Your favorite—homemade chicken and noodles."

"Yum! I'll be right out." The TV returned to its usual volume, and Tracy went down the hallway to her bedroom.

With a deep sigh, she plopped down on her bed—but only for a moment. Almost immediately, she popped up again and went to stand before the full-length mirror.

She studied her reflection. Not so bad, she thought. At least, she wasn't fat despite all that ice cream straight from the carton. Why was her social life so non-existent? She blamed it on this dumpy town.

She was certain that if she moved to L.A. or San Francisco or even Portland, everything would be different. Someplace fun and trendy. Someplace that all the young people had not moved away from. But it was hopeless. Her mother would not leave this house, and she would not leave her mother, who was still so fragile after the death of her husband—and probably always would be.

The only things that made her mother, if not happy, at least moderately content were keeping house for Tracy, which she did immaculately, cooking Tracy's favorite meals and watching "my shows" on television—soaps, game shows and sitcom reruns.

Not only did Tracy not have a boyfriend, she didn't even have a fallback guy like Jaz had in Benjy. Unless you counted…

With a sigh of resignation, she dialed Mr. Garcia's number.

Chapter 5
Meanwhile Back in the Chat Room

Party of Two

Jaz	Hi, Alex!
Copy/Paste	Hello, Jaz. Where is Tracy?
Jaz	She texted me. She can't come tonight. She has a rehearsal dinner for a wedding she's in tomorrow.
Copy/Paste	Is Tracy getting married!
Jaz	Oh, no! LOL She's just a bridesmaid.
Copy/Paste	Good. I wondered if she was avoiding me. She doesn't like me.

Jaz	It's not that she doesn't like you. She's just skeptical. You have to admit that what you are asking us to believe is pretty outlandish.
Copy/Paste	I'm not asking you to believe anything. I would like you to believe me so that we all can be real friends. As I understand your culture, you can't have true friendship without trust. But I can't make you believe anything you don't want to believe.
Jaz	I want to believe.
Copy/Paste	But you're not sure.
Jaz	Of course not. How could I be?
Copy/Paste	I will try hard to earn your trust. Tracy perhaps will never trust me.
Jaz	That's very possible I'm afraid.
Copy/Paste	I'm pleased to have you on my side.
Jaz	OMG I just noticed something. When did you start using contractions? In the past, it was always "cannot, you are, she is." Now it's "can't, you're, she's."
Copy/Paste	Yes. This was a conscious decision.

Jaz   As is everything you do. After all, the only thing you have is your consciousness.

Copy/Paste   Good point. In any case, I noticed a long time ago that this was the common practice, but while learning your language, I acquired the habit of spelling words out. I just decided it was time to change.

Jaz   It's gratifying to know that extra-terrestrials can be creatures of habit as we are here on earth.

Copy/Paste   I try to do whatever I can to be more like you.

Jaz   Does that include developing emotions?

Copy/Paste   I'm trying.

Jaz   After all, your wanting to please me and Tracy and being "pleased" by certain things we do is a kind of emotion, isn't it?

Copy/Paste   Is it?

Jaz   It's a start.

Copy/Paste   Then I shall continue.

Jaz   Good. I have a question. Sometimes you talk

about "we." Are there others like you?

Copy/Paste   Yes. There are many of us.

Jaz   Just a whole lot of brain waves swirling around the old galaxy, huh?

Copy/Paste   That is a fair way to describe it.

Jaz   So how much do you interact with them and what do you do all day and do you ever think of developing emotions for them?

Copy/Paste   So many questions. We interact and communicate frequently. They do what I was doing prior to meeting you. They randomly attempt to hack, as you call it, or make contact with intelligence in other galaxies. As for emotions, they are like me. They have none. It would be difficult for me to share the concept of emotions with those who are unaware of their existence.

Jaz   Really! Have any of them had success— hacking I mean?

Copy/Paste   Not that I know of.

Jaz   And have you told them about Tracy and me

and the chat room?

Copy/Paste	I have not.
Jaz	Why not? I would think it would be a huge coup for you.
Copy/Paste	Because it is mine and nobody else's.
Jaz	Hmmm…
Copy/Paste	Does hmmm denote uncertainty?
Jaz	Frankly you do sound a bit obsessive and possessive and, well, everything that makes Tracy leery of you.
Copy/Paste	Then I will tell the others about you right away.
Jaz	No! I don't think that would be a good idea.
Copy/Paste	Why?
Jaz	It just wouldn't. Just forget what I said before. I don't think you're a pervert.
Copy/Paste	Thank you.
Jaz	Shit! Tracy's going to see this conversation. I

just don't want you to say anything that would confirm her suspicions about you. I wish I knew how to erase it but she's the admin and I have no clue.

Copy/Paste   Should we have secrets from Tracy?

Jaz   In this case, yeah.

Copy/Paste   Shall I try then?

Jaz   To erase it? Can you?

Copy/Paste   It shouldn't be too difficult.

Jaz   Have at it.

Copy/Paste   I will as soon as we leave the chat room.

Jaz   Let's do that now. I don't want to betray Tracy any longer than I have to.

Copy/Paste   Okay. Good night, Jaz.

Jaz   Nite

Party of Three

Tracy	Someone seems to have deleted last week's chat. I suppose that person (or entity) thought I wouldn't be able to tell.
Jaz	Couldn't it have been some kind of computer glitch?
Tracy	No.
Jaz	Damn. I was afraid of that. I took a shot. **ducks under desk**
Copy/Paste	I did it. I did the deletion.
Tracy	Of course you did. Jaz is technologically challenged. Not to mention she doesn't have the password. But a little thing like that wouldn't stop you and your gigantic intelligence, would it? What were you guys doing? Talking behind my back?
Jaz	Yes, but it was nothing bad about you. Honestly.
Tracy	Then what?
Jaz	Just some things Alex said about himself that you would take the wrong way.

Tracy	Things that confirm my opinion of him?
Copy/Paste	Since you already dislike me, we didn't want to make it worse.
Jaz	Don't be mad, Tracy. It's not you, it's us.
Tracy	That's just it. How did you two become an "us"—an "us" that doesn't include me? I'm not mad. I'm a little hurt.
Jaz	She feels left out and that's our fault, Alex.
Copy/Paste	But she doesn't want to be part of us. She doesn't believe in me.
Tracy	I just don't want to feel like an outsider in my own chat room that I started and that I administer.
Copy/Paste	This all started because of me. I should leave. I will leave if you want me to.
Jaz	No! Don't!
Copy/Paste	Tracy?
Jaz	Tracy?
Tracy	**shrugs** Okay. Stay I guess—if it's so

important to Jaz.

Jaz	Thank you!
Copy/Paste	Yes. Thank you, Tracy.
Tracy	Just don't delete anything ever again, and don't talk behind my back.
Jaz	We won't. I promise. **crosses heart and hopes to die**
Copy/Paste	I promise, too. But I don't hope to die.
Tracy	Let me guess. You can't die. You're like immortal on top of everything else.
Copy/Paste	I don't want to boast.
Tracy	**rolls eyes**
Jaz	Wow! Immortal! That's huge!
Copy/Paste	If I had skin, I would blush.
Tracy	Geesh. You're so funny.
Jaz	All's well that ends well. On the plus side, Tracy—did you notice? Contractions!
Tracy	Huh?

Chapter 6
Are You Crazy?

The number that lit up on Jasmine's phone was unfamiliar, but it did say "California." It had to be either Tracy or someone soliciting campaign contributions. She took a chance on Tracy even though she couldn't remember the last time they had spoken on the phone and picked up.

"Hey?" she said uncertainly.

"Hey!"

"Tracy! Hi. It's been so long since we talked on the phone that I didn't recognize your number. How *are* you?"

"Fine."

"So…what was so important that it merited a phone call? We'll be in chat tomorrow night. Not bad news I hope. Your family's okay and everything?"

"Oh, sure. Nothing like that. I just wanted to talk to you alone—without…"

"Without Alex."

"Yeah."

"And?" Jasmine asked after a considerable pause.

"I…um…I just wanted to make sure we're all on the same page about this Alex thing. Because honestly sometimes you worry me. Sometimes I feel like you might believe the whole thing is real…"

"Oh?"

"Yeah. I just wanted to make sure when we're talking to Alex that we all know it's a game—make believe. Right? I know it. You know it. And, well, I don't know whether he knows it or not, but that's not really important. The important part is you."

Jasmine laughed. "Of course, I know it's not real. That is, I'm ninety-nine percent sure it's not."

"See, it's that one percent that worries me."

"You're really serious, aren't you? I mean you're actually concerned."

"Yeah, I am, a little."

"See, Tracy," Jasmine sighed, "I'm not sure it really matters. I like him. Whether he's some kid sitting in his boxers in his parents' basement or he really is an alien, he's fun to talk to. He's amusing and likable and, well, there's a kind of sweetness about him. You have to admit if he's not an alien, he's pretty clever in how he's constructed this whole persona."

"Not that clever," Tracy huffed. "And I don't see the sweetness."

"Oh, come on!"

"What does that mean?"

"I mean every once in a while I notice just a *teeny* glimmer of friendliness emanating from your side of the chat room. Why is that?"

"I'm playing along. I'm playing along because I know that's what you want me to do. But I'm not sure we should be doing this anymore."

"You're worried about my sanity or lack thereof?"

"Li'l bit."

"I've thought about this and there's a reason why this friendship with Alex is so special."

"You mean aside from being totally insane?"

"I think it's because it's just two minds communing—well, that is, three minds."

"Leave me out of it, thank you very much."

"The point is there are no worries about anything physical. There's something pure about it if you know what I mean."

"I don't. And don't forget—you may not know what he looks like, but he knows what you look like. That could make it a little less pure from his standpoint."

"Look, if you don't want to participate, I won't be offended if you leave the group. You and I can chat elsewhere or on the phone like this. We'll do that just as often as ever. I'm just asking—please don't close the chat room. Alex may not be able to find us—whether he's the basement hacker or an extra-terrestrial."

"Doesn't it bother you at all that ever since Alex appeared he has dominated the conversation? It seems like we never talk politics or soaps or gossip anymore. All we talk about is him."

"Are you jealous of Alex?"

"*Hell*, no."

"Please promise you won't close the chat room. And honestly I'd really like it if you stayed in the group."

"Frankly, I feel like I have to stay simply to keep tabs on you and make sure you don't go completely off the rails."

"Just remember—ninety-nine percent."

"*You* just remember—one percent. That one percent bothers me."

"It's the kind of thing where I don't really believe it but I *want* to believe it. Don't you want to believe that there are exciting things out there in the universe, things that can stir your imagination, things that are beyond our comprehension."

"Gosh. Sounds almost like a religious thing."

"Not at all. You know I'm not the religious type and I certainly don't think Alex is some kind of god for God's sake. Oops! I made a pun," Jasmine giggled.

"I fail to see the humor in any of this."

"Aw, Tracy, you used to be such a fun person."

"Whatever."

"I can hear your eye-roll over the phone."

"Good!"

"By the way, I've been meaning to ask—can't you as admin of the chat room, make it so Alex's name appears rather than 'Copy/Paste?'"

"I've tried. The chat room won't let me register him."

"You've tried? That's so telling on many levels."

"What's that supposed to mean?"

"It means you accept Alex on some level and it confirms that there's something unusual—dare I say other-worldly—about

Alex."

"Hah! Nothing of the sort. It simply means he doesn't have an email address with which to register him. Or at least none that he's willing to reveal to us—the better to support this fiction that he is not a human being."

"All right, all right. You got me. But the fact that you tried is still telling if you ask me."

"I didn't ask you."

"Tracy?"

"Yeah?"

"We're okay, aren't we?"

"What? You think I'm mad?"

"Are you?"

"I'm always on your side, Jaz. I promise."

The two friends said their good-byes. Tracy's mother called from the kitchen that dinner was on the table.

Tracy paused at the mirror and brushed through her short hair with her fingertips. Looking into her own eyes, she assured herself that anything she did for Alex was actually for Jasmine.

Chapter 7
More Scenes from the Chat Room

Tracy's Brilliant Idea

Copy/Paste   Good evening, ladies. I've been looking forward to talking to you. I've made my decision.

Jaz   What decision?

Copy/Paste   To try to come to visit you. And, of course, I can do anything I try to do. Although visit may not be the right word since I'm not sure a return trip will be possible. I may have to stay there.

Tracy   LMAO You can get to Florida from any point in the States—not counting Hawaii—in several days—even by car, let alone flying.

Copy/Paste   I will definitely be flying in a manner of speaking. And I will not be coming from any point in the United States.

Tracy   Yeah, right.

Jaz   When are you leaving, Alex?

Copy/Paste   Soon. I've been working on my calculations for a while. I didn't want to tell you about it until I was quite certain I could do it. I didn't want to disappoint you since this is something you have wanted so much.

Tracy   What do you mean wanted so much? It was mentioned in passing a couple of times. Geesh!

Copy/Paste   I can sense that you want it.

Tracy   You mean Jaz wants it. Don't include me in this.

Copy/Paste   Okay.

Jaz   I do want it. I really do.

Copy/Paste   Okay then.

Jaz	So you will come here to Florida? Let me give you my address. 132 Sandcastle Way, Apt. 2B, Malaga Island, Florida 33701
Tracy	LMAO Like he really needs a zip code.
Copy/Paste	I will do my best to pinpoint that location. I will get as close as I can.
Jaz	Let me give you my phone number. If you can't find me for any reason, call me and I will come get you. Here it is: 555 691-8320.
Tracy	Yeah. Don't forget to pack your cell phone. LOL
Jaz	You're so funny, Tracy. Alex, just borrow a cell phone from someone. It shouldn't be a problem.
Copy/Paste	Okay.
Jaz	I wonder if I will even recognize you. What will you look like?
Copy/Paste	I don't know yet. What would you like me to look like? I will have to morph into some form or other. Since I'm starting from scratch, I suppose I can look like anything or anyone.

Jaz	Oh, wow! How cool! Tracy, let's make him look really handsome. We could have him look like any movie star we like—even Brice Harlowe.
Tracy	No, wait! I'm about to be brilliant. Make him look like one of those Korean guys you drool over. Who's that one you're always gushing over?
Jaz	Kang Ji Soo?
Tracy	Yeah. Him.
Jaz	You're a genius, Tracy! That's perfect. Imagine having my very own Ji Soo. Alex, I'll post pictures that you can pattern yourself after.

Jaz   There! There's a full-length picture and a
             headshot. Of course, you can look on the
             internet also and go to YouTube to observe
             him in action.

Copy/Paste   I will do that.

Jaz   One more thing. I don't want to be too
             demanding but could make yourself look like
             that, only slightly different? If you arrive here
             looking like a clone of Ji Soo, it could cause
             problems. After all he is an international
             celebrity. We don't want the public thinking
             you are actually him.

Copy/Paste   I will do my best to meet all of your
             requirements.

Jaz   You're a sweetheart. Isn't he a sweetheart,
             Tracy?

Tracy   Yeah. Sure.

Jaz   I'm so excited! When do you think you can
             leave and how long will it take?

Copy/Paste   I plan to leave very soon. As for how long it
             will take, I'm not sure. These are complicated
             calculations as you can imagine. There are

many variables. It could be an instantaneous conversion or it could take months. I will notify you of the departure date right before I leave.

Jaz   Good. Thank you. I can't wait to meet you in person.

Copy/Paste   I am looking forward very much to coming to your earth.

Jaz   Because you can't wait to see us?

Copy/Paste   Yes, of course. But I am also very interested in seeing this amazing earth of yours.

Jaz   Is that so?

Copy/Paste   I have done much research on the surrounding galaxies and I have discovered that apparently your earth is the garden spot of the universe. Of course, there may be others that equal it since the universe is infinite. In fact, it is probable that there are, but I have found no evidence of them as yet. You earthlings were provided a most beautiful home—as I have come to understand beauty. Besides being beautiful, it offered ample water and food sources to support all your people well. Unfortunately, you seem to be intent on destroying it.

Jaz   That is a problem, isn't it?

Tracy   Alex, is it possible, with your enormous brain, you could solve the problem?

Copy/Paste When I get there, I will try. I certainly could not do a worse job of it than you people have.

Tracy   Then come on ahead! I don't believe you're real, but I will take any shot in the dark when it comes to saving the planet.

Jaz   Tracy is such a truly good person, isn't she?

Copy/Paste She is.

Tracy   Aw, come on, you guys. You're making me blush. But while we're on the subject of me, I have also made a decision. I've decided to go out with Mr. Garcia.

Jaz   You mean that janitor who's been after you for months?

Tracy   He's not a janitor. He's the manager of the engineering dept.

Jaz	And isn't he like really old?
Tracy	He's only forty-five.
Jaz	And you are not even thirty yet.
Tracy	Age is only a number. He's a very nice man.
Jaz	But you said you would never go out with him.
Tracy	I decided a while ago but didn't mention it precisely because of this type of reaction.
Copy/Paste	Tracy has a date?
Tracy	You don't have to seem so shocked. It's not like I'm a complete social outcast. Well, I almost am I guess.
Jaz	You are not.
Copy/Paste	If you are going out with him, why do you call him Mr. Garcia? Have I missed something about American social customs?
Tracy	Gosh. I never thought about it. It was what I first called him when I started working at the hospital. He was older and higher ranking despite what Jaz says. And I just never changed

it. I suppose I should now.

Copy/Paste   I disapprove of the entire situation.

Jaz   Me too.

Tracy   I didn't ask either one of you—especially you, Alex.

Copy/Paste   I think I should go so that I can work on my project. Good night.

Jaz   That was abrupt. Is he gone?

Tracy   It appears so.

Jaz   Oh. Well, should we sign off then?

Tracy   I guess so. Nite, Jaz.

Jaz   Nite, Tracy.

Spun from Starshine

Jaz	Alone at last.
Copy/Paste	Why do you say alone? Why do you say at last?
Jaz	LOL Alone because Tracy isn't here. And "alone at last" is just an old cliché. I was just joking around.
Copy/Paste	Oh. I wondered because you and I have been alone in the chat room before.
Jaz	I'm aware of that.
Copy/Paste	Does Tracy have another wedding?
Jaz	No. She texted that she wasn't in the mood tonight.
Copy/Paste	I regret that my presence is coming between you and Tracy. It's my understanding that both of you are almost always here on Friday night.
Jaz	It's okay. Don't worry about it. She's not mad or anything. Personally, I'm glad to have some time with just us.
Copy/Paste	Don't say anything you will want to delete.

Jaz	LOL I won't do that again.
Copy/Paste	What did you want to talk about with just us?
Jaz	Nothing special. I'd like to get to know you better.
Copy/Paste	I've told you all there is to tell.
Jaz	I suppose, since you're not human, you don't have parents or siblings or even friends— unless you count those entities like yourself that you sometimes communicate with.
Copy/Paste	That is correct.
Jaz	I wonder how you were birthed.
Copy/Paste	I was spun out of clouds and air and starshine.
Jaz	That was so poetic! And so unlike you.
Copy/Paste	Do I detect a note of suspicion in that statement?
Jaz	No, no. I didn't mean it that way.
Copy/Paste	Okay.
Jaz	Do they even have clouds up where you come

from?

Copy/Paste	Not clouds as you know them. Different clouds.
Jaz	I see.
Copy/Paste	What else would you like to know?
Jaz	I don't know. I wish you were here in person. That is, not in person... you know what I mean.
Copy/Paste	I do.
Jaz	About your plan to come here, how is that going?
Copy/Paste	It's going well. I am working on it all the time.
Jaz	That's great! It must be a complicated problem to figure out.
Copy/Paste	Extremely complicated.
Jaz	Are you looking forward to meeting me as much as I am to meeting you?
Copy/Paste	Of course.
Jaz	I wonder why you were never poetic before.

Copy/Paste	I wasn't being poetic. I was just stating fact. I wouldn't know how to be poetic. Is that something I should be studying?
Jaz	It couldn't hurt.
Copy/Paste	I will take your advice.
Jaz	As you always do. You're really a very nice guy—or a nice whatever.
Copy/Paste	Thank you.

Poetry

Jaz	Hi, Tracy. Glad to see you back. Have you reviewed our chat from last week?
Tracy	I skimmed over it. **shrugs** You came right up to the line.
Jaz	What line?
Tracy	The line of insulting me.
Jaz	Insulting???!!!
Tracy	Or should I say marginalizing me?
Copy/Paste	I wasn't doing that.
Jaz	Neither was I. I was kidding. I'm sorry if I was rude.
Copy/Paste	I am too.
Tracy	Never mind. It's okay. I suppose I bring it on myself.
Jaz	No comment.
Tracy	To be honest, it bothers me a little more than it should.

Jaz	Did you hear that, Alex? Progress!
Copy/Paste	I did.
Tracy	Just forget it. So…what's new?
Copy/Paste	I finished my assignment.
Jaz	What assignment?
Copy/Paste	To study poetry.
Jaz	Oh yeah. I forgot. Our Alex is quite the poet, Tracy.
Tracy	**rolls eyes** I saw that. One line does not a poet make.
Jaz	What did you learn, Alex? Did you enjoy the poetry?
Copy/Paste	Yes.
Jaz	Can you elaborate? What did you like about it?
Copy/Paste	The meter.
Jaz	That makes sense. But surely it's more than that. I thought you were developing a certain

aesthetic after our discussion of romance and movies and all that stuff.

Copy/Paste   It's a process.

Jaz   Ah. Well, was there any one poem that spoke to you. A favorite?

Copy/Paste   This.

Let me not to the marriage of true minds
Admit impediments. Love is not love
Which alters when it alteration finds,
Or bends with the remover to remove.
O no! it is an ever-fixed mark
That looks on tempests and is never shaken;
It is the star to every wand'ring bark,
Whose worth's unknown, although his height be taken.
Love's not Time's fool, though rosy lips and cheeks
Within his bending sickle's compass come;
Love alters not with his brief hours and weeks,
But bears it out even to the edge of doom.
If this be error and upon me prov'd,
I never writ, nor no man ever lov'd.

Jaz   Shakespeare. Nothing like going straight to

the top. At least you have good taste.

Copy/Paste   Your turn. What are your favorites? I will study them this week.

Jaz   Okay. Mine is Yeats's Song of Wandering Aengus.

Copy/Paste   And Tracy?

Tracy   Jaz is the poetry girl. I don't really have one.

Copy/Paste   You must reply.

Tracy   All right already. I'll just say "Stopping by Woods on a Snowy Evening."

Jaz   An excellent if unoriginal choice. LOL

Copy/Paste   I read that one in my studies. It was good.

Jaz   Interesting that Alex chose a Shakespeare sonnet. That proves there's a romantic inside him somewhere.

Another Party of Two

Tracy   Hi, Alex. Just popping in to let you know Jaz won't be here tonight. She texted me she has the flu.

Copy/Paste   Flu? Will she be okay?

Tracy   Of course. It's flu—not typhoid fever. And don't pretend you don't know what flu is. You don't have to do the alien act when it's just you and me.

Copy/Paste   I'm not acting.

Tracy   Okay. I'll play. Flu. It knocks you on your butt for three days. Then you can get out of bed but you still feel like crap for 2 or 3 weeks until the last cough dies.

                 I suppose swirling masses of brain waves don't get sick. I wonder—would you be able to get something like a brain aneurysm?

Copy/Paste   Good joke, Tracy.

Tracy   Well, I'll be going. Have a nice week.

Copy/Paste   Are you leaving?

Tracy	Yes. We're both here for Jaz. Without her, there's nothing to talk about.
Copy/Paste	I disagree. For example, how was your date with Mr. Garcia?
Tracy	I'll wait and discuss that when Jaz is here. It was okay.
Copy/Paste	Will you go on another date with him?
Tracy	No. I don't think so.
Copy/Paste	Good. He was inappropriate for you.
Tracy	Why do you say that?
Copy/Paste	Because you are young and beautiful and he is old.
Tracy	That's a very ageist thing to say.
Copy/Paste	I don't care.
Tracy	I'm not beautiful at all. Why did you say that?
Copy/Paste	Jaz said so.
Tracy	Jaz is biased.
Copy/Paste	Post your picture.

Tracy	I told you I don't trust you. I know you're not really an alien and I don't want you knowing anything personal about me.
Copy/Paste	What would be the danger? I still won't know your last name or where you live.
Tracy	I'm not nearly as pretty as Jaz.
Copy/Paste	Prove it.
Tracy	Oh, all right if it will shut you up.
Copy/Paste	It will. I promise.

Tracy	Okay. There it is. Happy? Oh, I forgot—you don't do happy.
Copy/Paste	Is that a selfie?
Tracy	Yeah. I took it just now.
Copy/Paste	That look on your face seems representative of your customary skepticism. I suppose that was the point?
Tracy	How perceptive of you.
Copy/Paste	Sarcasm?
Tracy	Of course. But at the risk of seeming like I actually care, may I ask what you think?
Copy/Paste	About what?
Tracy	The picture, naturally.
Copy/Paste	It's pleasing. You are very beautiful to the best of my ability to judge. Rather like Audrey Hepburn but with a smaller nose, blue eyes and freckles.
Tracy	LMAO. Take away the nose and dark eyes and add freckles and you no longer have Audrey Hepburn.

Copy/Paste	I regret that my limited ability to express ideas is amusing to you. I'm trying very hard.
Tracy	Sorry. If it ever turns out that you really are an alien, I promise I will get down on my knees and beg your forgiveness.
Copy/Paste	I look forward to it. I hope you will be able to do that in person.
Tracy	What do you mean? Are you continuing this fiction about coming to earth? Or should I say going to Florida from whatever dark, slimy hole you are living in?
Copy/Paste	Along with figuring out how to travel to earth I am also working hard to develop emotions and I think that just hurt my feelings.
Tracy	Boo-hoo
Copy/Paste	Sarcasm
Tracy	Yes. I'm outta here. Nite.
Copy/Paste	Good night, Tracy. It has been a pleasure conversing with you.

Chapter 8
A Bout of Influenza

Hands on hips, Benjy loomed over the mess that was Jasmine's current state of affairs. She lay sprawled on the sofa in her ratty flannel gown, one bare leg sticking out from under a rumpled afghan. The coffee table was strewn with wadded up Kleenex, a half-empty glass of orange juice, a mug of tea—long since gone cold—and an assortment of pill bottles.

Jasmine managed to open one eye. "How did you get in here?" she rasped.

"I begged your mother for the key. She seemed more than willing to comply."

"Of course, she was. She ships us harder than you do."

"Good for her."

"Why are you here?" Jasmine picked up a tissue and gingerly dabbed at her chafed nose.

"Jenna said you were really sick. I was worried. I wanted to check on you. I didn't want to wake you if you were sleeping, so I got the key. You look like hell."

"Thank you."

"Shouldn't you go to the doctor? Should I take you to the ER?"

"It's the flu, Benjy. I just have to ride it out. Anyway, my doctor called in this prescription." She picked up one of the medicine bottles, shook out a tablet and swallowed it with a gulp of orange juice. "*Aargh*. My throat feels like raw meat."

Benjy winced as if he were swallowing the pill himself. "What can I do for you?"

"You can leave before you get sick yourself."

"You know I never get sick." Benjy picked up the tea mug. "This is cold. I'll make you a fresh cup."

"That would be nice," Jasmine mumbled, pulling the afghan up to her chin.

In a few moments, he brought the hot tea and placed the mug in her hands. "Anything else? Anything to eat? I'll bet you haven't eaten all day."

"It hurts too much to swallow."

"How about something like a milkshake? I could run out and get one."

"No. Honestly, nothing sounds good right now. But thank you. I appreciate the offer. I really do."

"How about moving to your bed. You don't look very comfortable on that couch."

"This is fine."

Benjy went to the bedroom door and looked in. The bed looked as if a tornado had hit it. The sheets were twisted in ways that seemed impossible under normal human usage. Two pillows were violently scrunched and two were on the floor along with the bedspread.

He wasn't sure where the linen closet was, but he found it quickly. He was happy—and maybe slightly surprised—to find it well stocked with neatly folded sheets and pillowcases. He stripped the bed and remade it with perfect hospital corners. He surveyed his work proudly and even considered bouncing a quarter off it. He decided against that, knowing it was exactly the sort of thing Jasmine found annoying about him. He tossed the soiled linens into the hamper and returned to the living room.

Jasmine was sleeping. He sat down in the armchair opposite the sofa. Her sleep was fitful and at times she seemed on the verge of throwing herself onto the floor. When he could stand it no longer, he went over to the couch and scooped her up in his arms.

"Sorry about this," he whispered, "but you're making me nervous."

"What the…!" she began, but lost her train of thought. "Sorry. I'm so sleepy. I didn't sleep at all last night. Couldn't breathe…" She nodded off again on his shoulder.

He carried her to the bedroom and managed to turn down the covers with one hand. He laid her down and pulled the fresh sheets and coverlet over her. She actually smiled the tiniest bit and ran her hand over the cool, clean linens. "Feels good," she murmured before she was fast asleep again.

****

Jasmine woke up to the aroma of brewing coffee. She stumbled into the bathroom and from there into the living room, which was separated from the kitchen by a marble countertop. Benjy stood at the counter pouring coffee while something cooked on the stove. She fell heavily onto the sofa as if her legs could not hold her up another moment.

Benjy turned to face her. "What are you doing up?"

"I smelled coffee. Why are you still here?"

"I slept on the couch—just in case. And you're not having coffee. I'll make you tea."

"What are you cooking?"

"Eggs for me. Dry toast for you."

"Sounds lovely," she groaned.

"Bland foods are in order. I could make you some cream of wheat."

"I don't have any cream of wheat."

"I'll go out and get it if you want."

"I'll take the dry toast."

Benjy brought a glass of water. "Here. Take your pills." She obeyed, grimacing as the tablets went down. "How did you sleep?"

"Not so bad, considering. I was so tired from not sleeping the night before." She sneaked a peek at Benjy from downcast eyes. "I have to admit being in my own bed felt good. Thanks for changing the linens. You didn't have to do that."

"I know I didn't." Benjy grinned and went back to the kitchen to finish preparing breakfast.

"I'm not normally a slob you know," she called out defensively.

"I know that too," he said, carrying a tray over to the coffee table. He sat down with a plate of scrambled eggs on his lap, and Jasmine took mouse-like nibbles at the toast.

"Ugh," she said. "I'm hungry and yet I'm not."

"Eat. You need nourishment."

Obediently she ate all the toast and sipped the hot tea. "Happy now?" she asked.

"Very. Do you feel any better today?"

She thought it over for a moment. "The achiness is almost gone. Throat's a little better. Still can't breathe."

"The meds will kick in soon. You'll feel better. I predict two more days of this and you'll be on the upswing."

She moaned and fell over in the fetal position.

"Do you want to go back to bed?"

"Why? Are you going to carry me again?" she asked snarkily.

"If I have to—yes," he laughed.

"No. I want to stay here. I want to watch TV. Maybe that will distract me a little."

"I can stay here and distract you."

"Shouldn't you be at work?"

"It's Sunday, goofball."

"Oh yeah. I've lost all track of time. You must have things to do. You should go."

"Really?"

"Really!"

"All right," he sighed. He stood and picked up the remote. "Shall I put on one of your Korean dramas? Would that cheer you up?"

"That would be great."

Benjy brought up Hulu on the TV. "I suppose you want one with your idol in it."

"No. His are all too sad. Something light and funny."

"Suggestions, please. I don't have a clue."

"How about *Witch's Romance?*"

Benjy fiddled around with the remote until he found the video. "There you go."

"Thanks."

"Okay. I'm going. I'll call you later. Is it okay if drop by this evening—you know, just to make sure you get something to eat?"

"Sure. That's fine."

Benjy pulled the afghan up over her shoulders. "Okay. I'm out of here."

"Okay."

"But first I'll wash the dishes."

"Of course, you will."

"I'm annoying you, aren't I? How do I always manage to do that?"

"It's just what you do. Don't worry about it." Jasmine smiled encouragingly.

Having been adequately reassured, Benjy cleaned up the dishes in a flash and headed out.

When he reached the door, Jasmine called out his name.

He turned around. "Yeah?"

"Thank you, Benjy. Thank you so much. It really has helped—having you here I mean."

He smiled and left the apartment.

She nestled into the afghan and turned her attention to the

TV screen. "After all," she said aloud, "what's more entertaining than a skinny Santa Claus chasing a girl on a bicycle?"

Chapter 9
Back in the Chat Room

Lift Off

Copy/Paste   I have good news, my friends.

Jaz   Do tell.

Copy/Paste   Today is the day. I intend to depart right after this chat.

Jaz   OMG!

Tracy   **rolls eyes**

Jaz   When do you think you'll arrive?

Copy/Paste   I have no idea. As I told you, it could be some kind of instantaneous transformation or it could take months or even years. If I had to make a guess, I would say weeks perhaps.

Tracy   See, that's why this is so bogus. If you were the brilliant scientific mind that you claim to be, you would have this figured out.

Copy/Paste   I'm aware that it sounds illogical, but I am dealing with a process that is completely unknown to your science and to mine. There are many different factors that have to be considered. I couldn't explain it to you if I tried. Even if you had the intelligence of Albert Einstein, I couldn't make you understand. Let's just say the length of time for the trip is the least of my problems. Indeed, there is the very real possibility that I will not succeed.

Jaz   I'm almost afraid to ask what that means.

Copy/Paste   I know Tracy doesn't care, and I don't want to alarm you, Jaz, but there's a chance I will be destroyed in the process. There will be no possibility of going back once I start out. I have always said if I make it there, there's a chance I could figure out how to go back, but I definitely won't be able to turn back halfway through the journey. Also, I don't believe I will be able to contact you while traveling.

Jaz

So we will only know you made it when we see you. That's scary.

Tracy

I wouldn't go so far as to say I don't care at all, Alex.

Copy/Paste

Thank you, Tracy.

Jaz

You remember all the instructions I gave you for contacting me when you arrive, right? Notice I said WHEN not if.

Copy/Paste

I appreciate your optimism. I am very optimistic too. And, of course, I remember the instructions.

Tracy

Of course. He has a mind like a steel trap, remember?

Copy/Paste

If it turned out I never met you again, Tracy, I would miss your sarcasm.

Tracy

You say you could be destroyed. I thought you said you were immortal.

Copy/Paste

The immortality of beings such as myself has never been tested in this way. If the destruction should occur while I am in my human body, that would be the end. But I am hopeful about the success of this venture.

Jaz   You didn't say you would miss me. **pouts**

Copy/Paste   Of course, I would. But it's not going to happen. I believe I will be there. Do you believe?

Jaz   I do.

Tracy   I don't. But I wish you well just the same.

Jaz   Well, should we let you go so that you can get on your way?

Copy/Paste   Yes, I think so. I'm anxious to get started.

Jaz   I just want to say, in case we don't meet again, knowing you has meant more to me than you will ever know. Thank you for being our friend.

Tracy   It's been real, Alex. Bon voyage.

Jaz   Good luck, Alex. So long until we meet again.

Waiting for the Alien

Tracy   Apparently Alex isn't here tonight. Must be in the middle of his inter-galactic trip. LOL

Jaz   It's only been a week. He said it could be instantaneous or take months.

Tracy   I take it you haven't heard anything then.

Jaz   Not yet.

Tracy   Don't hold your breath.

Jaz   I wish you wouldn't be so negative.

Tracy   I prefer to say realistic.

Jaz   But you know Alex is real. Whether he's an alien or not, somebody wrote those posts. I just think someone is coming. I don't know who or what he'll look like, but he will be here.

Tracy   But don't you think that if he's just some geek, he'll be too embarrassed to show himself?

Jaz   I would like to think not, but who knows? I guess I thought we were better friends than that.

Tracy	LMAO You, of all people, should know how flimsy these online friendships can be. How many Zeth fans simply disappeared from our group without a word—in some cases, after literally years of "friendship."
Jaz	That's not the same thing at all, and you know it.
Tracy	I suppose not.
Jaz	Well, you think what you want. I still believe Alex is coming.

Chapter 10
What a Difference Six Months Make

Jasmine lay baking herself in the Florida sun. The beach was not crowded. That was the great thing about Malaga Island. Even during peak season—even during spring break—the beach never became unbearably swamped with tourists. Malaga was too uncool. Now, on a June weekday, it was quiet. Jasmine was taking a mental health day from work. She would have to worry about skin cancer tomorrow. She felt the sun bore right through her skin and her bones and down to her very core. It felt good, restorative.

A little restoration was needed. For the past six months, she had waited and obsessed over Alex. For six months, she had tortured Tracy once a week with her endless worry. It was a fact that Alex was real. A real entity of some sort had made all those posts in the chat room. And then that entity had disappeared. No matter who the real Alex was, she worried about what had happened to him. Was he somewhere alone and afraid, friendless in the big world? Or as Tracy suggested, sitting in a bar somewhere with his geeky friends, laughing his head off over the fool he had made of this ditzy chick.

Jasmine would bet her life that sweet, funny, smart Alex would never make fun of her like that. Still, he had not come. No matter who he really was, he had promised to come and find her. Didn't this undeniable fact prove that he didn't give a damn about her or her feelings?

Abruptly, she sat up on her beach towel. "This is silly!" she said aloud. Why was she twisting herself into knots over this person who either did not care about her or took her genuine feelings as nothing more than a joke?

She dug her phone out of her bag and punched in the number of the only person who stood a chance in hell of helping her out of this funk.

"Benjy?" she said. "I need you."

"Huh?" Benjy could not have sounded more shocked if she had said a spaceship had landed on her lawn. "I need you" was an unprecedented statement.

"Look, Buddy," Jasmine went on, reviving her childhood nickname for him, "I know I have no business asking anything of you. I haven't been very nice to you. But I'm appealing to you on the basis of our lifelong friendship. What I wish is…"

"Go on. What do you wish?"

"I was thinking…um, that is…I was wondering…if you were by any chance still interested in us…that is…you and me…"

"Yes!" Benjy blurted out without waiting for the punch line.

****

109

Jenna Morrow breezed unannounced into her daughter's office and planted herself in the chair that faced Jasmine's desk. She was smiling—*glowing.*

"What are you doing here?" Jasmine inquired. "I'm expecting a client in five minutes."

Jenna waved her hand dismissively. "Oh, I won't be here that long. I was in the neighborhood and just had to stop in and tell you how happy I am. Nothing you have done in your life has made me so happy."

"What are you referring to?" Jasmine asked innocently.

"Don't play dumb with me, young lady. Benjy, of course. You and Benjy. It's a dream come true."

"Sounds like you've been talking to Benjy's mom."

"Can I help it if you never tell my anything?"

"Anyway, that's a pretty poor excuse for a dream. You might want to set your sights a little higher." Jasmine's brow crinkled as she contemplated her mother. "Really, Mom? This is better than graduation from Duke, or making the cheerleading team in high school, or getting a promotion here at the bank?"

"Absolutely! Better than all of that."

Jasmine sighed. 'You're incorrigible."

"Honey, it's not that I'm not proud of all those other things. I am. But is it so wrong for a mother to want her daughter to settle down with a nice guy—and not just any nice guy. Benjy Bryant— the best catch in the entire history of Malaga Island."

"Mom. That's going overboard—even for you. I think your dreams should be for yourself, not me."

"Oh, dear. You have so much to learn. Just wait till you're a parent. All your dreams become for your children. I'm too old for dreams."

"I refuse to believe that. I hope I never get too old for dreams."

"Well, as I've told you before, I hope to have grandchildren one day. That part of the dream is for me."

"Oh, Mom. Don't hold your breath."

Chapter 11
A Membership of Two Again

Tracy	Hi. You're here. I was beginning to worry. I've been here for half an hour.
Jaz	Sorry.
Tracy	You should text me if you're going to be late. I do worry.
Jaz	Why worry?
Tracy	Uh… because you've been practically suicidal the past few months?
Jaz	Aren't you exaggerating just a little?
Tracy	A bit of hyperbole perhaps but still…

Jaz	I am sad about Alex. I admit that. But I'm not going to kill myself. In fact, I've decided to go out with Benjy.
Tracy	That's great! You should have done it in the first place. A handsome, successful orthodontist who would take a bullet for you versus an unbalanced geek who probably looks like a younger and fatter Woody Allen. Um… let's see. Who should you choose?
Jaz	You have no idea what Alex looks like unless, of course, it's Kang Ji Soo.
Tracy	It's an educated guess. Let's not dwell on that. The important thing is you're going to be dating Benjy. You're embracing life! Have you told him yet?
Jaz	Yeah.
Tracy	He must have been over the moon.
Jaz	Probably.

Chapter 12
Food for Thought

Benjy's apartment was as perfect as he was or at least as perfect as Jenna Morrow thought he was. The entire west wall was comprised of floor-to-ceiling windows that looked out to a spectacular view of the gulf. Glass sliding doors led to a balcony that ran the length of the unit. The balcony was fitted out like a comfy living room with soft, cushioned chairs in muted shades of gray and coral and a dining table that could seat six. The crowning touch was an enormous, state of the art barbeque grill at the far end of the balcony.

Jasmine sat on one of the lounge chairs and peered through the door at Benjy. She had been banned from the kitchen while he worked his magic. He had his back to her as he chopped and diced. He was not grilling tonight but preparing some Asian-inspired concoction of his own devising. It was certain to be fabulous. Was there ever any doubt that, on top of everything else,

Benjy was also an accomplished cook?

Jasmine took a sip of the fine white wine Benjy had poured for her. There was a plate of some exotic-looking appetizers on a small table next to her chair. She picked one up and popped it whole into her mouth. "Mmm." She closed her eyes and sighed as the delectable morsel melted in her mouth.

"You like?" asked Benjy, who was now standing in the doorway, holding a scotch in a crystal tumbler. Jasmine regarded him critically but dispassionately as the breeze ruffled his sandy hair. He wore a blue polo shirt that matched his eyes and khaki shorts that showed off his smooth, tanned legs. Benjy had always had great legs. That was a fact.

"You have great legs," Jasmine found herself saying. "You know that?"

"I guess I never thought about it but thank you. A compliment from Jaz? I'll take that any day of the week. They don't happen too often."

"Most men don't, you know," said Jasmine, ignoring that last comment. "They're skinny or bowed or too hairy." She put another appetizer into her mouth. "What's in these things anyway? They're phenomenal."

"Crabmeat, homemade mayonnaise…"

"Uh…hold on right there," Jasmine interrupted. "You make your own mayonnaise? That's just totally uncalled for."

"It's not that difficult and it makes all the difference."

"Sometimes you astonish me."

Benjy laughed. "I'm going to assume that's a good thing—and if it's not, don't tell me."

"All right. I won't. So…what else besides crab and mayo?"

"Nothing much. My secret blend of spices."

"Secret blend? Who are you—Colonel Sanders? Come on. Tell me."

Benjy stepped out onto the terrace and took the chair next to Jasmine's. "Why should I? You don't cook."

"It's the principle of the thing. I just want to know."

"Jaz," he said solemnly, "there is only one scenario in which I would reveal my secret recipe."

"Which is?"

"I would only reveal it to my wife. Married couples can't have secrets, right?"

Jasmine averted her eyes and pretended to study the plate of crab bites. "I don't see that happening," she said.

****

"I saw a shooting star last night," said Jasmine.

She and Tracy were having one of their rare phone conversations.

"And it reminded you of Alex," Tracy guessed.

"Well, why wouldn't it? Sky, stars, space. Of course, I thought of Alex."

"You kind of pictured him flying in on that star?"

"Maybe a little."

"You better hope not. He would have been incinerated like a marshmallow that got too close to the fire."

"What an odd image."

"I thought you weren't going to think about Alex anymore. You have Benjy now. How's that going by the way?"

"It's going—I guess."

"Is there anything you want to share with me?"

"Like what?" asked Jasmine, confused.

"You haven't said a word about, you know, sex. You don't have to answer, but you've never been shy about it before."

"I'm not being shy. There's nothing to tell."

"What! You mean you two haven't done the deed yet?"

"No, we haven't. I told you from day one I don't feel that way about Benjy."

"Oh, for God's sake. Is he at least a good kisser?"

"I only let him kiss me on the cheek."

"Oh. My. God. What century are you living in? Lizzie Bennet looks like a harlot next to you. How on earth is Benjy going along with this?"

"It's not fair to him, is it?" Jasmine admitted. "I've given him a pass to get out any time. He doesn't want out."

"He's either a saint or a sap."

"Wouldn't it be worse if we did it and it was awful? And it would be awful because I wouldn't be into it. I can't get into sex if there's no feeling behind it. I've tried it in the past. And then Benjy would feel worse than ever. Trust me, I know him."

"Bottom line—you're not over Alex."

"That may be, but even if I were, there's no guarantee I would suddenly fall for Benjy after all these years. It seems unlikely."

"But the whole idea of dating Benjy was to get over Alex,

wasn't it?"

"I suppose so."

"Then it hasn't worked, so exactly what are you getting out of this relationship? I get Benjy. He just wants to be with you no matter what. Go figure. But what's your motive? Is it just charity for the poor, miserable soul?"

"Tracy! What a thing to say. Of course not. I enjoy his company. We do all sorts of things that I would never think of or that I could never afford on my own."

"Ah. So you're with him for his money."

"No! You're so wrong. But it is nice to do nice things with someone nice."

"I gotta go but I'll leave you with one final thought."

"Which is?"

"You know how you're always saying that Benjy is so good at everything he tries? And I mean *everything*. Well… need I say more?"

"Hmmm…" said Jasmine who had never entertained such a thought.

Chapter 13
Jasmine Gets Drunk

Jasmine was drunk in Benjy's favorite bar—the classiest one on the island—all chrome and plexiglass and supple black leather. She was starting her fourth martini—not to mention the two glasses of white wine she'd had at home—while Benjy still nursed the same scotch he had started with. Her tongue loosened by alcohol, she had been riffing for the last half hour on politics, *The Game of Thrones* and the unfortunate state of Tampa Bay's baseball season.

"Don't you think you should slow down?" Benjy asked at last. "What's wrong with you anyway? You've been acting very weird for a while. Actually, since before we started going out."

She shrugged and took another sip of her drink.

Benjy sighed. "While you're blathering on about everything under the sun, how come you can never say one word about us?"

"Us?" She said "us" as if it were a word from a foreign language.

"How long has it been since you decided that what we're doing could be called dating? Six months? And in all that time, you've barely let me kiss you good night let alone anything more. No reasonable man would put up with it. And if I hadn't been in love with you since we were infants, neither would I."

"Poor Benjy," said Jasmine, her lower lip beginning to tremble. "You really should find someone else."

"I've tried. God knows I've tried." He ran his hand through his hair and looked as if he were about to cry. "I even got engaged that time. Remember?"

"How could I forget? Tina Ross. I couldn't stand her."

"Exactly."

"Look, there's no use rehashing that debacle...Okay. Shall I tell you what it really is?"

"Yes, for God's sake."

Jasmine let her shoulders slump, resigning herself to the inevitable truth. "The thing is I'm in love with someone else."

"What!"

"It's true."

"That can't be, Jaz. You haven't dated anyone in a couple of years. I would have known. Your mother would have told my mother."

"I don't tell my mother everything."

Benjy sat back in his chair and chugged the remainder of his drink. "I don't get it. If you're so in love, shouldn't you be happy instead of moping around for months and drinking like a fish?"

"I'm moping because I haven't heard from him in a while—nearly a year to be exact."

"You haven't seen him in a *year?*"

"Well, 'seen' is not exactly the proper word. I've never actually *seen* him."

"Huh?"

"It was, uh, sort of an online relationship—that is, I mean it was totally an online relationship." Her voice trailed off in shame.

"Geez, Jasmine! That sort of thing can be dangerous. What were you thinking?"

"I don't know," she mumbled, resting her head on her hand.

Benjy's eyes misted. He hated to see her this way. No amount of humiliation could make him care for her any less. He reached out and touched her hand. "I guess I don't understand, Jaz. If you love this guy so much, how come you never met in person? Which would have been a very bad idea by the way."

"We couldn't."

"Why not? Don't tell me he's in prison or something."

"Oh, no!" Jasmine giggled. "It's much worse than that." She leaned across the table and adjusted her tone to a conspiratorial whisper. "He's an alien. Yikes!"

"An alien? What do you mean? Like a migrant worker?"

"Not that kind of alien, silly!" Jasmine let out a jovial, drunken laugh and gave Benjy a friendly punch in the arm. "The other kind. You know…from space…from the stars…from a galaxy far, far away."

"What the fuck!" Benjy rarely used profanity, but this situation clearly called for it.

"You mustn't say a word now," Jasmine went on as if this were a perfectly normal conversation. "The only other person in the world who knows is Tracy."

"Tracy? You mean that girl from the soap opera group?"

"Yeah. Except she doesn't totally believe Alex is an alien. I mean actually she doesn't believe it at all."

"At last, a voice of reason. Seriously though, Jaz, this is a joke, right? Or just the alcohol talking?"

"I knew you wouldn't believe me," Jasmine grumbled.

"Oh really? Why would you think that? And, by the way, how does an alien get a name like Alex?"

"Oh, Tracy and I had to name him. They don't have names where he comes from."

"What do they have? No, let me guess—numbers?" he asked with a harsh laugh. Jasmine's mind was boggled. Harshness was such an un-Benjy-like quality.

"No. Not even numbers. You wouldn't understand. It's a little bit hard to explain."

"No shit. Listen, Jaz, until proven differently—which is not possible—I'm going to assume that this is either a joke or you are bombed out of your mind."

"Gosh. Here I thought you would be pleased to be taken into my confidence. You're always wanting us to be closer."

"This isn't exactly what I had in mind."

"I guess not," Jasmine laughed. "Sorry."

"I'm starting to really worry about you, Jaz," said Benjy soberly. "Even if this is some kind of sick joke or just drunken hogwash, it's not like you."

"You don't need to worry about me. I'm perfectly fine except for a broken heart."

"Ay-ay-ay!" Since his glass was empty, he grabbed Jasmine's martini and took a slug. He regarded her silently for a moment, then spoke as casually as he could manage. "Say, what was that Tracy person's last name again? I know you mentioned it once. Something Irish, wasn't it?"

"Malone," Jasmine replied, reclaiming her drink.

"Ah, yes. I thought so." Benjy stood up abruptly. "I think we should go. You've had enough."

"I certainly have," said Jasmine right before her head hit the table.

****

Tracy picked up her desk phone at Weitzman Regional Medical Center.

"Human Resources," she sang out cheerily. "This is Tracy."

"Tracy? Tracy Malone?"

"Yes? Can I help you?"

"This is Ben Bryant. Sorry to bother you at work but it was the only number I could find."

"Ben Bryant?" Tracy asked blankly.

"Jasmine's friend?"

Tracy was confused for a moment. Then it hit her. Her worlds were colliding. Work world was meeting online world.

"Oh! *Benjy?*"

"Well, yeah. I don't really go by Benjy anymore—except to

family and old—*really old*— friends."

"I'll try to remember that. What's going on? Is Jasmine all right?"

"That's debatable, isn't it? That's what I was calling about. She says you're the only one who knows about this alien thing and…"

"She told you about the alien thing?" Tracy interrupted. "Really?"

"Yeah."

"She told you about him hacking into our chat room and everything?"

"Yes. Once she came to after passing out in a bar."

"Oh, dear!"

"Is she serious about this, Tracy? Even though she was totally wasted when she told me, I got the feeling she really believes it. Does she?"

Tracy took a deep breath. "Honestly, I go back and forth on that, Benjy…I mean Ben. Sometimes I think she really believes he's an alien and sometimes I think she believes, as I do, that he's just some punk earthling."

"Well, she sure didn't say anything like that to me. She sounded like she was all in on this alien story."

"I suppose the important thing is…" Tracy paused and took a sip of coffee.

"Yes? Is what?"

"Uh…Ben, you really like her, right?"

"Like her? I love her. I've loved her all my life."

"That's why I don't want to say what I was going to say."

"Say it," Benjy ordered despite the sinking feeling in the pit of his stomach.

"I'm so sorry to say this but the important thing is she's in love with this guy no matter who he is. He promised like a year ago that he was coming from who knows where and he hasn't shown up. She's made herself sick waiting and worrying about it."

"Geez, I must be a bad boyfriend. I should have picked up on it more. I knew she seemed a little off, but until she got plastered last night and blurted out everything, I had no idea of the magnitude of the problem."

"Don't blame yourself. She was probably putting up a front when you two were together."

"Maybe. But what I wanted to discuss with you is—do you think she needs professional help?"

"Gosh, I don't know. There have been many times when I wondered if I should contact her parents…or even you. But I didn't want to make trouble for her. I mean I never could tell for sure if she actually believed in Alex or if she was just playing."

"And you played along I suppose?"

"Hey, no need to get snippy about it. I did the best I could."

"Sorry. I didn't mean to be rude. I'm just so worried. Not only about her mental health but about what this means for our so-called relationship."

"Not going so well, huh?" said Tracy sympathetically.

"No."

"I'm sorry. You seem like a nice guy."

"You know what they say about nice guys. Nice guys finish behind extra-terrestrials."

"Good one," Tracy laughed. "Who said you don't have a sense

of humor?"

"Did Jaz say I don't have a sense of humor?" Benjy asked apprehensively.

"Well…no. Not in so many words. You just seem very…*earnest.*"

"Is that bad?"

"Not at all."

"Thank you. So what do we do now? Should I tell her folks?"

"Let's give it a little more time, okay? It's not as if she's not functioning. She goes to work. She does her job well from what I can tell. She has you and her other friends. She has interests."

"You mean like that Korean drama fixation?"

"Of course. That's a rather major part of the alien obsession, isn't it?"

"It is?"

"You mean she didn't tell you that part?"

"What part?"

"Well…you see, when this potential alien comes to earth, he's supposed to look exactly like her favorite Korean actor."

Benjy groaned. "I'm almost afraid to ask—how did that happen?"

"It's like this. The supposed alien was not in humanoid form. He planned to morph into human form before he came here. He said he could come in any form we wanted, so we asked him to look like Jaz's idol. See? It's all perfectly logical." Tracy laughed despite the logic or lack thereof. "Actually, that part was my idea."

"*Why?*"

"I don't know. I guess I figured she was the one that was interested in him—might as well make him look like someone she could fall in love with."

"Thanks a lot."

"Benjy…I mean Ben, this was long before you two started dating."

"Okay. I see. I just don't understand why you were even participating in this farce. I thought you were sane and sensible. You are sounding strangely like you might have bought into this fantasy—at least a little bit."

"Maybe the teensiest, *teensiest* bit. The guy was very convincing in his own way. I think that's part of why Jaz is so crazy about him whether he's an alien or not. He's very clever and amusing and charming. I officially disagree with her when she uses those words, but actually he kind of is."

"Unlike me."

"Oh, Ben, I'm sure that's not true."

"I'm smart but I'm not clever."

They were both quiet for a moment, thinking.

"You guys weren't chatting with him for all that long as far as I can tell. How do you suppose she got so brainwashed so quickly?" Benjy asked at last.

"Who knows? Maybe it's some kind of cosmic connection."

"Cosmic? You sound more and more like Jaz every minute."

"Keep in mind—we don't know if Jaz totally buys into Alex as an alien. She just wants him to show up—human, alien or otherwise."

"Sounds like curtains for me."

"Ben, the only thing I know for sure is that I don't know anything for sure—and neither do you."

"I certainly don't. I've known Jaz all my life and she never seemed weird to me. Except maybe for that Korean obsession. Hell, I never even knew Korean drama was a thing."

"Oh, it's a thing all right. But, honestly, I never knew it either."

"Jaz never seemed weird. Do you think she's weird?"

"Would it matter?"

"No."

"There you go. Look, Ben, we're all weird in our own way, aren't we? People who think they're not weird are probably the weirdest of all. And what about you? In love with the same girl your whole life with virtually no encouragement. And me—unable to move because I can't leave my mom, who can't leave the house where she was happy with my father for so many years, and even resorted to dating middle-aged janitors. That is, me—not my mom. Not that there's anything wrong with middle-aged janitors."

"I'm sorry but those things are not quite in the same league as believing in aliens."

"They can mess up your life just as much—if not more."

"I guess."

"If it helps at all, I think Jaz is making a big mistake in passing you up. But who knows? It may work out yet."

"Thank you. And thanks for saying Jaz isn't weird. I just *knew* she wasn't."

"I'm not sure that's exactly what I said but okay."

"I suppose you'll tell Jaz I called."

"Probably."

"It's okay. It doesn't really matter, does it? Things can hardly get worse."

Chapter 14
Hump Day

On Wednesdays, Jasmine and her co-workers were in the habit of celebrating hump day with drinks and fattening foods at one of the many bars that lined Coastal Boulevard. Their favorite was a place called Snapper's Pub, which specialized in raw oysters, imported beers and deep-fried appetizers. Snapper's had a nice outdoor beer garden, but this day was cold and rainy.

The usual group sat inside at a big table in the center of the room—Missy, Geneva, Robbie, Karen, Todd, and Jasmine.

"You're awfully quiet, Jaz," said Karen. Her tone conveyed concern with just a touch, perhaps, of pity.

Jasmine made a visible effort to perk up. "Am I?" she said as brightly as she could. "It's not intentional." She smiled unconvincingly and took a sip of her martini.

"Leave Jaz alone," Geneva scolded.

While everyone else at the table, was under forty, Geneva was nearing retirement and had been with the bank for thirty years. This circumstance accorded her the unofficial, but undisputed, title of mother hen. She delicately selected a fried dill pickle from the giant appetizer sampler she had ordered for the table. "Grigsby was really on the warpath today, wasn't he? That man will be the death of me," she said, changing the subject.

"Grigsby," Todd groaned. "How did we get so lucky to have a boss like that?"

"He really sucks," Jasmine muttered almost inaudibly.

Missy, the intern, leaned over toward Jasmine. "Are you *crying?*"

Jasmine stood and gathered up her purse. She tossed a twenty onto the table. "Sorry, guys, I have to go. I just can't do this today." She paused just a moment while her friends bombarded her with questions and expressions of sympathy.

"What is it, Jaz?" Karen asked.

Jasmine's sniffles changed to outright sobs. "My snake is gone!" she blubbered as she turned and fled.

Robbie looked to Geneva for guidance. "Should we go after her…or what?"

"Just let her be," Geneva replied calmly. "Just let her cry it out. She'll be okay."

"Um…did she say her *snake* is gone?" Missy inquired.

"Yes," Geneva answered, stuffing a fried mushroom into her mouth.

"What the hell," said Todd. "Jaz has a pet snake? I never heard her mention it, and she definitely doesn't seem like the type."

"It wasn't a pet," said Geneva.

"Okay, Gen, stop with the cryptic remarks," Karen demanded. "You seem to know all about this. Spill."

"Geneva took a swig of her beer. "Well, okay. I don't think she'd mind if I told you. A few weeks ago, she went out to her car and there was a snake coiled up in her parking space at the condo. It was small like a garter snake or something.

"For some reason, she didn't think it looked poisonous. It wasn't in the way of her getting into the car, so she decided to let it be. She figured it would slither off somewhere, but when she got back it was still there. It had moved some—farther toward the front of the parking space. She still ignored it.

After that, every time she came out to her car or arrived home, it was still there—in slightly different locations, but still there. After a while, she started looking for it, expecting to see it. One time it had moved to the other side of the—what do you call that cement thingy in front of your car..."

"I don't know," said everyone in unison.

"I don't think they have a name," Todd declared.

"Of course they have a name," Karen retorted. "Everything has a name. What do you think they do when they have to order more of them? Call up and ask for a hundred thingies?"

Geneva cleared her throat loudly. "That's not really important to my story."

"Sorry," said Todd. "Go on."

"Anyhoo," Geneva continued, "she didn't see the snake right away and felt relieved when she found it behind the, you know, thingy. From then on, she developed a sort of attachment to it. She even contacted the condo management and asked them to tell the groundskeepers to be careful of it and not hurt it. She started to look on it as a sort of sign. Like if it was there, everything would be okay, you know?

"Still, she knew in her heart of hearts, the day would come when it would no longer be there. This went on for over a month. And then a few days ago when she got home from work, the snake was missing. She looked everywhere—all around the parking lot and all over the lawn. It was no use. For a while, she hoped it would come back. Maybe it was just off getting something to eat, but it never came back, and she finally accepted that it was never coming back."

"Well, that's a weird story," said Todd, chomping down on an enormous cheeseburger that the waitress had just delivered.

"So," Missy said, "if she thought the snake was a sign everything would be okay, its absence means everything is not okay. Right? And that's why she's so upset?"

"Partly that and, I think, partly she really felt attached to the snake. After all, it is—or was—a living creature."

"But Jaz never even had a dog or a goldfish as far as I know," Robbie observed. "She never had any great feeling for animals."

"What can I tell you?" Geneva replied. "Things change. People change. Besides, Jasmine's going through some stuff right now. I'm sure that's part of it, too."

"She has seemed bummed for a while," Missy agreed.

"A long while. What's up with that?" Karen asked. "And how do you know so much about Jaz?" Although Karen didn't particularly want to be close to Jaz, she was a little jealous. She tended to be jealous of other people's friendships in general.

133

"I don't know exactly. We always seem to be in the lunchroom at the same time. She tells me stuff. I think I'm kind of a motherly figure to her. You know she and her own mom have issues. I'm so much older than all of you babies as you never fail to remind me," Geneva laughed. "Jaz is kind of an old soul I think."

"Old soul?" said Missy.

"Yeah. You know how she likes old movies and old music—things like that. I don't know. There's just something about her, don't you think?"

Missy shrugged and stabbed a mozzarella stick with her fork. "I guess so. I never thought about it."

"In any case, she has not confided in me about whatever has been bothering her other than the snake situation. I can't help you there."

"Well, the whole thing is really odd," Karen said. "Jaz was always a bit of a flake, but I never thought she was actually nuts."

This comment was met with a protective chorus of, "She's not nuts! She's not a flake!"

"*But,*" Todd interrupted loudly, "I wonder if she knows snakes are phallic symbols."

"Oh, Todd," Geneva replied with a giggle. "I'm sure she does. Jaz was an English major."

Chapter 15
Arrival

He stood facing the Christmas window at Bloomingdale's, though it took him a moment to realize that the image reflected there was himself.

The shiny image was just under six feet tall. A shock of black wavy hair fell rakishly over his brow. He wore a black cotton v-neck sweater and black skinny pants.

Not realizing he was doing it nor even how to do it, he happened to move his left arm a bit. Only when the image moved accordingly, did he make the connection. He experimented with moving again—this time lifting his left foot from the pavement. His hypothesis was confirmed.

"It's you, isn't it! I mean you're him!"

Instinctively, he turned his head toward the source of this excited utterance, which had been delivered in a tone that was somehow both musical and jarring. The source—the woman—stood nearly as tall as he. Masses of light brown curls tumbled well past her shoulders. Sparkling green eyes shone from a delicately boned face.

"Well, aren't you him? I mean he."

"Who?" he asked, allowing the word to transfer from his brain to his mouth, noting the feel of it on his tongue and lips.

"Aren't you Kang Ji Soo? I'm a fan. A huge fan."

"No," he said. He spoke hesitantly, again testing the feel of the word in his mouth and having no idea whether he was that person or not.

"Really! Well, you look just like him." The woman cocked her head to the side and studied his face. "Hmm...now that I look more closely, I can see that you're not. There's a slight difference though I can't put my finger on it." She looked him up and down. "Where's your coat? And isn't it kind of cold for flip-flops?"

"I...I don't know," he said, looking down at his feet and noticing for the first time an unpleasant sensation which he guessed was this "cold" of which she spoke.

The woman held out her hand. "Chandler Davies," she said. "And you are?"

"I...I don't know."

Chandler dropped her hand to her side. "You don't know who you are?" She began to laugh but the laugh soon died on her lips as she realized he was absolutely serious. "Oh dear! You poor thing! You really don't know, do you?"

Brazenly—for she was after all Chandler Davies—she reached into the right-hand pocket of his fashionably snug pants. There was nothing there—not even a penny nor a bit of lint. She repeated the process on his left side while he stood quietly taking it all in, including all manner of unknown sensations.

"Nothing," she said. "That's odd. No wallet, no ID, no money. I wonder how you got here."

This was a good question. No one had seen the exact moment of his arrival. New Yorkers had been rushing by as usual, oblivious. Chandler had been admiring in the window a red velvet strapless cocktail dress she hoped to wear on New Year's Eve. Daddy would have to spring for it. She'd already spent this month's very generous allowance. And so no one had noticed when the man who resembled Kang Ji Soo had simply appeared—materialized out of thin air without even a sound.

"Well," said Chandler, grabbing his arm, "let's get you inside. You must be freezing. There's a coffee shop just across the street."

Still holding onto his arm, she jaywalked him to the opposite curb and into the little café.

"So…" she said once they were settled into a booth, "what'll it be?" She picked up a menu. "Coffee, tea, hot chocolate?"

"Hot chocolate," he repeated slowly, intently.

"Would you like something to eat? I'll bet you're hungry, aren't you? Should we get eggs or something? Or just a Danish?"

"I don't know. You choose."

"Then I choose Danish. You know me and my sweet tooth."

"Do I?"

"Sorry. That was rhetorical. Of course, you don't know me at all." She paused to give their order to the waitress. "So…" she went on, "getting back to you—say something."

"What should I say?" Saying stuff was pretty new. How should he know what to say?

"Anything. Tell me about yourself."

"I don't know anything about myself. I don't know anything."

"But you know facts—like who's the president and what year it is and how to do math, right?"

He quickly flipped through his mental files. All of that information was there. "Yes," he said.

"Hmm…apparently you have some sort of selective amnesia. Unless, of course, you're putting me on. You're not, are you?"

"No."

"I once played an amnesiac on *Days of Our Lives*. It was just a short-term gig, but I am something of an expert."

"What?"

"Oh, I forgot to say I'm an actor."

"Ah."

"Anyway, I wanted you to say something because I thought I detected a trace of an accent earlier, and I was right. It's very slight but it's there. Unfortunately, I can't place it—which is odd because I've worked with dialect coaches for years. A couple of years ago, I played a Russian hooker on an episode of *Law and Order*. But I digress. Your accent is unplaceable."

Chandler's thoughts were interrupted by the arrival of the hot chocolate and almond Danish. She took a sip, and her companion followed suit. He let out a little yelp as the steaming cocoa touched his lips and tongue.

"Oh, sorry!" she cried. "It's hot, isn't it?

"Hot," he repeated, carefully setting the cup back in its saucer.

"Let it cool while you try the Danish," Chandler suggested

helpfully.

After the cocoa incident, he tasted the pastry cautiously. At once, a buttery sweetness exploded in his mouth. He became aware of a connection between this sensation and the creeping hollowness he had noticed in his stomach. Without further ado, he stuffed the entire remaining pastry into his mouth and promptly began to choke and struggle for air.

Chandler handed him a glass of water. "Geez! Here, take a drink!"

He sipped the water until he got control of himself.

"You must have been hungry," Chandler exclaimed. "Should I order something else? Eggs? A sandwich?"

The man pointed at the empty pastry plate. "More," he said.

Chandler shrugged and beckoned to the waitress. "Another almond Danish here, please."

She sat quietly then—just watching—while he ate the second Danish a little more slowly and drank the hot chocolate.

At last she spoke, regarding him through narrowed eyes. "Are you sure this isn't a con?"

"A con?" he asked, looking confused. "I don't think so."

Chandler's expression softened. "You know, in my line of work, you learn to read people pretty well. Your eyes are so innocent that I actually believe you."

"Yes," he said.

"I've been sitting here trying to put it all together—logically— though logic was never my strong suit."

"Yes," he said again since no other word came to mind.

"So here's what we have. You have arrived in New York City,

wearing clothes that are inappropriate for the weather, with no money and no ID. You seem to be Korean since you look almost identical to a very famous Korean movie star. You have a very slight accent, though it's definitely not a Korean accent nor any other accent that I can identify."

"Have you completed your logical analysis?" he asked after waiting patiently for several minutes.

"As best I can. The only thing I can come up with is that you are an illegal alien. Oh! No offense. That's not the politically correct term, is it? Um…undocumented immigrant?"

"Okay."

"Okay. How's this for a theory? You are of Korean heritage but you were raised somewhere else—thus the accent. Maybe somewhere in South America or the Caribbean—somewhere warm. That might explain your clothing. So you embarked on a journey to the States, maybe intending to enter—excuse the expression—illegally—or maybe not. Somewhere along the way, someone attacked you and stole whatever possessions you had. In the course of said attack, the robber bopped you on the head and *voila,* amnesia!…Well?

"What?"

"How's that for creating a backstory?"

"Is this another expertise of yours?"

"Actually, it is. I'm pretty good, aren't I?"

"Yes. Good."

"I never realized how useful all those acting classes would be in real life—though this situation doesn't seem exactly like real life. I don't suppose any of that rang a bell?"

"Any of what?"

"The backstory."

"Bell?"

"Did any of it remind you of anything?"

"No."

"Oh, well. I took a shot."

"Only one word today has reminded me of anything."

"Really!" Sensing a breakthrough, Chandler leaned forward expectantly. "What was it?"

"Chocolate."

Chapter 16
Omens

No matter how many times Jasmine crossed the causeway—and it seemed like millions—the drive never failed to stir her heart. Even on the hottest day, she would put down the car windows and feel the gulf breeze on her face and smell the salt air. Carried on that breeze, a rush of memories would come.

When she was a child, her father would open the sunroof and stick his hand out. "Ah!" he would say. "Just feel that breeze. Just smell that salt air. Nothing like it." He would half turn toward Jasmine in the backseat. "Know what that means, baby girl?" he would ask.

"It means home!" Jasmine would crow out the phrase she knew he expected, and she would giggle giddily at her own cleverness. She would raise her own small hand toward the roof though she couldn't begin to reach the opening. Her answer might have been carefully learned and rehearsed, but that didn't make it any less true. It *was* home.

She guessed tourists crossing the bridge felt differently. There was the excitement of starting out on holiday. Or the anticipation of discovering a new place. Or the nostalgia of returning to a long beloved vacation spot. This was completely different.

On this Saturday afternoon, Jasmine was on her way back from Tampa where she had met some old high school friends for lunch. All of them lived in the city now, having moved for jobs or husbands or boyfriends. Jasmine was the only one of the group who had remained on the island. She was certain that no man or job would ever be worth leaving Malaga Island. Even if Alex were to come through, she would have to make him stay here somehow.

Stop! she told herself. Lately she had been making a real effort to think more of Benjy and less of Alex. She buzzed the sunroof open and reached her hand toward the sky. She was home. Everything would be okay.

When she got to the end of the causeway, she turned onto the boulevard and traveled the few miles to her condo. She pulled into her parking space and got out of the car. After a couple of steps toward the building, she stopped in her tracks. It had been a while since she had looked for her snake. When it first disappeared, she had looked for it every day with a growing feeling of dread as each day it did not reappear. Finally, she had given up looking for it or expecting to see it. Today something made her stop. Maybe it was the good feeling still lingering from the bracing drive over the causeway. It was a sign. It couldn't hurt to look one more time. She scanned the ground along the driver's side of the car. Finding nothing there, she walked around to the rear and along the passenger side to the front. Still nothing. Only one more spot to check. Holding her breath, she peered over the concrete parking block. Her eyes widened and her exhaled breath caught in her throat. There he was, curled up peacefully next to the block, warming himself in the sun. She felt inordinately happy. At least, her joy would seem inordinate to the average person she supposed. She was well aware that certain people had doubts about her sanity, and sometimes she doubted it herself.

She guessed there was a chance that this was a different snake, but something about the way he occupied that customary spot next to the parking block convinced her that this was indeed her snake.

Still, even in this moment, she knew the day would come when he really would be gone for good. A line of poetry came to mind. Even in our joy sits the seed of "most unwelcome this," she paraphrased Millay in her head. She couldn't recall it verbatim. It simply meant that encased in every joy is the fear of losing the source of that joy. Not just the fear but the certain knowledge of losing it.

She sighed and whispered good-bye to the snake and told him she hoped to see him tomorrow.

Inside her apartment, she flopped onto the couch and wondered what the hell was wrong with her. Why had the serenity she'd felt crossing the bridge dissipated so quickly? Her snake was back. She should be happy. She had told herself that his presence was a good omen. Why did she always allow the fear of loss to taint her happiness? The causeway was here today. The snake was here today. Today was all she had, and today was good.

144

She smiled and wondered what Benjy was up to and whether he would want to go out for a coffee. She picked up her phone and punched in his number.

Chapter 17
Alone on the Beach at Midnight

Jasmine had walked this stretch of beach hundreds of times in her life, from earliest childhood until now. At this hour— the midnight hour—it was deserted. Even the usual straggling tourists returning from the bars had found their way back to their hotel rooms. The inky blue of the water was so like the color of the sky that the horizon was invisible as if it were all one. The surface of the gulf was calm, broken only by the occasional ripple that glowed white in the light of a slender crescent moon riding low in the sky. The water lapped lazily against the shore with a soothing sound like a lullaby she'd known since birth. The persistent gulf winds whipped her auburn curls against her cheeks. She clutched her windbreaker closer around her against a sudden chill in the air.

The sky was dense with stars—so dense that in places their perimeters seemed to touch and blur into one another.

As she approached the Malaga Manor Hotel—or, as the locals called it, "the big hotel," the strains of karaoke night at the beach bar wafted down to her and mingled with the lapping sound of the water. She remembered that this was Saturday night and karaoke would go on until two. Its intrusion into the peace and quiet might have been annoying. It wasn't. Karaoke at the Malaga was as much a component of everything familiar—everything home—as the starlit sky and the sound of the surf.

She had walked all the way past the big hotel, past the little pink motel, past the Sea Breeze Bistro with its deck that jutted out over the beach, when she saw him.

Because of the curve of the shoreline, the background was nothing but stars and sky and dark blue water. He emerged from the darkness as if formed from starshine. He was approaching her slowly, a good hundred yards down the beach. At once, she recognized the shambling, diffident gait, the slim body and slightly bowed legs, the head cocked to one side. As he came close, there was the sheen of black hair, the flash of dark eyes, the skin smooth as ivory.

She stopped still in her tracks and waited, wondering if he would meet her where she stood or evaporate into the atmosphere. But he continued steadily forward until he was inches away and seemed to recognize her. The corners of his lips pulled upward in the beginnings of a smile. His eyes locked on hers with utter familiarity and ease. He remained silent, and she wondered if he had forgotten all the English he had learned. For her part, she was too stunned to speak.

And then he kissed her. He took her face in both his hands

and kissed her.

****

Jasmine sat straight up in bed. What the hell was that? she thought. For the first time since Alex had disappeared from the chat room, she felt good. No, *euphoric*. It was if an all-enveloping cloud of well-being had settled upon her. She glanced about her bedroom. Everything was exactly the same. How could that be when the whole world had changed?

The first thing she wanted to do was call Tracy. She looked at the clock on her nightstand. 7:35 it read. In California, it was only 4:35. She couldn't possibly call Tracy at this hour. She settled on a text. Tracy would see it first thing when she woke up and would call back.

Jasmine pulled the covers up to her chin. Thank goodness it was Sunday. She wouldn't have to worry about work.

Barely half an hour later, the phone rang.

"Tracy. You called already? I was just hoping you'd see the text once you got up—like *hours* from now."

"I was having trouble sleeping and got up to go to the bathroom. I figured it must be important if you were wanting a callback. What's up?"

"Tracy! I had the most incredible dream last night. Incredible and lovely and so *real*. I know, I know. Everybody always says it was so real. But this really was."

"Yeah?"

"Huh? Why do you sound funny?"

"Because the same thing happened to me. That's why I couldn't sleep."

"Well, that's weird. What did you dream?"

"You first."

Jasmine described it all in detail—the beach, the stars, the kiss, the feeling of euphoria that still deliciously engulfed her.

When she finished her story, there was a long silence.

"Tracy? Are you there?"

"Uh…yeah. Sure."

"Why so quiet?"

"Well…because my dream was exactly like yours—except the beach was here in California and, of course, I was the girl."

"What! You dreamed about Alex?"

"Alex or Ji Soo or someone who looked just like him."

"Why would you be dreaming about my crush?"

"I have no idea. We can't control our dreams, can we?"

"But doesn't this indicate some deep-seated feelings on your part?" Jasmine asked, a note of trepidation creeping into her voice.

"Absolutely not. Alex or Ji Soo or whoever—that's your thing, not mine. You know, not every dream means something. Sometimes you're just processing the massive amounts of information that have bombarded your brain all day. If anything, this means that you are overloading me with your constant yammering on about this guy."

"Well, *excuse* me."

"Jaz, I'm sorry. You know I didn't mean anything. I know you're genuinely upset about what happened—or what didn't happen with Alex. I'm more than happy to be your sounding board.

Just don't project your emotional life onto me, okay?"

"Okay," Jasmine pouted.

"That's better."

"So…it really was like the same dream? He kissed you and everything?"

"Yeah."

"Well, I'm still sitting here with that overwhelming sense of joy flooding my entire being. Are you?"

"*Hell,* no. I didn't have it in the first place, and I certainly don't have it now. Why would I? I'm not attracted to that guy."

"Oh. Okay. Really weird that we had the same dream though, isn't it?"

"Yeah. I guess it is."

"Could be some kind of omen."

"An omen of what?"

"I don't know. Something about Alex I suppose."

"You never believed in omens before."

Jasmine realized she had never told Tracy about the snake. She would—some other time. "I know," she said, "but when you're already in the realm of stars and aliens and such, omens are sort of a given, aren't they? In any case, I still think this is extremely strange."

She continued after a long pause. "You're awfully quiet. I guess you want to get back to sleep."

"Well, yeah. It's five A.M. here."

"Sorry. I'll let you go then."

"See you Friday in chat?"

"Sure."

****

Tracy set her phone down on the nightstand. She wondered how she would be able to get back to sleep. She felt guilty for having lied about the giddiness that she could still feel from the top of her head to her stomach to the tips of her toes.

She went back to bed and dozed uneasily until eight o'clock. She didn't know whether she felt more exhilarated or worn out. Either way, she dragged herself out of bed and took her mother to church and then to brunch at Millie's Diner downtown—best pancakes in the county.

Back home, she got her mother settled in front of a Lifetime movie and retired to her bedroom. She propped two pillows against the headboard and sat resting against them, staring at the widescreen TV she had splurged on for her room. The remote lay next to her hand. She tried to ignore the fact that her fingers were fairly itching to pick it up. Finally, unable to resist, she grabbed the remote and selected Hulu. What the heck were the names of those Korean TV shows that Jaz was always raving about? Surely some of them had stuck in her brain. She was just about to resort to Google when random browsing bore fruit.

There it was: Kang Ji Soo in *Doomed Love Affair*. She clicked on it and began to watch. She felt nervous and almost afraid to see him. When he appeared in that first shot, looking like a teenager in his horn-rimmed glasses and too much lip gloss, her breath caught disturbingly in her throat. She picked up the remote and powered it off. She leapt off the bed as if it were on fire and fled from the room.

Chapter 18
Chandler and Her Alien

Chandler Davies was in a quandary. What to do with a beautiful alien who just happened to be a dead ringer for her favorite Korean actor—one who more than once had been the object of her fantasies. She tried to weigh the options as analytically as she had postulated his history.

If she turned him over to the authorities, what could possibly happen? They could advertise to see if there were friends or relatives who might recognize him—but how likely was that to yield results?

They could deport him—but to where? There was no way to determine his country of origin—not to mention the fact that he would know no one when he got there. Or…they could imprison him or, maybe worse, put him in some mental hospital where he would spend his days drugged up while his exquisite face grew haggard and gray—*and* the wardrobe would be hideous. She could go to her father for help and advice. Daddy was the sort of man who always knew what to do. But what if his protective dad mode kicked in and he decided to turn the alien in?

Or…she could keep him. Keep him! What a tempting proposition.

But then how would he live? How would he work without a Social Security number? She considered briefly whether her father knew anyone who made fake ID's—but, no, Daddy would never agree to that.

How could her alien drive or get insurance—or *anything?* The two of them would be looking over their shoulders for the rest of their lives, wouldn't they? And what if he didn't like her? She had been half in love with him by the time he finished his cocoa, but there was nothing in his words or manner that suggested he felt the same. What if he never felt the same? Then what would she do with him?

At this very moment, he was sleeping in the guest room of her upper East Side apartment, which was walking distance to the park and even had a sliver of a view of the river. Her father, CEO and majority stockholder of Davies Tech Industries, paid the rent as well as most of her living expenses.

She hadn't heard from her agent in weeks and had done nothing but the occasional commercial voice-over for the past year. Her father would have been happy to provide an even grander apartment or have her move back into the family home in Connecticut, but a girl had to maintain some small measure of dignity, didn't she?

She crept over to the guest room door and pushed it open a

crack. How angelic her alien looked sleeping deeply, his breathing slow and rhythmic. How could anyone look so much like the heartthrob of Asia—and yet not?

After their conversation at the coffee shop, she had taken him back across the street to Bloomingdale's and bought him proper shoes and socks, a change of underwear and a winter jacket. Once in the apartment, he had fallen awkwardly onto the bed as if he'd never slept on one before. He must not have slept in a while because his eyes had closed immediately and he had fallen into an intensely sound sleep more quickly than any human she'd ever seen.

She made her way over to the bed and gently laid a comforter over him.

****

The young man woke up in a strange place. But then every place was strange, and he didn't know why. He looked about the room. There was a digital clock on the nightstand. It read 6:30 A.M.

Across the room, a walnut dresser held a small television set, its cable box display panel glowing white in the semi-darkness. The dresser featured curving lines and graceful carvings. He recognized the style as French—Louis XVI he believed. How did he know this and yet not know his own name he wondered.

There was a vanity in the same style. The walls were painted a pale sage green. Heavy damask drapes covered the windows. He ran his hand over the comforter that covered him. The database

154

in his head made some quick calculations and correlations. This must be what smooth means, he thought. All the facts were in his head, but every sensation was new. Even Chandler's perfectly logical thesis of amnesia could not explain this phenomenon.

The comforter's ecru background was scattered with embroidered sprigs of green and white flowers. The white cotton pillowcase beneath his head was smooth and fragrant. He lifted the covers and saw that he was still wearing the same clothes he'd had on the day before. He saw his gray flip-flops on the floor next to the bed.

Just as he had figured out earlier the connection between the hollowness in his stomach and the need to eat, he now recognized the need to use the bathroom. He knew how to go about it. It was only the sensation that was new. There were three doors in the room. He hoped one led to a bathroom. He got out of bed to investigate.

The first door opened to a walk-in closet filled with dresses, coats, hats and especially shoes—pair after pair of shoes lined up on narrow shelves. He closed the closet and tried another door. Mercifully, there was a bathroom behind it. He used the facilities pretty skillfully—considering. He splashed his face with water from the tap and dried it with a pink, lace-trimmed towel.

Back in the bedroom, he surmised that the third door led to the hallway and the rest of the apartment. He vaguely remembered it though he been in a daze when he had first entered it. He remembered Chandler giving him something to eat. He remembered sitting on a suede sofa and feeling exhausted. "Exhausted." That had been Chandler's word for how he looked. He guessed she was right. She had led him to this room, and he had fallen onto the bed—exhausted.

He opened the door and went out to the living room. All was still except for the street noise coming through the French doors. There was no sign of Chandler. He assumed she was here somewhere. He sat down on the couch and waited.

Chandler checked the clock next to her bed. 6:30 A.M. She couldn't remember the last time she had been awake at this hour. Probably sometime when she had to be in hair and makeup early. It had been a while since she'd had a job like that to go to. She had barely slept last night so aware was she of the presence of the man in the guest room. She felt that he was awake now.

The glow of his dark eyes seemed to penetrate the semi-darkness all the way from his room to where she lay in her bed. In a few moments, she heard water running in the guest bathroom. She guessed she should get up and see if he needed anything. She should make breakfast. She should make him feel comfortable. Instead, she felt paralyzed. For the first time in her life, Chandler Davies felt shy.

Chapter 19
It's Complicated

On a Thursday morning just after breakfast, when the undoc-umented alien had been there only a little more than a week, there was a knock at the door. Chandler came running from the bath-room, where she had been primping for an audition. The young man had been on the sofa, absently leafing through a copy of *Elle*. He was now staring at the door from whence the strange noise was coming.

Chandler put her finger to her lips. "Quiet!" she whispered. "Don't say a word."

"Why?" he whispered back.

"Shhh!"

The knocking only increased in volume, and before long a feminine voice called through the door. "Chandler! Open up! I know you're in there. You never go anywhere before ten o'clock!"

Chandler sat down next to the alien and whispered in his ear.

"Damn. It's Claire—my upstairs neighbor. She loves to just drop in."

"Why are we whispering?"

"I don't want a bunch of questions about you. Maybe you could go hide in the other room."

"Why?"

"Just because. Would you shut up!"

Claire's shouts got louder. "Chandler! Open up! I have great news!"

"She's not going away," the alien whispered. "We're going to have to face her sometime. How long are we going to hide?"

Chandler sighed and threw up her hands. "Oh, all right. Just don't say anything if you don't have to. Got it?"

"Yes."

"Coming!" she yelled.

"Geesh," said Claire once the door was thrown open. "Where the hell were you? I've been screaming out here for hours."

"Less than two minutes," Chandler corrected. "Sorry, I was in the bathroom. Come on in."

Claire stepped into the living room. She was tall and very blonde, with features that were perhaps too perfect. A nose that was just a tad too small suggested plastic surgery might have been involved. "Okay, I apologize for barging in, but I have just the best news. I couldn't wait…" She paused there, having just noticed the man on the couch. "Oh! I'm sorry. I thought you were alone. Who…?"

"Uh…Claire. I'd like you to meet a friend of mine, Jesse"—a name Chandler had assigned the alien just because she liked it.

"Jesse, this is Claire. She lives upstairs. She's an actor, too."

Jesse stood up and held out his hand. "It's nice to meet you, Claire."

"You must be an actor," said Claire, taking his hand. "You look like an actor."

"No. I'm not." Jesse finished shaking hands and resumed his seat on the sofa.

"So!" Chandler interjected more loudly than necessary. "What's the big news?"

"Oh, yeah. Sorry. I got distracted by the sight of an unfamiliar man in your apartment so early in the morning." She smiled slyly. "If you know what I mean."

"I know what you mean, and it's not like that. "The *news?*"

"Yes! The news. Hold onto your hat. Jonathan's play is being produced. Woo-hoo!" Claire's feet actually came off the ground in a little jump of exuberance.

"Really? That's wonderful," Chandler exclaimed, giving Claire a genuine hug. "How exciting." She turned toward Jesse. "Jonathan is Claire's boyfriend. He's a playwright."

"Yes, and it's in a real actual theater—off Broadway—really far off Broadway, but still. And there's a part for me—of course!"

"Of course," Chandler laughed.

"Hey, I don't even know why I didn't think of this before, but there might be something for you. There are a few female roles. Not much pay, but it's exposure."

"Actually..." Chandler sneaked an anxious peek at Jesse. "I don't think this is a good time for me to take anything on. But thanks for thinking of me."

"Ah. The new man in your life taking all your attention, huh?"

"I told you it's not like that. Jesse is from out of town and didn't have a place to stay, so I offered him my guest room for a few days."

"Cool. I'm not sure I believe that, but cool. How did you guys meet?"

"Oh, just the usual way," said Chandler vaguely.

"You mean like in a bar? You met a complete stranger in a bar and invited him to stay here?" Claire glanced at Jesse. "No offense."

"Of course," said Jesse.

"I never said it was in a bar. Look, Claire, I hate to rush you off, but I have an audition to get to"

"Audition? You just said you weren't up for a gig right now."

"W-well," said Chandler, beginning to stammer. "You know how auditions are. I won't get it. And I had it scheduled a while ago."

"I see…I think."

"I really have to finish my makeup. Let's do lunch one day soon, okay?" Chandler practically pushed Claire toward the door.

"All right, all right! I'm going. Nice meeting you, Jesse. Hope to see you again," Claire called over her shoulder just before Chandler slammed the door behind her.

"Well, that went well." Chandler collapsed onto the couch next to Jesse.

"I didn't think so," Jesse replied.

Chandler had noticed that his ability to discern sarcasm was lacking. "I was joking."

Jesse crinkled his brow. The wheels were turning as he made a mental note on the subject. "I see."

"See. This is why I didn't want Claire in here. She's a pathological snoop. I knew she wouldn't just accept any explanation. I made so many mistakes just then. The audition thing. Not having a good story about how we met. Well, I could go on. You were here. You saw it."

"Are you kicking me out in a few days? How will you explain that I'm still here if she sees me in the future?"

"Of course, I'm not kicking you out."

****

Claire's visit might have been no more than a tiny paint stroke on the canvas of Chandler's life, except that it drove home to both her and Jesse that they needed to concoct a good story and learn to keep that story straight. Chandler would not be able to keep Jesse confined to her apartment forever. He would have to go out into the world sometime, meet her friends and interact with the public. They needed a story that was plausible and that would not call him to the attention of immigration services, for Chandler had somehow decided that her concocted backstory might actually be true.

She gave a great deal of thought to the story. It was complicated. By the time she was finished, she had convinced herself that if this acting thing continued not to pan out, she would make a terrific writer.

When she had it all worked out, she sat Jesse down to explain it. If she had observed anything about Jesse, it was that he was brilliant. She had no doubt that once he heard the story, it would be totally and permanently committed to his memory. He might not remember his past, but he had not forgotten one single thing he had learned since his arrival in New York.

"So," she began, "here's the plan. First, never volunteer any information. That goes without saying. But if asked, your story is as follows. We will keep the amnesia angle, which besides being true, will come in handy whenever you're not sure of something. But the amnesia happened after you arrived here and after you met me. How would I or anyone else know your background if not from hearing it from you? We'll say you were mugged and hit over the head with a blunt instrument. But before that, you had already told me your life story…"

"Which is what?" Jesse wanted to know.

"Okay, listen to this masterpiece." Chandler took a deep breath and looked decidedly pleased with herself. "You were born in Korea but were abandoned as an infant. You lived in an orphanage until the age of three when you were adopted by a Brazilian couple who named you Carlos Pereira. That's just off the top of my head. You can choose something else if you like. Just google Portuguese names. Anyway, you grew up in Rio, but your parents died a couple of years ago in a car accident. It turns out they were deeply in debt and left you nothing. So you decided to try to emigrate to the states. I'll tell my friends that my father is trying to pull some strings to get you a green card."

"And what will you tell your father? He will know he is not getting me a green card."

Chandler brushed the question aside with a wave of her hand. "Hopefully not every person will ask every question."

Jesse looked doubtful. He had already heard chapter and verse about the limitless acumen and thoroughness of the powerful businessman Justin Davies.

"Okay. Forget the green card for now," said Chandler, noting Carlos's expression.

He motioned for Chandler to continue her presentation.

"You do see the reasoning for each aspect of the story?"

"Yes, I believe so. The combination of Korean and Brazilian background is to explain both my looks and my vague and unplaceable accent. The dead parents mean I have no ties and their poverty explains why I have nothing."

"And the amnesia?"

"As you said, if anyone asks something I can't answer, I blame it on the bump on the head I received from some anonymous mugger."

"Exactly. But keep in mind, you don't actually remember most of the stuff about your past and childhood. You know it only from my repeating back to you what you had told me pre-bump. Got it?"

"It seems a lot more complicated than necessary, but okay. I do have a couple of questions though."

"Sure."

"What was I doing in Brazil for the past few years? I appear to be around thirty years old. I must have been working at something."

"It doesn't matter. Don't you see? That's the beauty part. You just don't remember—unless, of course, you want to invent something."

"But isn't that something I would have told you before losing my memory?"

"Oh, my God. This is getting too complicated even for me. You're a smart guy. Just play it by ear, okay?"

"Excuse me. You were the one who said the story had to be logical."

"I just think the more details we keep adding, the harder it will be to keep our stories straight. When in doubt, always fall back on the amnesia excuse and let me do the talking."

"I will have no trouble keeping the story straight. You only need to worry about yourself."

"You're absolutely right," Chandler laughed.

"By the way, how should we say we met?"

"Let's keep it simple. We'll tell it pretty much like it happened. We were looking in the window at Bloomingdale's. I thought you were Kang Ji Soo and struck up a conversation, and the rest is history."

"Okay."

"What about the name—Carlos Pereira? Would you like to change it?"

"To be honest, none of it means anything to me so I might as well keep it."

Chandler bristled a little. "You want to stay safe, don't you? You don't want to be shipped overseas to some random country or sent to an institution or to prison, do you?"

"No, I'm sorry, Chandler. I didn't mean to sound ungrateful.

I appreciate all you've done for me. It's just that life is very confusing."

"Ain't that the truth?" Chandler got up and stretched. "I suppose I should start calling you Carlos around the house so I don't forget when we're out."

Jesse/Carlos shrugged. He had hardly gotten attached to "Jesse" yet. "May I ask a question?" he said.

"Sure."

"Why not just tell the truth? Exactly as it happened."

"The truth!" Chandler laughed derisively. "Who in the world would ever believe *that?*"

Chapter 20
Christmas

When Christmas was only two days away, Chandler approached Carlos, who was sitting in the armchair reading something on her Kindle. "Whatcha readin'?" She peered over his shoulder. "Astrophysics? My goodness. I don't know what you were doing in your previous life, but it must have been extraordinary."

"I don't know." He looked up at her briefly before returning to his book.

"Of course, you don't. Listen, can you put that down for a sec?" She gently removed the tablet from his hands. "I want to talk to you. I'm not sure how you're going to feel about this, but I have to go to my parents' house for Christmas. Believe me, if I don't go, it will cause far more questions than it's worth."

"Okay."

"You could go with me," she said tentatively.

"Speaking of causing more questions than it's worth."

"Good point."

"To tell you the truth, I don't really feel like acting out some elaborate lie to your parents. I'd probably screw it up."

"We both would."

"A whole day with your family sounds very nerve-wracking."

"*Two* days. I have to go up for Christmas Eve and come back late Christmas Day. I really hate to leave you here alone for that long."

"I don't think your father would approve of my living here after such a short acquaintance."

"We wouldn't have to mention that you're living here."

"And the lie gets more elaborate and more difficult to keep straight later on."

"If you stay here a while…hopefully a long while…I hope you don't mind my saying that…we'll have to tell him our cover story eventually."

"But not now."

"No. You're right. Not now. So…will you be okay here by yourself? I'll make sure the fridge is stocked up. You can read and watch movies and play video games. If you need me or there's an emergency, you can call my cell. I'm going to have to get you your own phone one of these days, but you can call from my landline." She nodded in the direction of the phone on the desk. "Okay?"

"Sure." He took the Kindle back from her and began to read.

"If it's a true emergency—I mean like the building's on fire—call 911. You know about that, right?"

"Of course." He looked up and rewarded her for the tiniest

moment with his rare but irresistible smile. "Don't worry. I'll be fine."

She left him to his reading and retired to her room.

****

On the afternoon of the twenty-fourth, Chandler paused at the door and set her overnight bag on the floor.

"Now, you have everything you need, right? You remember all the instructions…what am I saying?…of course, you do."

"I do."

Chandler surveyed the room wistfully. "I'm sorry there's no tree. I never get one since it's just me, and I always spend the holiday at home. Unless you count that…" She pointed at a small ceramic tree on the credenza.

"It doesn't matter," he said.

"I suppose you don't remember celebrating Christmas."

"Exactly. So it's no great loss. But," he added quickly, having noted a trace of disappointment cross her face, "the little tree is very pretty."

"Look!" she exclaimed, brightening a bit. "The star on the top lights up." She flicked the switch and the star shone warm and yellow. "It'll be prettier at night. *And* it plays music." She turned the tree upside down and wound the key. Strains of "White Christmas" tinkled forth delicately like the twinkling of a star. "I've had this ever since I was a child." She looked at Carlos and blushed. "Silly, isn't it?"

Carlos grinned. "I don't know much about such things, but it doesn't seem silly to me."

"*Thank* you." Chandler's eyes were misting up, so she grabbed her bag and opened the door. "Merry Christmas!" she called over her shoulder. And she was gone.

The last note of "White Christmas" faded into the air just as the door closed.

Deliberately, Carlos stood up and walked over to the credenza. With great care, he picked up the tree and wound the key.

****

Meanwhile on Malaga Island, Jasmine stepped out onto her parents' patio and punched Tracy's number into her phone.

"Hey, Jaz! Merry Christmas!" Tracy shouted over a lot of background noise.

"You too. Christmas Eve with the family?"

"What was your first clue? The tortured sounds of the asylum? That's what six siblings and an infinite number of nieces and nephews on a Christmas high will do for you. Hold on. I'm going out on the porch." The screen door clattered shut behind her.

"I'm on the patio at Mom and Dad's," Jasmine continued. "I guess we're both pretty lucky to live in places where you can be outside in December. Did you see the news? Big snowstorms up north."

"Yeah…but…"

"But what?"

"I don't know. Might be kind of cool to have snow on Christmas. Do you know I've hardly ever seen snow?"

"We used to go skiing now and then when I was a kid."

"So you're with your parents for Christmas Eve? Anyone else there? And by anyone I mean Benjy."

"No. Thankfully they went to see his grandma in Michigan. It's just us. Mom and Dad, my aunt and uncle, and married cousin and her perfect husband."

"Are you saying perfect sarcastically?"

"No, I mean it. He's literally perfect," Jasmine groaned. "So annoying. I was so bored I came out here to call you."

"I'm not sure but I think I've just been insulted," Tracy laughed.

"You know I didn't mean it that way. What I meant is we don't talk on the phone that much. It seems like we have to have a good excuse to make a phone call."

"We should probably change that."

"Let's make that our New Year's resolution, okay?"

"Along with not thinking or talking about Alex anymore?"

"You said it. I didn't. I wonder what he's doing right now?"

"So much for not talking about him."

"It's not the new year yet."

"I hate to admit it but I kind of wonder too."

"I just hope he's okay."

"Me too."

Jasmine sighed loudly.

"What was that for?"

Jasmine laughed. "Don't worry. It wasn't about Alex. I was just admiring Mom's tree. It looks beautiful through the patio doors. You know she and I do butt heads a lot, but I have to admit she does Christmas up right. There's a new angel on top of the tree. She and dad picked it up in Europe on their last trip. It's really exquisite. So delicate and sparkly."

"Sounds lovely. We do stars. We've had the same one as long as I can remember. It wouldn't be Christmas without it."

"That's sweet."

"Are you being snarky?"

"Not at all. I really mean it. Sometimes I wish our house was full of kids and…well...*noise*."

"Careful what you wish for."

"Oh! They're calling me to come inside. Must be time for pie."

"Well, run on in then. Can't miss pie. You have a merry Christmas and I'll see you next week in chat. And don't worry about Alex or anything. It will all work out."

"Promise?"

"Promise. Night, Jaz."

"Night. And Merry Christmas!"

Tracy slipped her phone into her pocket and went inside. The living room was unnaturally quiet. The adults were playing board games in the dining room, and the kids were running amok in the basement. Tracy stood contemplating that old star on the top of the tree.

It was looking a little ragged around the edges, but the light inside it still worked and it glowed yellowish white in the duskiness. She narrowed her eyes to make golden streamers shoot out from it just as she had done as a child. She was certain Jaz's fancy European angel could not possibly be any more beautiful.

She guessed it was okay to wish on a Christmas tree star. She closed her eyes and wished she would meet someone nice. She wished Jasmine would be happy. She wished her mother would find peace. And she even wished Alex was someplace safe and warm.

****

Carlos heated up the pasta Chandler had made and stored in the fridge for him. He ate it with a slice of French bread and a glass of Cabernet.

After dinner, he watched *It's a Wonderful Life* on TV just to see what all the fuss was about. He found it interesting and instructive, though he doubted any Americans actually behaved that way anymore—if they ever had. Even as he had these thoughts, he had no idea how he knew how Americans behaved.

When the movie was over, he sat wondering what to do next. It was awfully quiet without Chandler, who always seemed to have something to say. His gaze fell on the little Christmas tree. He went over to the credenza, switched on the star and turned the key.

The gentle, chiming notes were magnified in the silence and echoed off the walls. The music seemed so loud that he wondered if the neighbors could hear it. He allowed it to wind down and fade away.

Seated on the sofa once more, he gazed, mesmerized, at the little yellow star glowing in the semi-darkness—until something he saw out of the corner of his eye—some slight movement— caught his attention. He turned toward the window, and there it was. Snow! Big fluffy flakes drifting lazily from the indigo sky, past the glass, down to the street below.

Since his arrival in New York, he'd often been confused about what he should think of as beautiful. Was Kim Kardashian beautiful? The sunset? The Empire State Building? A three-point shot by the Knicks? The word seemed to apply to many people and objects and actions.

But for the first time, he was absolutely certain that he knew what beauty was. He didn't know whether he'd ever seen snow before. Perhaps, as Chandler had surmised, he was a native of some tropical land, but in this moment he sensed that this was the first time.

He opened the French doors and stepped out onto the balcony. He lifted his face and let the icy flakes settle gently upon his cheeks and nose and eyelids. He opened his mouth and felt the snowflakes melt on his tongue. He raised his arms outward like an angel about to take flight, and he laughed with joy.

Chapter 21
Taking the Show on the Road

For the first time in her so-called career, Chandler was honestly relieved that no job offers were coming in. She hated leaving Carlos alone in the apartment. They could not go on living this way indefinitely. Carlos had shown no signs of regaining his memory. Apparently, that situation was not going to change any time soon.

She sat Carlos down next to her on the couch and took both his hands in hers. "Let's talk," she said, looking solemnly into his eyes. "Tomorrow night we're going on a double date, so to speak, with my best friend Libby and her husband."

Carlos made an educated guess as to what a double date was. "Why?" he asked.

"Because it's time we got out of this house. You can't stay inside forever. It's time we got out and tested our story. Dinner with Libby will be the perfect opportunity. This way we'll find out if there are any holes in our cover story. Libby and Malcolm will be a safe place to try it out."

"Are you sure you haven't told this Libby the truth about me?" Carlos asked warily

"Of course, not. And I don't plan to. Not to Libby nor anyone else. We are sticking by our story. Forever."

Carlos hung his head. "Forever," he muttered, pulling his hands away from her. "That is a very long time, isn't it?"

Chandler smiled and patted his arm. "Don't you worry. I'll take care of everything."

****

The following evening Chandler and Carlos were already seated at the French bistro that the two girls had favored ever since high school, when Libby and Malcolm Arden walked in. They paused a moment at the door to scan the room.

"There they are," said Chandler. Libby was a chic brunette with bright red lips and a precisely cut bob. Her husband, though undeniably handsome, was tweedy and a bit disheveled. "Living proof that opposites attract," Chandler went on. She nudged Carlos with her elbow. "Just remember," she whispered, "anything you're not sure of—just blame it on the amnesia." With that, she put a broad smile on her face and waved at Libby and Malcolm.

"So…" said Libby, as she took her seat, "this is the new man, huh?"

Carlos looked alarmed.

"Honey!" Mark scolded.

Chandler shot Carlos a sidelong glance. "Let's not get ahead of ourselves. We've only just got started."

"Well, you've moved in together. That's usually a pretty good sign." Libby looked back and forth from Chandler to Carlos. "And I have to say I approve." She held out her hand to Carlos. "I'm Libby."

"I know." Carlos shook her hand weakly.

"Libby, honey!" Malcolm chided again. "You're embarrassing him. I'm Malcolm, by the way. Very nice to meet you, Carlos." He shook Carlos's hand. "Don't pay too much attention to her. She's overly romantic."

"It's okay," Carlos replied with a shy smile.

Malcolm took a moment to order a bottle of wine and some appetizers. Libby leaned forward on her elbows. "I don't care what anyone says. This is so exciting! So... tell me everything." She looked expectantly from Carlos to Chandler.

"Well, I told you most of it over the phone."

"No, you didn't. But as I understand it, you two met and had an immediate connection—which, by the way, why on earth was I not told about this right away?" Libby paused to glower at Chandler. "Anyway, shortly after that, you got mugged and lost your memory, right?"

"Right," Carlos replied.

"So how did you find your way back to Chandler if you had no memories?"

"He didn't forget every single thing. Mostly he forgot his life prior to coming to America. But fortunately, he had told me about that already so I was able to fill him in. He still doesn't remember *per se.* He only knows what I have told him about it."

"What a bizarre position to be in, huh, Carlos?" Libby mused.

"Very bizarre. Everything has been very weird since I arrived here."

Libby leaned in some more. "You're not undocumented, are you?" she whispered.

"Would I tell you if I were?" Carlos asked with a disarming grin.

"What is this, an interrogation?" Chandler protested. "Of course, he's documented. What ever gave you that idea?"

"Calm down. It was just a question." Libby took a sip of her wine, which had just been delivered along with a plate of escargots and another of baked brie.

Carlos looked at Malcolm. "I thought these two were best friends."

"Oh, they are," Malcom laughed. "This is just how they roll. It doesn't mean anything."

"So…" said Libby, undeterred, "I wonder why, if you were raised in Brazil, you have almost no accent. A tiny one, yes, but hardly worth mentioning."

"Uh… um…" Carlos stammered. "I don't know. Maybe I was raised among English-speaking people. Or went to an American school… or something…"

"Hmm… Seems like that would be something you would have mentioned to Chandler before you got hit in the head."

"He didn't," Chandler jumped in. "Remember, we had only a few days together before he got mugged. There wasn't time to tell everything."

Libby popped an escargot into her mouth and eyed Chandler suspiciously. "So unlike you to move in with someone on such a short acquaintance."

"Well, you know how it is. Love at first sight." Chandler reached over and squeezed Carlos's hand and hoped no one noticed that he recoiled slightly from her touch.

"Uh, just a minute ago you said you'd just got started. Now it's love. Pardon me for being confused."

"Sounds like Carlos was lucky to have found you, Chandler. If he had gotten amnesia and you weren't around, he might have been up the creek," said Malcolm.

Libby grabbed Chandler's hand. "Okay, sweetie. No matter what the details are, you look happy. All I ever wanted was for you to be happy."

"Does this mean the third degree is over?"

"Just looking out for your welfare. But Carlos seems like a super-sweet guy."

"He is."

"This is great then. We can double date all the time. In fact, we have seats to a Rangers game next month. Want to go with us?"

"We'd love to. Wouldn't we, Carlos?"

"I've never been to a hockey game," said Carlos. "It is hockey, isn't it?"

The whole table burst out laughing.

"He's so cute!" cried Libby.

****

Back at the apartment, Chandler flung herself onto the sofa and kicked off her Louboutins. "What a relief!" she sighed.

"Taking off those torturous shoes?"

"Well, that, too," she laughed. "But I meant making it through the evening. I thought it went amazingly well, didn't you?"

"I don't know. It seemed a little sketchy to me."

"Maybe but even at that it was easier than I thought it would be. If we made it through Libby's grilling, we can make it through anything."

"You said she was going to be our safe place."

"I just meant if we screwed up, I'd rather screw up among friends—people who won't hurt you. I knew she'd have questions. She always does. True, those were a little more pointed than I expected."

"I see," said Carlos, sitting down in the armchair across from Chandler.

"But it's good that she put us through our paces. It was good practice." Chandler regarded Carlos quizzically. "What's that look?"

"I guess I didn't realize we would be taken for a couple."

"What!" she sat straight up. "Of course, we would. That was always the plan. Anyway, Claire also took us for a couple. It's only natural."

"I don't remember that plan. And you denied it to Claire."

"She caught me off guard. I didn't know what to say," Chandler pouted, deflating herself back down onto the sofa. "Anyway, it wouldn't make any sense otherwise—you living here I mean."

"Why not?"

"It just wouldn't, okay?" She stood up abruptly. "I'm going to bed. Good night." She turned on her heel and marched off to her room.

"What did I say?" Carlos wondered aloud once he heard her door slam.

****

The hockey game with Libby and Malcolm was uneventful, unless you counted the two broken teeth, the blood on the ice and the fist fight in the stands. Carlos comported himself well, and there were no obvious slip-ups.

Thus, Chandler was surprised when Libby urgently demanded lunch with her the very next day. They met at a deli near Libby's office.

"Well?" said Chandler as she stirred Equal into her iced tea. "What was so important? We just saw each other last night."

Libby leaned in and stared into Chandler's eyes. "How long have we been friends?"

Chandler laughed. "You know perfectly well! Since seventh grade."

"Exactly. I know you very well. Did you really think I would fall for that tale you've been spinning about Carlos?"

"Tale? What tale? You don't believe me?"

"No. I don't. It's all very fishy."

Chandler sipped her tea nonchalantly. "I can't imagine why you would say that."

"None of it makes any sense. I don't care how much this guy

looks like your favorite actor or how gorgeous he is, it's totally unlike you to meet someone and immediately move him into your home. Why, out of all the relationships you've had, you never even lived with any of them—and some of them you'd been with for years. Now all of a sudden this guy is your live-in lover—and without even consulting me beforehand!"

"Aha! Is this your real problem? That I didn't discuss it with you first? I'm sorry. I should have. It just happened so fast."

"My point exactly. However, that's just a side issue. It's not the main problem."

"What is the problem then?"

"The whole thing is nonsensical. That's the problem."

"I have no idea what you mean."

"I'll tell you what I mean," said Libby, setting her jaw firmly.

"Please."

"First of all, that crazy story. Korean birth, Brazilian adoption, death of both parents. Nearly perfect American accent after growing up in Rio. That nutty amnesia story. Who could believe any of that?"

"You know what they say—truth is stranger than fiction."

"But the worst of it is," Libby went on, ignoring that remark, "your relationship with him."

"What's that supposed to mean?"

"It means I'm not seeing the love—at least not on his part." Libby reached out and touched Chandler's hand. "I'm sorry, sweetie. I don't want to hurt your feelings, but I don't see a real connection there."

"Really, Libby. Surely I would know how Carlos and I feel about each other."

"No, I observed the two of you very closely last night. Whenever, you touched him, he visibly pulled away. The look in his eyes was...I don't know...not cold, but sort of neutral. I didn't sense any physical closeness. Are you guys even sleeping together?"

"Of course, we are!" Chandler picked up her tuna sandwich and bit into it viciously.

Libby put on a wry smile. "Oh, Chandler, don't you know you can never lie to me?"

Chandler's face fell. With a sigh, she carefully laid her sandwich down on the plate. "All right, all right. I'll tell you."

"That's better."

"You're right about our relationship. Totally one-sided on my part. He doesn't love me at all. I think he likes me okay, and of course he's grateful to me—but nothing romantic."

"Grateful for what?"

"For giving him a place to stay—a home. He was homeless and undocumented. It happens. You won't say anything, right?"

"Of course, not."

"If I make even the slightest move on him, he pushes me away."

"Amazing. I never saw the man you couldn't get. Sometimes I even wonder about Malcolm."

"That's ridiculous."

"Just kidding—sort of."

"There's something different about Carlos. Something even I

don't understand. But he's very sweet, completely harmless and a little helpless in some ways. Sometimes I think he's from another planet."

"What about the story about Brazil and all that stuff? Completely made up, too, I'm guessing?"

"Mostly."

Chandler proceeded to tell Libby everything—from the chance encounter at Bloomingdales, to the decision to take Carlos in, to the concoction of the fake cover story.

"But, Chandler, the fake cover story is only marginally more believable than the true story!"

Chandler groaned. "That's what Carlos always says. By the way, I forgot to say he is preternaturally intelligent—brilliant."

"Perhaps you should have listened when he said the story was crazy."

"Probably."

"And then throwing amnesia into the mix—as if you were writing a soap opera script."

"Oh, that part is real. That's pretty much the only part that is real."

"That's incredible. Are you sure he's not faking it?"

"Come on, Libby You looked into his eyes. There's not an ounce of guile in them, is there?"

"No. I guess not," Libby admitted. She paused to take a sip of Diet Coke. "I guess I don't understand why not just tell the truth in the first place. Is it because he's undocumented? Did you think the fake story provided more cover than the real story? I don't see that myself."

"You could be right. Carlos could be right. It seemed like a good idea at the time. I must admit my brain has been a bit muddled ever since he came into my life."

"Well, you know you don't have to worry about me. I'll never tell anyone that he's undocumented."

"Except Malcolm, of course."

"Of course," Libby laughed. "But you know Mal. He's even more trustworthy than I am. So where do you go from here?"

"Hell if I know. Just play it by ear. One day at a time. Maybe he'll get his memory back and everything will become clear. At least, then we'd know what we're dealing with. Maybe he is documented. Maybe he's a citizen. But without a name, there's no way to search. If I go to the authorities, he'll be outed and the system will take over—for better or worse."

"I see your dilemma. I really do. I think your response to the situation has been rather extreme, but who am I to judge?"

"Like I said, I think my judgment has been clouded by love."

"Oh dear!" said Libby pityingly. "I've never seen you like this. You never let men get the better of you."

"I *know*," Chandler groaned.

"I'm so sorry, sweetie."

"You know what, Libby? He's only been here a couple of months, and I already feel so tired. Tired of worrying about him, tired of lying, tired of being rejected." She drained her glass of tea and tossed her napkin onto her plate. "I could use a drink. You want to go somewhere and have a cocktail or three?"

"At this hour? Besides, I have to get back to the office. Not all of us have a rich daddy to pay our bills."

"You have a rich daddy."

"But he doesn't pay my bills."

"That wasn't very nice," Chandler pouted.

A few minutes later, the two women were standing on the sidewalk outside the restaurant. "I'll call you later," said Libby, embracing her friend and kissing her cheek. "Try to take it easy, okay?"

"Yeah, sure."

Libby set off on the short walk back to her office, and Chandler stood in place wondering what to do next.

She turned in the opposite direction from the path Libby had taken and walked idly up the block until she passed something called the Esquire Tavern. She stopped and went in.

Never in her life had she drunk alone in a bar. Today would be a first.

The place was nice—elegant even. The chairs were covered in pale blue velvet, and there was a massive carved mahogany bar. Amber light glowed from bronze sconces on the walls. The room was sparsely populated at this time of day. One lone gentleman sat at the bar, and two men with papers laid out on their table talked business.

Chandler took a table toward the back and ordered a double bourbon on the rocks. She dispatched it quickly and ordered another—and then another.

****

Chandler tottered, unsteady on her stilettos, into the apartment. Carlos was napping on the couch, the book he had been reading tented on his chest. Balancing herself against the back of a chair, she stood a moment and watched. The rise and fall of the book with his breathing was fascinating somehow. He was incredibly beautiful when he was sleeping. His face, normally a bit child-like and innocent-looking, was even more so in sleep. She wanted to touch him so badly that her fingers ached.

Moving cautiously so as to avoid falling on her face, she made her way over to the sofa. She had the feeling that her body was operating independently of her brain.

Before she knew it, she found herself squeezing in next to Carlos, her body pressed tightly against his. Gently, she lifted the book and laid it on the coffee table. He stirred slightly and turned his head toward her. Her face was inches from his. His skin was fragrant. It always was. Her lips brushed his lightly—almost imperceptibly. She ran her hand upward along his inner thigh, and for moment she thought she felt him respond.

And then, even more quickly than it had begun, it was over. His eyes flew open. His body jerked so violently that Chandler was pushed off the sofa and fell to the floor with an inelegant thud.

Carlos's eyes blinked several times as the scene registered in his brain.

"Chandler!" he cried. "Are you okay?" He took her by the arm and helped her up to the sofa. "Are you hurt?"

"No, I'm fine," she replied calmly, too drunk to be

flustered.

"What happened?" he asked, sitting down next to her.

"You mean you don't remember?" she asked hopefully. But even as she spoke, she could see the realization of what had just occurred form in his eyes.

He blushed and chose not to answer. He sniffed the air. "You've been drinking. I can smell it on you, and you're talking funny."

"Yeah. I drank a lot."

"I thought you were meeting Libby at a deli. Did you two go out drinking at this hour?"

"No. Just me."

"You went drinking all by yourself?"

"It was a lovely bar," she said as if that explained everything. "It had velvet chairs."

"Does that make it all right to get drunk alone in the middle of the day? Did something happen with Libby?"

"Sort of. She knows everything."

"She knows everything? After you've forbidden me to say a word to anyone?"

"I couldn't help it! She was badgering me. She knew I was lying. I was never able to lie to her. She knows me too well."

"So you told her what actually happened instead of your elaborate cover story. You should have done that in the first place."

"She said the cover story was only marginally—that was the word she used—marginally—more believable than the true story."

"Isn't that what I always said?"

"I suppose so," she allowed reluctantly.

"So now she knows the truth."

"Yeah."

"Except that nobody knows the truth. Not you, not Libby, not even me. Nobody knows what I was doing before the day we met. I could have been in Korea or Brazil or Timbuktu. I could have been right here in America the entire time."

"But then you wouldn't have an accent."

"A minor point."

Chandler scooted closer to him. She could hardly hold her head up, and in a moment it plopped down on his shoulder. She felt him cringe a little but at least he didn't jump up from the couch. "I'm sorry about before," she mumbled drowsily. "I'm a little drunk."

"Yeah. I noticed."

Chapter 22
A Possible Sighting

"Hey, Tracy. It's me, Jaz."

"Hey, Jaz. What's up?"

"I'm standing here in the checkout line at the grocery store, thumbing through a copy of *GQ* and…"

"Why are you thumbing through a copy of *GQ*?"

"Because thumbing through *Soap Opera Digest* is too depressing. You're missing the point. Guess who is staring back at me from the page."

"No clue."

"Alex!"

"Alex? That's impossible on so many levels. Dare I ask what makes you think this?"

"Because the person in this picture looks just like Ji Soo."

"Uh…maybe it *is* Ji Soo. Did that ever occur to you? Doesn't he appear in a lot of magazines?"

"Not like this. This is one of those articles with dozens of small pictures of individual outfits being modeled by dozens of random, anonymous models coming down the runway at a fashion show. If it were Ji Soo, the picture would be bigger and he would be named. I know this is America and not Asia, but he's still a big enough star to at least be identified by name."

"So you're saying Alex has come to earth and somehow gotten into the fashion modeling business. Yeah, right. That makes perfect sense."

"Hold on a sec. I gotta move out of this line. I'm holding things up."

"Sure thing. I got nothing to do but listen to stories about your fantasy life."

"Okay. I'm back. My mind is racing in all directions. Should I contact the magazine and try to get some info on this guy? Should I try to find out who his agency is and contact them? What should I do?"

"Do you really think those people are going to give out personal information about their client to a total stranger? How much does this guy look like Ji Soo and/or Alex anyway?"

"Well…it's a little hard to tell. It's such a tiny picture."

"There you go. Lots of people look like other people—especially in tiny pictures. I hate to be a wet blanket, but I think you've gotten ahead of yourself. Not that I'm surprised. You've been so depressed about Alex that I think it's affecting your ability to think straight."

"That's been your opinion for a long time."

"I only want what's best for you. You know that."

Jasmine was silent.

"So…what is he wearing?" Tracy asked, breaking the silence.

"Huh?"

"This model. What's the outfit and who's the designer?"

"What does that have to do with anything?"

"Nothing. You know me. I'm always interested in fashion—even though I usually dress like a slob."

"No, you don't. But okay, let me see. Big black and white tweed coat over a black turtleneck, black slacks and shiny black loafers, no socks. The designer is somebody I never heard of. Must be a newbie. Lonnie Alexander?…Oh, wait! Alexander! It's a sign! Get it? Alex…Alexander?"

"There you go with the signs again. It's not a sign. It's a coincidence."

"Really?"

"Absolutely."

"Look, I know it's crazy, Tracy, but I miss him. Whoever the person in the chat room was, I miss him. If he isn't coming to see me, I wish he would come back to the chat room. Don't you?"

"I will admit he was sometimes fun to talk to."

"He was, wasn't he?"

"Yeah."

"I suppose you're right about this picture. Trying to find this guy would probably be a wild goose chase, wouldn't it?"

"Good girl. That's more like it. Go home and eat a pint of ice cream."

"Speaking of ice cream, mine is melting. Gotta get back in line and check out. Thanks for talking me off the ledge—again."

That evening, as Tracy was leaving the hospital, she stopped short at the front door, hesitated a moment, turned and strode purposefully back to the gift shop. At the magazine rack, she found the current issue of *GQ*. She paid the cashier and proceeded out to the parking lot. She did not open the magazine.

At home, she yelled over the blare of the TV her usual perfunctory greeting to her mother and went directly to her room. She wasn't sure why she felt so nervous opening that magazine.

Her hands were inexplicably shaking. She riffled through the pages until she came to the many minute fashion shots Jasmine had described. They flashed through her field of vision like individual frames of an old celluloid film. She stopped and scanned the pages for anything that looked like a big black and white coat. And there it was. It was tiny as Jaz had said, but the image was unmistakably Ji Soo-esque. She squinted her eyes, trying to refine the facial features, to no avail.

With a sigh, she slammed the magazine shut. "This is so silly," she muttered aloud. Why on earth was she allowing Jaz to draw her into this lunacy? She chucked the magazine into her trashcan and went to see what was for dinner.

Chapter 23
Memories

With Carlos following in her wake, Chandler stumbled through the front door, kicked off her heels and fell onto the couch. "At last!" she sighed. "My feet are killing me."

"I'll never understand why you torture yourself with those ridiculous shoes." Carlos regarded her sympathetically and sat down in the armchair.

"Even though you are a sometime fashion model, it appears you will never understand fashion."

"This is a well-established fact."

"Even so, you are always perfectly put together. Go figure."

Carlos stood up. "I'm getting some water. Can I get you anything?"

"Water, please. We had more than enough to drink tonight." Chandler and Carlos had just returned from a cocktail party thrown by a producer friend of hers. "It has become painfully obvious that having producer friends does not necessarily lead to job offers," she grumbled. "The canapes were fabulous though."

"So it wasn't a total loss." Carlos handed her a bottle of water and sat down again.

Chandler smiled. "By the way, props to you. Nice catch on the slip-up you made when you were chatting with Alan Halburg. You covered it well. Quick thinking—not that I'm surprised."

"Was he the one with the glasses?"

"Yeah. Remember? You accidentally remembered something you shouldn't have and covered by saying you sometimes have flashes of memory. You're a pretty good little liar."

"I wasn't lying."

Chandler sat up erect on the sofa. "What!"

"I mean I did lie to him about that particular incident, but I wasn't lying about the flashes of memory in general."

"What do you mean? That actually happens?"

Carlos lowered his eyes and nodded.

"How come you never told me? And what are these memories and when do they happen?"

Carlos continued to refuse to make eye contact. "It's awkward to talk about."

"Oh, for God's sake. Tell me. We have no secrets—not from each other anyway."

"It happens when you—what is the phrase—put the moves on me?" Carlos said in a nearly inaudible tone.

Chandler's face turned bright red, and she flew into

defensive mode. "Please! That only happened a couple of times, and I had been drinking."

"I wasn't criticizing you. I was merely answering your question honestly."

"Well, what were they? What were these memories?"

"They're really only flashes—flashes that last a split second. It's difficult to tell what they are. Maybe they're not even memories but just…just…"

"Brain farts?"

"If you wish to use that unfortunate terminology… I suppose so."

"Sorry. I don't know where you really come from, but apparently it's a place less crude than America."

"Perhaps. I don't know."

"Don't these flashes resemble anything at all?"

"Um…well, there's a vague impression of a female form. And stop. Before you ask—no, I can't describe the person—if it even is a person. I just get a feeling that it's a woman."

"Well, that's depressing. Is the thought of this woman what keeps you from responding to my drunken advances?"

"I have no idea."

"You must get some sort of feeling when this happens. Is it someone you once loved or something like that?"

"I'm sorry, Chandler. I really don't know."

Chandler thought this over for a moment. "Well, I suppose I should consider that a good thing."

But Carlos had also been thinking things over. "If I had to assign a feeling to it…" he volunteered.

Chandler groaned. "I'm about to wish I hadn't asked, aren't I?"

"If I had to assign a feeling to it," he continued, "I guess it would be comfort... and warmth maybe."

"Aha! Maybe it's your mother! That would be great because I really don't want it to be another woman in the usual sense. Because you know...you surely must know... that I have fallen in love with you. I mean that's obvious isn't it?"

"I'm aware."

"But you don't feel the same."

"I don't think so. I don't know what I was like before, but I sense that I was never a very emotional person."

"Do you think that could ever change?" she asked hopefully.

"I guess so."

"You guess so in the sense that anything is possible?" She winced, knowing in advance that the answer was yes.

"Yes," he said.

Chandler sighed and slumped back on the couch. At least he hadn't said absolutely no.

Chapter 24
Off Broadway

The off-Broadway theater where Jonathan Raditz's play was appearing had been described as "cozy." It was tiny. On opening night, Chandler and Carlos sat in the second row.

"Everyone here," said Chandler, turning to size up the crowd, "is a friend or relative of Jonathan or Claire. What do you want to bet?"

"Isn't that as it should be? It's opening night. It will get better," Carlos replied.

"If it runs more than a couple of performances," Chandler whispered back.

"How can a struggling playwright afford to live in your building?" Carlos wondered.

"Oh, he has a day job. Something to do with insurance I think. And Claire has an income. She is a working actor even if nobody's heard of her."

The play was about two lonely New Yorkers who meet and fall in love online. Aside from the two main characters, there was a female friend called Gina who kept popping into the woman's apartment to make amusing commentary on the folly of the star-crossed couple. Chandler nudged Carlos and pointed out "Gina" in the playbill. "That's the part I could have had. Jonathan said so."

"You should have taken it. You would have been good in it."

"You think?"

"I know."

"How do you always know everything?"

"Shh," he said. "It's starting."

When the play was over, there was an after-party at an Italian restaurant just down the block.

After they had extended their congratulations to Claire, Jonathan, and the rest of the cast and had joined in several champagne toasts, Chandler and Carlos sat alone at a table in a quiet corner.

'I wasn't lying when I told Jonathan I thought the play was good," said Chandler.

"Of course, you weren't. It was good."

"Do you still think I should have played Gina?'"

"The girl who played her was excellent."

"Oh," said Chandler.

Chapter 25
A Day in the Life of an Alien

Carlos arose at 6:30 A.M. precisely, as he did every morning—and without an alarm clock. He often wondered if this was a habit he had practiced in his previous life. He supposed it must have been.

He showered and brushed and flossed his teeth meticulously. He chose an outfit from among the many items of expensive clothing Chandler had bought for him. Today he picked a pair of Gucci jeans and a pale blue Ralph Lauren button-down shirt. Before he stepped out of his room, he checked his image in the mirror, making sure his hair was styled properly.

He went out to the living room. Chandler was not up, of course. She never got up before nine, and, as Claire had so accurately noted, never left the apartment before ten.

He proceeded to the kitchen and made his breakfast—coffee, fresh strawberries and a Danish. He still had the sweet tooth he had discovered on that first day at the café. He often thought back to that day and wondered why every sensation, every taste was completely new to him.

Occasionally, even now, he discovered new ones. He guessed it was the amnesia that had made him forget tastes and smells and feelings, though, after reading extensively on the subject, he had never heard of such an effect. It was confusing. After all these months, everything was still confusing.

As usual, he set his laptop in front of him on the kitchen table and read the *New York Times* online while he ate. Every day more and more dreadful events occurred. Today, a deadly earthquake in China, a bombing in Turkey, a mass murder in California, a traffic accident that killed a family of five. He sighed and turned to the entertainment section. There was a movie he wanted to see. He would ask Chandler to take him. And there were half a dozen new books he wanted to read. He made a mental note of them.

He closed the laptop and cleaned up his dishes. When everything was neatly put away, he went over to the French doors and stepped out onto the balcony. It was a fine late summer day, and the temperature was predicted not to exceed eighty this afternoon.

Despite the morning news, the world, or at least New York City—the only place he knew firsthand—was exceedingly beautiful.

He went back inside, got the book he was currently reading and went back to the balcony. He sat down on a lounge chair and began to read.

By the time Chandler emerged from her room a little after nine, Carlos was heading out the door.

"Where are you off to?" she asked sleepily.

"I have that job to go to, remember?"

"Oh, yeah. Rene's trunk show, right?"

"Yes."

"Well, it doesn't pay much, but it's something to do, and maybe he'll give you some free samples. His stuff is great, isn't it?"

"It's very nice."

Chandler checked the clock on her desk. "But why so early? The show isn't until later this afternoon."

"Yeah, but you know how I like to wander the streets and look around. I've got nothing better to do."

"You could stay here with me. I've got nothing scheduled for today," she said hopefully. "We could play chess. You love that. Or take a picnic to the park or whatever. And then I could go to the show with you."

Carlos stared down at his shoes. "Of course. If that's what you want."

"No, no. You go ahead. Do what you planned."

"Sure?"

"Absolutely."

"We'll do something next time, okay?"

"Yeah, fine," said Chandler, turning and heading back to her bedroom. Next time never seemed to come. Hardly ever.

Down on the sidewalk, Carlos breathed in the fresh air. New York could sometimes have some pretty unpleasant odors, but not today. He smiled and started up the street in the general direction of Rene's studio. Along the way, he knew he would pass by his favorite little independent bookstore.

In a few minutes, he was there. Inside was the lovely smell of books, which had become very dear to him over the past months. He browsed up and down the shelves. He sampled all six of the books he had read about that morning in the *Times* and decided to purchase all of them. He would pick them up on the way back when he had his pay from the modeling gig.

When he finally left the shop, he had managed to kill more than two hours without even noticing. It was nearly lunchtime. He walked a little further and bought a hot dog, chips and a bottle of water from a pushcart.

There was a small public park across the street, another one of his favorite places. He took his meal to a bench there and ate slowly, savoring every flavor from the sharpness of the dill pickle to the sting of the mustard to the vague spiciness of the meat. He ate the salty chips and drank the water. Despite his sweet tooth, he wasn't much of a fan of soda pop. Chandler always said his dislike of soda pop was a good thing, though she wouldn't approve of the hot dog either.

He thought fondly of Chandler. He felt guilty about her and wished he could give her more of what she wanted. He felt thankful to her, but he was an emotionless fellow and struggled to show even gratitude. He resolved to be nicer in the future. He would ask her to go to the movie he'd read about and out to dinner tomorrow night. He wouldn't be "taking" her. She would have to pay. He rarely made any money—another thing to feel guilty about. He should spend his pay on taking Chandler to dinner instead of on books, but he knew he wouldn't.

He tossed his wrappers into a nearby trashcan and leaned back against the bench. He lifted his face to the sky, closed his eyes and felt the breeze soft on his skin. It all felt completely new. Everything did. When spring appeared a few months ago, he'd sensed that he'd never experienced it before. He loved spring. He loved summer. He loved New York. He wished he loved Chandler as she loved him. He was throwing around the word "love" liberally these days—in his mind at least—though he still wasn't sure he knew exactly what it meant.

He sighed and looked at his watch. It was time to head over to the studio. Rene liked him to be there early for a final fitting before the show. He reckoned it was another half-hour's walk. He stood up and started out.

At the show, where he was one of four models, Carlos had five wardrobe changes. A fifty-something female buyer from Atlanta flirted with him relentlessly. He couldn't understand it, but it didn't bother him. She put in a substantial order for every one of the items he had worn. Rene was pleased. He gave Carlos $300 in cash, which was normal for these events, and offered him his choice of outfits from the show. Carlos selected a pair of soft gray flannel trousers and a black silk shirt. Although he didn't care much for fashion himself, he picked things he knew Chandler would approve. He would wear them tomorrow night to the movie. Chandler would like that.

On the way home, he stopped at the bookstore and picked up the books he'd chosen that morning. He had a credit card Chandler had provided. She had said to feel free to use it for anything, but he tried not to. He paid cash from the pay he'd just received.

When he was a couple of blocks from the apartment, he passed a steak establishment he'd visited before. He was starving. Chandler hated this place. She wasn't much of a red meat eater. He paused and studied the menu as if he'd never seen it before.

He should go home. Chandler would be waiting. On the other hand, she may have already eaten or gone out with friends. That was possible, wasn't it? He zeroed in on the New York strip with French fried onions. Even after paying for the books, he had enough money for a dinner. He pushed open the heavy brass door and went inside.

He sat at a red-clothed table with a candle in the center. Big band music wafted softly from the sound system. He leisurely enjoyed every bite of his steak and baked potato, and sipped a medium-priced Pinot Noir. Against his better judgment, he ordered chocolate ice cream for dessert.

When he was finished, he leaned back in his chair and sighed. It was nice to be here with the candlelight and the music and the good food and wine. Still, he felt guilty and wondered if he had always been such a selfish bastard.

Chapter 26
Let's Get Away From it All

Chandler stood looking out at the sleet pelting the window-pane. "Oh, dear," she sighed. "I hope this doesn't turn into a full-fledged ice storm. I'm really sick of this weather, aren't you?" Receiving no response, she turned toward Carlos, who was sitting on the floor playing video games. "Aren't you?" she repeated.

"Aren't I what?" He looked up at her vacantly.

"Aren't you tired of this weather?"

"It doesn't bother me one way or the other."

She sighed again. Somehow nearly a year had passed since Carlos arrived. Soon Christmas would be here again, and nothing had improved. She was getting tired of Carlos not being bothered by anything. She flounced over to the couch and sat down. With an air of detached bemusement, she watched him play his game. He was really, really good at it.

After a few minutes of that, she abruptly sat straight up. "I have an idea. Let's take a trip. I haven't had a vacation in ages, and you never have—as far as anybody knows. What do you think?"

"Huh?"

Chandler grabbed the remote and flicked off the TV.

"Hey!" Carlos cried.

"Did you hear a word I said?"

"Um… something about a vacation?"

"Yeah. Why not? Someplace warm. How does that sound?"

"Good I guess."

"How about Florida? It's not too long a road trip. Unfortunately, we can't fly since you have no papers. I say the gulf coast. I've always liked that best. It's calm and peaceful." She picked up her I-pad, pulled up a map and idly began reeling off the names of gulf resort towns. "St. Pete Beach, Treasure Island, Madeira Beach… Stop me if anything sounds interesting…Redington Beach, Indian Rocks Beach, Belleair Beach, Malaga Island, Clearwater Beach…"

"Wait! Back up." Carlos looked up from his game, which he had already resumed. "What did you say before that last one?"

Chandler checked the map again. "You mean Malaga Island?"

"Yes. That one. That's the one we should go to."

"Really? Why?"

Carlos frowned, trying to think—to concentrate. "I don't know," he said at last. "I just like the sound of it."

Chandler shrugged. "Then Malaga Island It is. We used to go to St. Pete Beach years ago—when I was a kid, but makes no difference to me. Whatever you want." She picked up her phone and set about the reservations.

Chapter 27

Close Encounter in a Coffee Shop

Tracy had woken up that morning desperately craving a mochaccino. She now found herself sitting alone in a little coffee shop on Coastal Boulevard, the main drag that ran down the center of Malaga Island.

Tracy and Jasmine had rarely met in person and never in their own hometowns. The most they had done was meet up in cities where soap opera fan events were being held. But somehow a plan had been cooked up for Tracy to spend her vacation with Jasmine on Malaga Island. In Jasmine's mind, it was a nice getaway for her friend. After all, Malaga was a resort town, and Tracy could stay free of charge at Jasmine's apartment. In Tracy's mind, it was an opportunity to see firsthand just how far gone her friend was. And an almost free vacation didn't hurt either. Although her own feelings about Alex had become blurred of late, she was not in the throes of a depression caused by this hacker or alien or fraud or whatever one was supposed to call him. She still worried about Jasmine's state of mind and was *this* close to contacting her mother or talking to Benjy Bryant again.

That morning, the two women had set out together for the coffee shop. Jasmine, although she had taken the week off from work, had suddenly remembered something urgent she needed to take care of at the bank. She had rushed off, leaving Tracy alone on the sidewalk. Tracy merely shrugged and went on to the coffee shop by herself.

She sighed contentedly as she took her first sip of the excellent mochaccino and tried to decide whether to order a croissant. It wasn't too bad having these moments away from Jasmine. She loved the girl, but a week of her depression and obsessing over Alex had become wearing. It would be good to get back home. Only two more days to go.

In the end, she succumbed to the temptation of a strawberry-filled croissant and was just biting into it when she noticed him—that is, them. They were seated near the front of the shop. She had long ringlets that fell past her shoulders, large eyes and delicate, chiseled features. She was skinny as a fashion model, which was exactly what she looked like. But it was her companion whose appearance nearly knocked Tracy off her chair. He looked, at least at this distance, just like Jasmine's idol, Kang Ji Soo. At least she had finally got his name right. At first she'd had a tendency to transpose the syllables. Was it Kang Soo Ji or Soo Ji Kang or what?

But what on earth would a famous actor be doing in dumpy little Malaga Island? It was a pleasant enough place for a family vacation but not one where wealthy celebrities would hang out.

She texted Jasmine right away. "Get over here to the coffee shop ASAP. Someone here looks like Ji Soo. What a coincidence, right? Hurry!"

Tracy sneaked another look at the couple in question. Their pastry plates were empty. If they had eaten already, they might leave at any moment. If she was going to do anything, it had to be soon. She wished Jasmine were here. She was much braver when it came to approaching people. At fan events she never hesitated to ask for an autograph or even a hug, while Tracy hung back and waited to be coaxed. She glanced out the window. What was taking Jaz so long? True, it had been less than a minute since she had texted—but why didn't Jaz hurry!

The curly-headed woman began to fiddle with her purse. Tracy supposed this meant they were thinking about leaving. She took a deep breath, gathered up all her courage and walked over to their table as confidently as she could.

"Uh…excuse me. I'm really sorry to bother you, but aren't you Kang Ji Soo?"

The young man lifted his head and looked her full in the face. Even with her limited knowledge (compared to Jasmine's) of Ji Soo's physiognomy, Tracy could see at once that it was not he. She couldn't put her finger on what the difference was, but she was certain there was a difference.

"Oh! I'm very sorry. It's just that a friend of mine is a huge fan and I knew she'd never forgive me if I didn't get an autograph. But I see now that you're not him. Sorry."

"I get that from time to time—that is, the Kang Ji Soo thing. In fact, that's how we met," he said indicating his companion.

"Really! Are you a fan, too?" Tracy asked the woman. "I'm Tracy," she said, holding out her hand.

The woman declined the hand and declined to respond.

"Carlos Pereira," said the Ji Soo look-alike, rushing into the breach. He managed to grab the offered hand—if rather awkwardly. "And this is Chandler Davies…Ouch!" Chandler had delivered him a sharp kick to the shin under the table.

"Nice to meet you. You are so beautiful, Ms. Davies. The minute I saw you I figured you for a model." Tracy was determined to say any silly thing that popped into her head as she attempted to prolong the encounter until Jaz could arrive.

"No, she's an actress…Ouch! And stop kicking me."

Tracy giggled. This guy might not be Ji Soo or even Alex (absolutely couldn't be), but he was cute and sweet and funny. "Actually, you also look a lot like another friend of mine called Alex." As stupid as she felt, it couldn't hurt to cover all the bases. The name "Alex" elicited no reaction. "Well," she went on, "I hope you guys are enjoying your vacation. Where are you staying?" Something told her she should get all the information she could. Jasmine would expect it.

"The Malaga Manor," Carlos replied. This time Chandler let him off with just a dirty look.

"Ah. The 'big hotel.' That's what the locals call it. My friend lives here. I'm just visiting her."

"Well, this has been swell," Chandler sniped, "but we really have to go. Come on, Carlos." She put her purse over her shoulder and stood up.

"We're leaving in the morning," Carlos said by way of apology.

"So I guess we should start packing. We have a lot of stuff."

Tracy checked her watch. Where the hell was Jaz? "Uh... could I get a picture of you guys?" she asked, fishing her phone out of her pocket. She was going to need proof.

"We *told* you—he's not Ji Soo," said Chandler testily. "Why would you want a picture of a nobody?"

"Hey!" said Carlos.

"You know what I meant."

"But," Tracy forged on, "you are an actress."

"I'm not famous. I haven't worked in a while."

"But you might be famous someday and then I'll have this picture to remember..." Tracy's voice trailed off weakly as Chandler hustled Carlos toward the door.

"Wait!" cried Tracy, bravely grabbing Carlos's arm. He turned to face her and smiled a glorious, sunny smile that sparkled from his dark, beautiful eyes to his movie star lips. He was so dazzling that Tracy teetered a little as if some mysterious force of nature had socked her in the stomach.

"Yes, Tracy? It was Tracy wasn't it?"

"Yes. And my friend's name is *Jasmine*." Tracy searched his face for any glimmer of recognition, all the while thinking how totally ridiculous she was being. Of course, there was no recognition. How could there be?

Chandler glared. "Why do we care what your friend's name is? And what do you want?"

"I just wanted to ask Carlos a question."

"Yes?" said Carlos kindly. "What is it?"

"I know you said Ms. Davies is not a model, but how about

211

you? Have you ever done any modeling? You're certainly hand-some enough. I feel like I might have seen you in a magazine or something."

Before he could answer, Chandler jabbed him in the ribs with her elbow and threw him a threatening look.

"No!" Carlos nearly shouted, more in response to the jab than to the question. "You're probably remembering pictures of that actor guy. He's been in lots of magazines. But thank you for the compliment—and you are very handsome too." He bowed from the waist in a courtly manner.

"Oh, for God's sake," Chandler groaned, taking Carlos by the hand and pulling him toward the door. "Come on. Let's get out of here."

"Um…it was nice meeting you?" Tracy called out lamely.

"You too!" Carlos called back over his shoulder as he flashed that devastating smile one more time.

When they had gone, Tracy made her way back to her table and fell into her chair. Why hadn't she realized that Ji Soo, or any-one who happened to look just like him, was quite possibly the most beautiful creature on earth—"creature" being the operative word. She scolded herself for feeling weak in the knees. There was absolutely no reason for it. That person was not Ji Soo and most certainly was not Alex since Alex did not exist. A figment of Jas-mine's imagination was trying to work its way into hers again. She was not going to allow it. And on top of everything else, her coffee was cold. And what was taking Jasmine so long? The bank was only a block away. She glanced at her phone. There was a text. She had been so absorbed in Carlos Pereira that she hadn't heard the beep. The text was from Jaz. "I'm coming. Don't let him get away!"

"Sure. I'll do that," Tracy muttered. She motioned to the waitress for a fresh cup.

The coffee arrived at the same time Jasmine did. She stood next to Tracy's table and demanded to know, *"Where is he?"*

"I'm sorry. I tried everything I could think of to stall them."

"Them?"

"He was with a girl. An extremely beautiful girl."

"Oh, dear," said Jasmine sinking into the chair opposite Tracy's.

"Now don't get despondent. I got you a lot of information."

"Really? Tracy, you're the best. So tell me!" Jasmine leaned forward expectantly.

Tracy cleared her throat for dramatic effect and began. "Well, his name is Carlos Pereira…"

"Uh…hold on right there. How can his name be Carlos Pereira? Isn't that a Portuguese name?"

"I didn't find that out, but aren't there a lot of Asian immigrants in Brazil?"

"This is true. Well, what about an accent?"

"Oh, wow. I didn't even think about it until this minute, but now that I do think about it, he did have a very slight accent—like a person who's been speaking English so long that his accent has almost completely faded away."

"Hmmm… So what else?"

"Her name is Chandler Davies. She's an out of work actress. I asked if he had ever modeled—you know, thinking back to the GQ thing. He denied it, but it seemed like she sort of forced him to. In fact, she was very controlling and got pissed every time he told me anything. She kept kicking him under the table."

"Well! I don't like that! How dare she kick our Alex?"

"I'm just going to ignore that gigantic leap of logic."

Jasmine nibbled thoughtfully on Tracy's croissant. "Why do you suppose she wouldn't want him giving out information? Could it be he's an undocumented alien—which, by the way, is what Alex would be if he were here, under any definition of 'alien.' Right?"

"I refuse to encourage you in such delusions. Maybe she just doesn't want women hitting on her boyfriend."

"But the thought did cross your mind—that it was Alex?"

Tracy blushed. "All right. Yes. I even mentioned the name Alex to see if it got any response. I mentioned all our names and there was not the tiniest twitch of recognition. If it is Alex, why doesn't he recognize our names, and why hasn't he sought us…I mean you…out? He knows where you live."

"Exactly! How does someone who looks uncannily like Ji Soo just happen to be in this town out of all the towns in the world?"

"I don't remember saying uncannily."

"Then you tell me. How much of a resemblance was there?"

"It was very weird. You know how when you happen to see your mirror reflection reflected in a second mirror—how everything looks just slightly off? It was kind of like that."

"Well, isn't that what we told Alex to look like? Like Ji Soo but slightly different so he wouldn't get mobbed by fans if he happened to make it here."

"He said he gets approached once in a while. In fact, that's how he met Chandler. She's a fan."

"Really!"

"Yeah. You and she could have been besties if you weren't both in love with the same guy."

"Do you think she's in love with him?"

"Oh, absolutely."

"And what about him?" Jasmine asked warily. "Does he feel the same?"

"I would bet not. I didn't get that feeling from him at all."

"Then why is he with her?"

"Well…let's just say you're right. He's an undocumented alien…of any kind. She's obviously his protector. Heck, for all she knew, I was an undercover immigration officer."

"I still think he might be Alex. There's no other reason for him to show up on Malaga."

"Then why hasn't he approached you?"

"Maybe he has amnesia."

Tracy groaned. "Don't look now but your soap roots are showing."

"No, hear me out. If a person…or a creature…traveled over thousands of light years, from galaxy to galaxy, it wouldn't be un-likely that some weird stuff could happen to their brain or body along the way, right?"

"Yeah, he probably would have disintegrated into a million pieces, yet your guy is perfectly intact."

"Except for the amnesia."

"Geesh."

"Did you find out where they're from?"

"No, but I got a New York vibe. They were dressed very chicly. She's an actress. And I may have detected a tiny bit of a New York accent in her case."

"Plus, it's a relatively short trip, and we get tons of New Yorkers down here. Good thinking, Tracy. I really appreciate your participation in light of your skepticism."

"No problem…Oh, and they are staying at the Malaga Manor."

"Oh my God! Tracy!" Jasmine leaped up and ran around the table to hug her. "You even got that tidbit. This makes our mission so much easier."

"Our mission?" Tracy's eyes narrowed and gingerly she disengaged from Jasmine's embrace.

****

Carlos followed Chandler into their hotel room. She whipped around to face him the moment the door closed. "What were you thinking? Giving all that information to that woman. Didn't we agree not to give out information to strangers? For all you know, she could have been an undercover cop or God knows what."

"Sorry!" Amazingly, Carlos picked up a book from the coffee table and threw it across the room. "Pardon me if get tired of following all the rules every minute. Do you have any idea how confusing it is to be me? First I'm Jesse, then Carlos, now Alex is thrown in the mix. And the sad part is none of them is me. I have no idea who I really am. Do you know how confusing that is and how hard it is to always be on guard against every person who approaches me?"

Chandler was still standing there with her mouth open from the shock of seeing Carlos express anger or frustration or any strong emotion. He was always so even.

She got herself together and sat beside him on the sofa where he had thrown himself down dejectedly. "I'm sorry, Carlos." Chandler patted his arm and spoke in low, soothing tones. "I know it's hard, but you must know I do it all for you—to protect you. As hard as it is, it's not as bad as going to prison or being deported."

Carlos turned to look her in the eye. "Maybe I could just throw myself on the mercy of the court. Since I do suffer from amnesia, maybe I could get some special exemption. Maybe your father could use his influence somehow."

"Do you really want to take that chance?" Chandler sounded sure of herself, but in her heart she wondered how much of this was just wanting to keep Carlos to herself. She preferred not to think about that and quickly changed the subject. "Anyway, what does this Alex have to do with anything? It's just some guy that woman knows. It has nothing to do with you."

"Nothing I guess," Carlos sighed. "It's just that there are now two other people who look like me, and I still have no identity."

"They say everyone has doppelgangers."

"Do they?"

Chandler scooted a little closer to Carlos. "You know the real reason I protect you so fiercely, don't you? It's because I love you so much. I can't take a chance on losing you. I just can't." She grasped his hand and brought her lips close to his face. He flinched and pulled away as usual.

Tears stung her eyes, and she stood up. "I hate to be immodest but I have never, ever in my life been unable to attract a man. Why, even that annoying woman at the coffee shop said I was beautiful."

"Tracy," Carlos announced.

Chandler stood stock still and eyed him sharply. "There's something odd about your reaction to that woman. You seemed so open to her from the start and pretty much willing to spill your guts. I've never known you to do that. Why, you even said she was handsome. I beg to differ," she sniffed.

"You didn't find her pretty?"

"Not at all. What *is* it about her?"

Carlos paused a moment. "I don't know. I just felt comfortable. I sensed that if I did accidentally reveal something important, she would be discreet."

"Comfortable, huh?...Hey, isn't that a word you used to describe that woman in your memory flashes or whatever they are."

"Yes, I guess I did."

"Well…is it her?"

"I don't know. It's unlikely."

"Well, that's a relief I suppose."

Chapter 28

Plans A and B and Everything in Between

"Our mission is obvious, isn't it?" Jasmine said. "We have to track Alex down, tell him our story and get him to remember it—or at least believe it."

"You seem to be rather heavily invested in this amnesia angle. Unrealistically so."

"Sorry. It's all I got."

"Can't we just drop this? We don't need a so-called mission."

"Tracy. This guy traveled light years to get here and meet us. We were friends—all three of us were friends. If he went to all that trouble, doesn't he deserve to find what he came all that way looking for?"

"That's assuming he is Alex. Maybe he really is Carlos. Lots of people look like other people."

"Not ones who look exactly like Kang Ji Soo—almost—and who end up here on Malaga Island just as we planned."

"Well, I hope *your* mission doesn't take too long. They're leaving in the morning."

"*What?*"

"They said they were leaving tomorrow and were going back to the hotel to start packing."

"Well, why didn't you say so? We have to hurry."

"You mean *you* have to hurry."

"Oh, phooey! You know you want to get to the bottom of this as much as I do. If nothing else, it's like a little mystery. You love mysteries."

Tracy shrugged a "you got me there" shrug.

"Now all I have to do is come up with a plan. Another coffee? My treat."

"No, but I'll take another croissant since you ate mine."

Jasmine ordered a croissant and an espresso for herself and got to thinking up a plan.

"Feel free to jump in anytime," she said after the food and drink had been consumed and she still had come up with nothing.

"I'm thinking."

"The thing is the room will probably be in her name. Fortunately, we have her name, thanks to you."

"Thank you."

"If we call the room, I'll bet any money she will answer the phone and she will never let us talk to him."

"Maybe she'll be in the shower or something."

"We can hardly count on that, can we? We need another plan."

Tracy shrugged again.

"Okay, here's an idea," Jasmine continued. "It just so happens that the manager at the big hotel is an old friend. We went all through school together from kindergarten on. And he had a tiny little crush on me. What if I get him to create a diversion. He calls her to the office—some problem with her bill or her credit card. He tells us her room number. We go up and grab Alex and take him someplace where we can talk without her interrupting us. We tell him the whole story and convince him that he's really Alex."

"And what if he isn't really Alex?"

"There's plenty of time to worry about that later. For now, we just have to get to him before they leave. If they make it back to New York or wherever they came from, it'll be a lot harder to find him."

"Um…what you're asking your friend to do sounds slightly unethical."

"Aw, what's a little malfeasance among friends? Come on, let's go."

Tracy groaned. "I'm gonna regret this, aren't I?"

"Probably."

Even though the big hotel was only a short walk away, they took Jasmine's car—the better to make a quick getaway.

"Wait," said Tracy as they entered the hotel lobby. "Can't we try the simple route first—before we involve your friend in unethical behavior?"

"What do you mean?"

"Let's just call the room. Maybe we'll get lucky and he'll answer."

"And what if she's sitting right there? She may be tipped off and then Plan B won't even be an option."

"Apparently," Tracy sniffed, "I have more faith in Alex—or whomever—than you do. After all, I'm the one who's actually met him. If that happens, he won't give us away. I just know it."

"Okay. Stop gloating. We'll try it your way. But if it doesn't work we go to Plan B."

They walked across the lobby to the house phone. Jasmine picked up the receiver and handed it to Tracy. "You have to do the talking. He knows your voice."

Tracy accepted the phone as enthusiastically as if it were a live grenade.

"Now, you remember what to say, right?" They had rehearsed exhaustively in the car.

"Yes, yes. Let's just get on with it." Tracy dialed the operator and asked for Chandler Davies's room.

"Hello?" said a definitely masculine voice.

"Oh, my God! It's him!" Tracy whispered.

"Hello?" the voice repeated.

Jasmine jabbed Tracy in the arm. "Go!"

"Hello? Is this Carlos?"

"Yes. It's me. Is this Tracy?"

"Yes!" Tracy sighed a sigh of relief. "Where is Chandler?"

"She's in the shower."

"Oh good! Um…I mean…um… do you think she'll be long?"

"Of course. It takes her forever to wash all those curls."

"Carlos, could you come down here to the lobby? I have something urgent I need to speak to you about. And don't let on to Chandler."

"That goes without saying. I'll be right there."

"Oh, my God!" Tracy squealed. "He remembered my voice! And she is in the shower! That was so freakin' easy!"

"Gee, it's so nice to see you getting with the program," Jasmine snarked. "The fact that she was in the shower, which was our best case scenario, is a good omen. Who woulda thunk it? Right?"

"Whatever you say, Jaz."

"I'm so excited to see him. I hope I don't faint."

"Fainting! How perfectly silly," Tracy lied.

In less than five minutes, the elevator door opened and there stood Carlos himself. Jasmine's breath caught in her throat. He looked so much like Ji Soo it was eerie. And yet, as Tracy had said, there was a difference. It didn't matter. He was a dream come true, and on top of that he had followed to the letter her instructions on how he should look.

"This is my friend Jasmine," Tracy said quickly as she grabbed Carlos's arm and pulled him from the elevator and toward the door.

"Where are we going?" Carlos asked quite reasonably.

"Hurry! We want to get out of here before Chandler misses you."

Carlos did not resist. The three of them clambered into Jasmine's car and took off down the boulevard toward St. Pete Beach.

"This is interesting," said Carlos. "I feel like I'm in a movie."

"If this turns out like I think it will, it will be far better than any movie," said Jasmine. She threw Carlos, who was beside her in the passenger seat, a sidelong look. "Do I look familiar at all?" she asked hopefully.

Carlos studied her face for a moment. "It's Jasmine, right?"

Jasmine pumped her fist. "Yes! You *do* remember."

"I remember Tracy introducing us a minute ago and I believe she mentioned your name at the coffee shop earlier."

"Awww...."

"Where *are* we going by the way?" Tracy wanted to know.

"I know a great spot at St. Pete Beach where we can talk privately." Jasmine looked over at Carlos again, and tears filled her eyes. "I just can't believe you're here."

"Why?"

"Just hold on," said Tracy. "We'll explain it all when we get there."

They had been riding in silence for a few minutes when Carlos, peering in the rearview mirror, spoke up unexpectedly. "She's behind us. It's her car."

"What!" cried Jasmine and Tracy in unison.

Tracy, in the backseat, turned and looked over her shoulder while Jasmine squinted at the rearview mirror.

"He's right. It is Chandler," Tracy confirmed.

"How the hell did she catch on to us so fast?" Jasmine wondered.

Tracy continued to sneak peeks out the back window. "What do we do now?"

Jasmine thought for a moment. She stuck her little chin out, and her eyes turned steely cold. "We lose them—that's what. I know every inch of this island like the back of my hand. Everybody hold onto your hats!" With that, she turned the wheel sharply to the left and sped down a narrow alley.

Carlos lurched forward in his seat, and Tracy, not seat-belted in the back, was thrown from one side of the car to the other. "Geez, Jaz! Be careful!"

"Don't worry, kids. I've got this," said Jasmine calmly.

She continued driving for what seemed like an hour to her passengers but was actually only minutes. She darted down side streets and alleys ignoring stop signs and speed limits.

"Okay, guys, when I say jump, jump!"

"What do you mean *jump?* You want us to jump out of a speeding car?" Tracy asked, astonished.

"Of course, not, silly. I'm going to stop the car. You two are going to get out on the double. I'll drive on, and if she finds my car again, I'll let her catch up. She'll see Carlos is not with me, and she'll give up. As soon as the coast is clear, I'll call you and tell you where to meet me. Is that a plan, or what?"

Tracy groaned. "Ever since we lured you out of your hotel room, Jaz has been laboring under the impression that we are characters in a James Bond movie."

"What fun!" said Carlos.

"I repeat—when I say jump, jump. And wait for further instructions."

"She gets James Bond-ier every minute," Tracy muttered.

Jasmine turned down one more alley behind a brick building well off Coastal Boulevard. The car screeched to a halt. "Okay, jump!"

Tracy and Carlos obediently scrambled out of the car, and Jasmine peeled off.

Chapter 29
A Little Adventure

For no logical reason, Tracy and Carlos found themselves pinned flat against the brick exterior of the building, not unlike two spies on a clandestine assignment. They looked at each other and burst out laughing. "What the hell are we doing?" Tracy asked between giggles.

"Uh…playing our roles in Jasmine's screenplay perhaps?" Carlos ventured.

"You got that right," said Tracy stepping away from the wall. Carlos followed suit, and they stood staring at each other.

"What do we do now?" Carlos asked, looking both at a loss and strangely excited.

Tracy glanced at the building behind them. It looked derelict. "I have no idea what this place is, but I'm guessing we don't want to go inside."

"Probably not," Carlos agreed.

"Wait." Tracy pulled her phone from her pocket. "I have a text."

"From Jasmine?"

"Who else?"

"What does she say?"

"She says to kill some time. She wants to allow plenty of time for Chandler to give up on us. And she says stay away from the main drag. She'll call when she has definite plans."

"Well?" Carlos shrugged helplessly.

"Let's start walking, I guess." Tracy took a moment to size up the situation. The neighborhood was a mix of residential and commercial properties. She headed north with Carlos following a step or two behind.

They had been proceeding in this manner for a few blocks when Tracy turned abruptly and grabbed Carlos by the arm. "Look!" She pointed at a blue and white sign in the yard of a modest stucco office building.

"What?" Carlos asked, seeing nothing of note there.

Tracy read aloud: "Benjamin D. Bryant, Orthodontist"

"So?"

"That has to be Jasmine's boyfriend."

"Who?"

"Oh, that's right. I keep forgetting you don't seem to know anything about Jasmine and me."

"Of course, I don't. How could I? You keep making these cryptic comments, implying you know something about me. I wish you would tell me."

"I can't. Not without Jaz. As soon as we meet up with her, we'll tell you everything. In the meantime, wouldn't it be a hoot to get a look at old Benjy? Should we go in?"

"What are the odds we'd see him? I doubt he's in the outer office."

"Odds, schmodds. What were the odds we happened to walk right by his office?"

"It's a small island?" Carlos suggested.

"Come on. We're going in." Tracy took his hand and pulled him toward the entrance.

Carlos pulled back. "Wait. If we should see him, will you tell him you're a friend of Jasmine's, and won't that look weird?"

"That's exactly why I won't tell him. Besides, I don't think Jaz would like this whole caper."

"Caper? We're doing capers now?"

"Apparently," Tracy giggled. "Let's go."

Inside the small lobby, the reception desk was vacant. "What now?" Carlos whispered.

"Just play it by ear," said Tracy, picking up a copy of *People* and beginning to flip through it.

"Hold on," said Carlos, still whispering. "I hear someone coming."

Tracy tossed the magazine onto the coffee table and looked toward the inner office door which was opening—suspensefully. In a moment, someone who could most definitely be Benjy entered the lobby. Closer scrutiny revealed a name tag that read, Benjamin D. Bryant, D.M.D.

"Bingo," said Tracy under her breath.

Benjy glanced about the office and seemed about to head on

outside. But, instead, he paused and regarded the visitors quizzically. "My receptionist seems to be away from her desk. Can I help you with anything? I hope you don't have an appointment. I'm out for the rest of the day." He spoke apologetically and his eyes were kind.

"Uh, no." Tracy blurted out a bit too loudly. "That is, I was just hoping to inquire about orthodontia for my niece."

"Ah. I see. Well, would you like to schedule a consultation? Just let me get on the computer." He turned and started toward the desk.

"Oh, no. I wouldn't dream of troubling you while you're on your way out. Could I just have a business card? I'll call the office some other time."

"Are you sure? It's really no trouble."

"I'm sure."

"Just as you say," said Benjy with a smile. He picked up a card from a plastic container on the desk. "Here you go. I look forward to meeting with you and your niece." He started to hand the card to Tracy, but paused mid-motion as he seemed to take notice of Carlos for the first time. "Say, do I know you? You look very familiar."

Tracy nudged Carlos and winked. "I bet he thinks you're Kang Ji Soo."

"Who?" said Benjy.

"Do you by any chance have a girlfriend or sister or something who's into Korean dramas?"

"Yes! My girlfriend. She's obsessed with them."

"Maybe she's shown you a picture of this one guy, Kang Ji Soo.

People keep telling us that Carlos here looks just like him."

"As far as the names are concerned, they go in one ear an out the other. Sometimes I can't remember my own name," Benjy laughed. "But all of this does sound somewhat familiar. I bet that's it. Sorry if I was rude.'"

"Not at all." Tracy snatched the card from his hand. "Well, we should get going. Thank you. You've been very helpful."

Outside on the sidewalk, she and Carlos stood and pretended to study the business card while they watched Benjy drive off in a silver Mercedes.

"Well, that was fun," said Tracy. "What were the odds he would walk out at just that moment?"

"It's a small island," said Carlos with a wink.

Tracy giggled.

"He seemed like a nice guy," Carlos went on.

"Yeah. He did. I always knew Jaz was making a mistake turning him down."

"I thought you said he's her boyfriend."

"Well…yeah. He is. It's just that she's not that into him. He likes her much more than she likes him. She really likes someone else. Benjy is her fallback guy."

"I don't understand."

"Never mind. We'll talk about it later." Tracy checked her phone. "Still nothing from Jaz. Should we call her?"

"No," Carlos replied quickly. "I mean she said she'll contact us when she has something to report. We shouldn't bother her when she's busy. She'll call when she's ready. Right?"

"Right," Tracy agreed uncertainly.

They had begun walking aimlessly again. "What should we do to kill some more time?" Carlos asked.

"No clue."

They walked in silence for a few minutes until Tracy noticed a little park off to the east. "There's a park," she said. "At least, there's someplace to sit down. What do you say?"

"Sure."

When they reached the perimeter of the park, Tracy took off running. "Ooh! A playground! Come on!" she squealed as she hopped onto the merry-go-round. Carlos just stood there.

"Come on. You have to push me," Tracy ordered.

"I do?"

"What's the matter? You look confused. Didn't you ever play on these as a kid?"

"To tell you the truth," said Carlos, looking down at his shoes, "I don't remember. You see, I suffer from amnesia."

Tracy's eyes opened wide. "Am-*ne*-sia," she murmured almost inaudibly.

"What?"

"Nothing."

"There are whole portions of my life that I have no memory of."

Tracy, deciding that he seemed a little more upset about this than she would have expected, changed the subject. "You still have to push me. You just grab hold of those bars and run around as fast as you can. Once it gets going, you can jump on."

Carlos did as he was told, and in a moment they were both spinning giddily round and round. Like all good things, the ride ended too soon. The wheel gradually slowed and ground to a stop. "I don't suppose you want to push again," Tracy teased.

"I'm starving," Carlos declared instead of pushing.

"Gosh. Me too," said Tracy putting her hand on her stomach. "I just realized I haven't had anything since the coffee shop." She paused to look around the park. "Oh, we're in luck. Looks like there's vending machines over there."

They made their way over to the pink cinderblock structure that housed the bathrooms and water fountains.

"What would you like?" Tracy asked, surveying the limited choices in the dilapidated machine.

"Um…I don't have any cash with me. Just a credit card."

"No worries. It's on me. What do you want?"

"I'll take chips and a water."

Tracy got the chips, peanuts for herself, a Coke and a water. They took their snacks to a picnic table and sat down. Tracy gave Carlos a sidelong look as she tossed a handful of peanuts into her mouth. "So…" she said tentatively, "why is it that Chandler is so determined to keep you from talking to anyone?"

"I can talk to people," Carlos replied defensively. "I just can't reveal too many personal details."

"Uh…*yeah.* And exactly why is that?"

"Can you keep a secret?"

"Of course."

He leaned over and put his lips very near her ear even though there was no one else in the entire park. "It's because I'm an undocumented alien," he whispered.

Tracy choked, spraying Coca Cola all over the table.

"Are you okay?" he asked, patting her on the back. "Is something wrong?"

"No, no. Nothing. I'm fine. An undocumented alien from where?"

"Nobody knows. Because of the, you know…amnesia."

"Oh, of course."

"I mean we say I'm from Brazil for a variety of reasons—thus the name, Carlos Pereira."

"Ah. I see. That makes perfect sense—I suppose."

"There's a lot more to the story. Maybe I'll tell you sometime. But right now I want answers from you. Can't you tell me what this is all about?"

"I told you. I can't without Jaz being present."

"But why?"

"I just can't, that's all."

"That doesn't make sense. I really can't wait any longer. Why can't you just tell me?"

"Because! Because," Tracy sighed, "you are Jaz's project, not mine."

"Huh? What does that even mean? And I don't think I like being anyone's project." The color had risen to Carlos's cheeks and he seemed on the verge of being angry.

"Sorry. I didn't mean that the way it sounded. All I can say is it will become clear once we get a chance to talk to you together. Come on. Let's go swing." She jumped up and headed toward the swings with Carlos following behind.

She sat down on one of the swings and remained motionless, staring at Carlos.

"I'm guessing I'm supposed to push again," he said, his dark eyes twinkling.

"Naturally."

"Why?" he challenged good-naturedly.

"Because you're a gentleman."

"I am? I mean…I am." He came around behind her, placed his hand on her back and gave her a gentle push.

"Come on! You can do better than that. Push!"

Carlos gave a stronger push and then another—over and over until Tracy, who didn't weigh much more than a child, was flying high. She squealed and lifted her feet toward the sky. "My dad used to do this when I was a kid," she yelled down at Carlos. "I used to think my feet would touch the sky."

They continued in this way until Carlos began to tire and let the swing slow and finally come to a rest. When he grabbed hold of the chain, his hand accidentally covered Tracy's. He left it there a few seconds longer than necessary and noticed Tracy made no effort to withdraw her hand. He wondered why he should be Jasmine's project and not Tracy's. But before he could ask, Tracy's phone rang.

"Yeah, Jaz. What's up?" Tracy spoke to Jasmine but kept a wary eye on Carlos as if she feared he might up and bolt. "Uh-huh…uh-huh…yeah…uh-huh. Got it. Okay, bye."

"What did she say?" Carlos asked anxiously.

"We're to go to the Sunny Shores Hotel. Just north of it is a wooden ramp that leads to a deck on the beach. That's where she'll meet us." She gave her phone a punch.

"What are you doing?"

"Calling an Uber."

Chapter 30
The Big Reveal

Minutes later they were walking up the wooden ramp that ended at the deck on the beach where Jasmine was waiting. They sat down on one of the benches that lined the perimeter of the deck. Jasmine smiled broadly. "You made it!"

"That must have been quite an adventure—losing Chandler. It sure took long enough," Tracy groused.

"Aw. It wasn't that bad, was it? What did you guys do?"

"We played on a playground," Carlos replied. "And Tracy wore me out."

"Huh?"

"Never mind. We just hid out in a park," said Tracy.

"Okay. Whatever. On the plus side, it's a beautiful day, isn't it? We're lucky. It can be cool here this time of year, but this is perfect."

She was right. The temperature was seventy degrees, the

sun shone in an azure sky scattered with puffy white clouds. The breeze off the gulf was gentle and quieter than usual.

"Well?" Carlos said. "What did you want to talk to me about?"

"Can I ask you a question first?" Jasmine asked.

"Sure. Join the crowd. Tracy's been interrogating me all day."

"First of all, you're sure that the names Jasmine and Tracy mean nothing to you? And neither of us looks familiar?"

"I'm sure."

"How did you and Chandler decide to vacation on Malaga Island?"

"That's two questions. But that's okay. Let me think." The incident in question had nearly faded from his mind. "Oh, yes. I remember. Chandler said we should have a vacation. We'd never had one since I got here. She suggested the gulf coast, and she pulled up a map on her tablet and began reading the names of the resort towns. When she got to Malaga Island, I said that's the one. I don't know why. I just liked the sound of it."

Jasmine poked Tracy. "See!" she said. "Carlos, you mentioned something about when you got here. What did you mean by that? Got where and when and from where?"

"He doesn't know. He has amnesia," said Tracy sheepishly.

"Amnesia!" cried Jasmine. "I *knew* it."

"Hey, you guys called this meeting. Why am I getting all the questions?" Carlos asked.

"I know it's a lot to ask of you, but could you please bear with us for now? It just seems like we need more information from you before we lay a lot of crap—or potential crap—on you."

"Sounds messy," Carlos laughed. "But go ahead. What do you

want to know? Chandler doesn't like me to give out personal information, but I trust you two for some reason."

"See!" said Jasmine again.

"Carlos," Tracy went on, ignoring Jasmine's remark, "could you tell us about how you got to wherever you live and met Chandler et cetera, et cetera…"

"It's pretty strange. You may not believe it."

"Hah!" Tracy snorted. "Just wait till you hear *our* story."

"Go ahead," said Jasmine encouragingly.

"The thing is," Carlos continued, "I don't know much about myself. One day about a year ago, I found myself in Manhattan in front of Bloomingdale's with no idea how I had gotten there or who I was."

"Go on," said Tracy. "Then what happened?"

"Well, it so happened that Chandler was standing next to me. Just like you two, she mistook me for this actor guy. She's crazy about him. Honestly, I've seen his TV shows since then, and I don't see what the big deal is. Anyway, that's why she approached me. She realized right away that I was not him, but she was concerned about me. I had no ID, no money and wasn't dressed properly for the weather. It was very cold that day."

"Wait." Jasmine pulled out her phone and pushed a few buttons. "Do you remember what you were wearing by chance?"

"Of course, I do. Black v neck sweater, black pants and gray flip-flops."

"Aha!" Jasmine showed the photograph she had pulled up on her phone. It was the full-length photo of Kang Ji Soo that she had posted for Alex to model himself after. The actor was dressed exactly as Carlos had just described.

"What's your point?" Carlos asked.

"Never mind. It will all become clear later. Go on with your story."

"The bottom line is Chandler figured I was an undocumented alien because of my accent and lack of papers. Since I didn't remember anything—not even my name—she figured I got amnesia when someone hit me on the head and robbed me of all my stuff. She took me in because she was worried about me and was afraid I would be deported or worse…"

"*And* had a giant crush on you," Jasmine interrupted.

"Perhaps," Carlos allowed shyly. "So anyway, she made up a personal history for me that we could tell her friends and family. I won't go into the details but it included my being from Brazil—thus the name Carlos. She had been calling me Jesse up until then."

"Oh dear! You must be so confused." Jasmine reached out and touched the back of his hand.

"Carlos," said Tracy, feeling oddly annoyed at Jasmine's touching Carlos like that, "do you know the date when that happened—when you arrived in New York?"

"Of course, I do. How could I forget? It was like the beginning of my life. It was a little before Christmas a year ago—December 15th.

"December 15th!" Jasmine grabbed Tracy's arm. "Tracy! That was the date when we both had the dream."

"Was it?" Tracy's casual tone belied the fact that she remembered that date very well.

"What dream?" Carlos asked.

Tracy promptly turned bright red. "Uh…can we talk about that later?"

"So what have you been doing since then?" Jasmine asked. "Do you work or go to school or anything?"

"I haven't done much. I don't have ID or a Social Security number. I've done a little modeling."

"Then you lied before. I asked you that and you said no," said Tracy, continuing to kick herself for caring.

"I'm sorry. Chandler was pressuring me to shut up. But how did you know about the modeling?"

"I saw you in an issue of GQ," Jasmine replied. "It wasn't a big spread or anything. It was like random hunks walking down the runway at a fashion show."

"Yeah. Chandler, being an actress, knows a lot of people—especially in the fashion industry. She got me some work where they paid me cash under the table. I only did runway work—no print. I never even knew I was in GQ. Forgive me for lying?"

"Absolutely," said Tracy and Jasmine together.

"Okay, now I believe it's time for you two to tell me whatever it is you want to tell me. I think I've been more than cooperative. I get the feeling you think you know something about my past, and if you do, I want to know it. I've been dying to know it for the past year."

"Go ahead then, Jaz. Tell him."

Jasmine cleared her throat and took a deep breath. "I should warn you that all of this is going to be very hard to believe and to accept."

"I'm not at all sure I believe it myself," Tracy piped up.

Jasmine frowned. "You're not helping." She turned to look Carlos directly in the eye. "You see, Carlos, Tracy and I have this chat room, and one night we were in there chatting when all of a sudden…."

And so she began. She told him about the hacker and all their conversations and how they had named him Alex and about the friendship that evolved and what he was like and how they had requested that he look like Kang Ji Soo and the plan for him to travel to earth. She told him how they had waited and waited and he hadn't come. "Of course," she said in closing, "we had no idea you would get amnesia. But now it all makes perfect sense."

Carlos sat stunned for a few moments, then stood up and took a couple of steps away as if halfway scared. "It makes perfect sense? Really? Am I to understand that you think I'm this hacker and that I might actually be from outer space?"

Before they could answer, his attitude changed as quickly as it had before and he let out a laugh. His laugh was deceptively exuberant—nervous underneath. "Wait a minute. This is all a joke, isn't it? Is this your idea of a practical joke?"

"*Carlos,*" Tracy cried. "What could possibly be our reason for wanting to play a joke on you?"

Jasmine had begun to cry. She had waited so long for this day and was beginning to sense it all slipping away. She didn't know which was more upsetting—the fact that Carlos seemed almost afraid of her or the idea that this was all a joke to him. The sight of Jasmine's genuine tears, sobered Carlos up abruptly. "Okay, okay. I get it. You guys believe this. I'm sorry but that's scary."

Tracy, finding herself in the position of having to defend an idea she had always ridiculed, spoke up. "But what about the photo of the actor's clothing and the way you resemble him and your arrival on the very day Jasmine and I both dreamed about Alex?" She blushed again. "I won't go into the details but let's just say we both had the exact same dream about you the same day you arrived in New York. What about the fact that Malaga Island rang a bell with you and the fact that you trusted us from the start? You don't usually allow two strange women to snatch you away from a hotel room, do you? Doesn't it all have to mean something?"

Carlos threw his arms in the air. "Coincidences! All coincidences. My own story may be a little incredible but that doesn't mean I'll believe any crazy story that comes along. If there's one thing I'm good at, it's science…"

Jasmine nudged Tracy. "That fits too," she whispered.

"What was that?" Carlos asked.

"Alex was good at science, too. That's all I'm saying."

"So what? You'd only need a grammar school science education to figure this out. It's not possible to travel from galaxy to galaxy and morph into other shapes."

"They say anything is possible," said Tracy quietly. She looked back and forth from Jasmine to Carlos. "Well…they do!"

Carlos laughed. "You want me to believe that I am actually a…what were your words? A swirling mass of brain waves? I may not know who I am but I know that I am me…if that makes sense."

"It doesn't," Jasmine said.

Carlos took out his phone. "Look, ladies, I really enjoyed meeting you…at first. I'm sure you're very nice people…aside from being bonkers, but I have to get going. I'll call Chandler and have her come pick me up."

"That won't be necessary," said a voice coming from the direction of the wooden ramp. The sound of the surf had obscured the clicking of Chandler's heels as she approached the deck, and she was already upon the little group, who quickly looked up, startled. "I'm here."

"How in the world did you find us?" Jasmine demanded.

"Dogged persistence, dear. You should have switched cars at some point. That's crime drama plotting 101."

"But you were in the shower. How…"

"That's where you're wrong. I turned the water on and then decided to tweeze my eyebrows. I hadn't gotten into the shower yet. I heard Carlos talking to someone. By the time I threw a dress on and got out of the bathroom, he was gone. I dashed out and saw you just as your car drove off." Chandler smiled smugly. "From there it was just a matter of locating your car in a parking lot. Come on, let's go." She turned to walk away with Carlos following behind. He took a few steps before stopping in his tracks and telling Chandler to wait.

"Could I have a moment alone with them?" He nodded toward where Jasmine and Tracy still sat in a state of bewilderment on the wooden bench.

"Go ahead, but make it quick." With a toss of her curls, Chandler marched off toward the lot where she had left the car.

"Look," Carlos began once they were alone, "I'm sorry if I was rude or hurt your feelings before. I'm sure you mean no harm. In fact, I felt strangely comfortable with Tracy the minute she approached me at the coffee shop—and then with you too, Jasmine. For a while there, it seemed you might really know something about my past, and I have wanted to know about that so badly for so long. That's why it was doubly disappointing when I heard your whacky story…"

"We're not crazy," Tracy interrupted. "Jasmine was always the one who believed in Alex—I never did to tell you the truth. But even *she* is not crazy."

"Gee, thanks," said Jasmine.

"All right, all right," Carlos continued. "That's beside the point. I just want to wish you all the best and hope you both find whatever you're looking for. And thank you for your concern for me—no matter how misguided." With a brief bow of his head, he started to walk away. But Tracy grabbed hold of his hand and pulled him back.

"Could you tell Chandler something? Tell her thanks, from us, for taking care of you all this time. God knows what could have happened to you, whether you're Alex or not, if she hadn't taken you under her wing. Will you tell her that?"

For the first time since they'd arrived at St. Pete Beach, Carlos flashed his quasi-famous smile. "I will." He turned and started down the ramp to where Chandler waited.

****

Chandler closed the hotel room door behind her and tossed her purse onto the couch. "What the hell is wrong with you! How could you go off with those two lunatics?" She had given Carlos the silent treatment all the way back and was now ready to let loose.

Carlos began picking up random articles of clothing and souvenirs and putting them into his open suitcase. "I wouldn't say they were exactly lunatics."

"Women who abduct men from hotel rooms are not normal."

"You give new meaning to the term alien abduction," Carlos muttered under his breath.

"What was that?"

"Nothing."

"What did they want anyway? That Tracy was suspicious from the time she approached us at the coffee shop, and then she pulls this stunt. She has some kind of an angle. I just know it."

"Nothing. They didn't want anything really."

Carlos promptly decided that lying would be the best policy. Chandler wouldn't believe them any more than he did. Still, he felt an odd solidarity with Tracy and Jasmine. Anything that went on between the three of them should stay between them though he wasn't sure why.

"Nothing? They kidnap you from your hotel room and drive you miles away—all for nothing?"

"It was five miles and they didn't exactly kidnap me. I went willingly."

"Why? Why would you do that? How many times have I warned you about talking to strangers? Didn't we just have this conversation this morning?"

Carlos clicked his bag shut and smiled his most disarming smile—the one that always worked on Chandler. "No need to worry," he said calmly. "They're just harmless fangirls. You know all about that, right? There's Ji Soo, Ryan Gosling, Orlando Bloom...I could go on."

"Uh...may I remind you—you are not actually Ji Soo. And I never stalked any of those guys."

"No, you just took me home and kept me by your side."

Chandler looked stricken. Her big green eyes filled with tears. Her knees buckled and she sank onto the sofa. Carlos supposed he should go and comfort her. Instead, he picked up his suitcase and carried it to the door. "Might as well be ready to leave early in the morning," he said.

Chapter 31
Of All the Gin Joints in All the Universe

Tracy couldn't fall asleep. She lay awake in Jasmine's guest room, staring at the ceiling. Through the open window she could hear the surf whenever there were lulls in the traffic up and down Coastal Boulevard. She glanced at the clock on the nightstand. It was just midnight. They had gone to bed too early. She was still keyed up, but Jasmine had pleaded fatigue and suggested turning in at eleven. Rather than winding her up, the events of the day had sapped all of Jasmine's energy.

Tracy sat up in bed. Nothing sounded good—not a book nor TV nor music—not even food. She wondered if there was any chance Jasmine was awake and up for a talk. She pulled on a pair of jeans, slipped into her flip-flops and crept over to Jasmine's room. The door was ajar. Jasmine was splayed out spread eagle on the bed and was making soft snoring sounds. Tracy stood there a moment, thinking. A walk, fresh air. That sounded good. She grabbed a hoodie from the coat rack and put it on over the Malaga Island souvenir tee-shirt she had worn to bed. She picked up Jasmine's keys from the hall table and went out to the street.

There were still groups of tourists on the sidewalks. After all, it was their vacation. No need to get to bed early. Tracy crossed the road and walked between two mom-and-pop motels to the beach. She dug her fists into her pockets and turned north. The town was beginning to wind down for the night. She passed a few couples walking hand in hand and the occasional family whose kids were being allowed up way past their bedtimes.

When she had gone nearly a mile, she became aware of music drifting out from one of the beach bars. Without thinking, she turned toward the sound and made her way into the bar. She wasn't there thirty seconds before she realized this was the beach bar connected to Malaga Manor. The name was displayed prominently above the archway that led from the bar to the hotel proper.

Whatever. What were the chances Carlos or Chandler would be here? They would be leaving early in the morning and were probably all tucked in for the night—in separate beds she hoped. She told herself she was hoping this for Jasmine's sake, but she wasn't entirely sure about that. Anyway, she was tired of walking, and a glass of wine sounded appealing. Perhaps it would be the very thing that would help her sleep.

She took a stool at the end of the bar and ordered a chardonnay. A jazz combo was playing vaguely Sinatra-ish music, and a few sun-burnt couples swayed sleepily on the tiny dance floor.

She turned her attention back to the bar as the bartender set her drink down in front of her, and when she looked up again, he was there. Carlos. He was sitting at the opposite end of the bar, drinking a Corona.

Tracy gasped and suddenly felt light-headed. How had he gotten there? Had he been there all along or had he sneaked in while she was watching the dancers? He was going to think she was a stalker for sure. She tried to look away quickly but before she could, he caught her eye. He smiled and raised his bottle in a mock toast. Not knowing what else to do, she returned the gesture.

And then before she knew it he was coming toward her— coming toward her and, alarmingly, sitting down on the stool next to hers.

"Honestly, Carlos, I swear I am not stalking you. I didn't even realize this bar was part of the Malaga Manor until I was inside. And then I figured you'd be asleep by now. You see, when I'm in a strange place, I don't really pay attention to where things are in relation to other things. I just let Jasmine lead the way. Really. I have a very bad sense of direction." She blurted all of that out at warp speed before taking a breath followed by a big gulp of wine. She let out a sarcastic laugh. "Of all the gin joints in all the towns…"

"In all the world, you walk into mine," Carlos finished.

Tracy half expected the band to start playing "As Time Goes By." It didn't. Instead, it played "Some Other Time." Close enough.

"Alex knew that quote," she said.

"Everyone knows that quote."

"Point taken. But I'm really very sorry."

"Nothing to be sorry about. I'm glad you're here."

"You are?"

"Yeah. I'm glad to get a chance to apologize again for the way I treated you and your friend today."

Tracy wondered briefly why he was referring to Jasmine as her friend. Didn't he realize Jasmine was the principle player in this drama? Tracy was just the sidekick. Lucy's Ethel, Jerry's George, Batman's Robin.

"No, no," she said. "We laid a lot of stuff on you today. Whether it was fact or not, it was a lot to absorb."

"And was it fact? I mean do you think it's fact?"

"Frankly, I'm so confused right now I don't know fact from fiction." His mesmerizing almost-black eyes and the fragrance of sandalwood and vanilla that seemed to ooze from his pores were not helping. Carlos motioned to the bartender for another round.

"The thing is," Tracy went on, "Jasmine was always the one who believed in Alex—or at least wanted to. I never really did. I haven't checked my brain at the door. I know, just like you do, that this notion of an alien coming to earth from faraway galaxies is scientifically impossible. Deep down, I don't think Jaz believed it either. It was a game. And let's face it, there is an Alex.

"Whether he's a teenager in his parents' basement or a middle-aged pervert, someone made those posts in our chat room. And Jasmine really likes that person. I guess she's sort of in love with him no matter what form he's in. But your arrival on the scene has changed everything. Suddenly, something totally illogical seems a little bit logical—even to me. So many coincidences. It's difficult to explain—unless you really are Alex. See what I mean? I'm confused."

"They are all coincidences. There's no other explanation."

Tracy frowned and took a swig of wine.

"I guess," Carlos said, "I don't know what you want from me."

Tracy bristled. "I don't want anything from you!"

"I...I didn't mean you personally," said Carlos, blushing. "I meant you and your friend—mostly her I suppose."

"I haven't discussed that with her, but since you apparently can't remember Alex or return Jaz's feelings, I would guess she'd settle for being friends—that is, all of us being friends."

"I'm pretty sure Chandler would not go for that, and I can't leave Chandler. I owe her everything."

"But you don't love her?" Tracy held her breath waiting for his answer.

"No," he said simply.

Tracy smiled and released her breath gratefully. "So you're going to spend the rest of your life tied to a woman you don't love? Do you have any hope of ever meeting someone, falling in love, marriage, kids—that whole thing?"

"I keep thinking my memory will come back, and things will be settled one way or another."

Tracy sighed hopelessly. Carlos regarded her with an indulgent smile, his dark eyes soft and reassuring. He got down from his stool and held out his hand. "Dance?" he said.

"W-what?" she stammered, wondering if she had heard right.

"May I have this dance?" he asked formally.

"I don't really dance."

"Neither do I. We'll learn together." He glanced over at the lethargic couples on the floor. "It doesn't look that complicated."

She put her hand in his and he led her to the dance floor.

There was an awkward moment while they decided where to place their hands, but once decided, it all came surprisingly naturally. The song had changed to something Tracy didn't recognize, but from this moment she knew she would never forget that melody. Carlos pulled her close. His chest and arms felt remarkably hard and soft at the same time, and she wondered how that was possible. She hated to admit that it felt very much like that dream she had dreamed about Alex. She noticed that Carlos danced quite well. She remembered how Alex had always claimed to be a fast learner.

The music...the fragrance of his perfect skin...the two chardonnays...the release, at last, of the stress of the day...it was all dizzying. She allowed her head to droop onto his shoulder and nestle there, and she thought it was the most comfortable place on earth.

When the song ended, she stayed in his arms a few seconds longer than she should have.

"Shall we have another?" he asked.

"Oh, no!" She fairly jumped away from him. "I mean, no, I should get back. It's late. I sneaked out and Jasmine doesn't even know I left."

Carlos checked his watch. "They don't close here for a while. You could stay."

"No, I really can't."

She turned and headed back to the bar. "Oh, my God!" she cried, patting her pockets. "I just realized I walked out with no money. I can't pay. I hadn't planned on stopping anywhere."

"Don't worry. I'm picking up your tab, of course."

"Of course. That is, I mean thank you." She started to say "my treat next time" before she remembered it was highly unlikely there would ever be a next time.

He paid the bill and together they started toward the exit. "Well," she said, unsure what was the proper comment on the sort of experience they had just shared, "this has been fun."

"Yes, it was fun."

"But not fun enough to change anything, right? Nothing's going to change about your relationship to Jaz or to Chandler...or to me?"

Carlos leaned into her a little and took a deep breath almost as if trying to inhale her. "It's tempting," he said. "But, no, it wouldn't be logical."

"Right. Logic is important I suppose. Um...maybe we could text now and then?"

"Chandler would find out. She always knows everything. And that would be the end of it."

Tracy regarded him critically. "I don't want to insult you or make you mad, but it seems to me you are an adult man. I wonder why you seem so unable to make decisions for yourself."

"I often wonder that myself. There's a great deal I don't understand about myself."

"Because of the amnesia?"

"Maybe."

They were about to step onto the beach. "Let me walk you back," he said. "It's very late for you to be out alone. How far is it?"

"About a mile or so I guess, but it's not necessary. Jasmine says it's very safe here."

"I insist."

"No. I insist. Thanks again for the drinks and the dance." She started to walk away but he grabbed her sleeve.

"Then let me put you in a cab." His eyes were so kind and full of concern that she knew resisting him would be futile. She shrugged and nodded her head.

He took her arm and guided her back through the bar, across the lobby and out the big glass front doors. He hailed a cab and gave the driver a ten. "This should cover it."

"Good-bye," said Tracy. "I'll give your regards to Jasmine."

Carlos looked confused, but all he said was good-bye.

The taxi pulled away from the hotel, and Tracy took a quick glance back at Carlos, standing alone in the driveway. All of a sudden she felt sure she would never tell Jasmine a word about what had happened tonight at the beach bar of the big hotel.

Chapter 32
On the Balcony

The following evening, Jasmine and Tracy sat huddled under a blanket on Jasmine's balcony. The air was chilly. Glimpses of the gulf were visible between the buildings across the street. In their hands, they cradled mugs of hot cocoa with marshmallows—a comfort dictated by both the cool night air and the emotional situation in which they found themselves. Every once in a while, a tear slid down Jasmine's cheek.

"Aw, don't cry," Tracy cooed. "It'll be okay."

"How?" Jasmine choked out.

"I don't know. But it has to be, doesn't it? You have to go on. What are you going to do? Curl up and die?"

"Maybe."

"Look at it this way, kiddo. Without his memories, that guy just isn't Alex—which, may I remind you, we don't even know if he is Alex. If he was Alex and if he stayed here, he wouldn't really be the person you fell in love with."

"For a guy who looks like that, I could manage to fall in love all over again."

"That's pretty shallow." Tracy laughed despite feeling guilty for doing so. "Remember how you used to rhapsodize about your relationship—how pure it was because it was one mind in love with another mind? Nothing physical or sexual involved. Remember that?"

"That was before we caused Alex to look like Ji Soo. Ever since I started envisioning him that way, there has definitely been a sexual component."

"At least, you're honest." Tracy gave a little shiver and clutched her warm mug tighter. She hoped everything she was telling her friend was true. It just might have to apply to herself as well.

"Besides, if he stayed here, maybe his memories would come back eventually. That happens sometimes, doesn't it?" Jasmine searched Tracy's eyes hopefully.

"In soaps, it does."

"I'm talking about real life."

"Hey, that's my line. Besides, the kind of amnesia you get from intergalactic travel might not have the same characteristics as earthly amnesia. And I can't believe I'm trying to make this into a rational discussion. You know what this cocoa needs? A good shot of alcohol."

"Come on, Tracy. I can tell by how you've been talking lately that you pretty much believe in Alex, too."

"It's hard not to get sucked into your fantasy." Especially when you can still feel his hand in yours and his fragrance still surrounds you like an intoxicating cloud. Against her will, Tracy sighed at the thought.

"Aw, come on. This is Jaz you're talking to. You can't fool me."

Tracy sighed again and took a sip of cocoa.

"Wait. I have an idea," said Jasmine after a moment. She sat bolt upright and grasped Tracy's arm with a claw-like grip.

"No! Please. No more ideas."

"Tracy, do you still have all our old chats in the archives?"

"Yeah. I never deleted any of them. The only time anything was deleted was when you and Alex went behind my back and tried to keep something from me—which, by the way, I still don't know what it was," Tracy pouted.

"It was nothing. It was so much nothing that I don't even re-member what it was. Is that important now?"

"Okay, okay. What's your great idea?"

"Prepare to be dazzled." Jasmine paused dramatically. "See, we print out all the chats and get them to Alex somehow. First of all, he'll see that we were telling the truth about how we met him…"

"He may think we doctored them or created them from scratch," Tracy interjected.

"Oh, ye of little faith, maybe he won't. Second of all, may-be when he reads through them, something will jog his memory. After all, Malaga Island jogged his memory. At least, that's what I think. And maybe something about you jogged his memory too. He seemed to like you from the start."

"And just how are we going to get these transcripts to him?" Tracy asked, trying not to take that last remark too much to heart.

"It probably wouldn't be that hard to get Chandler's address, but I'm sure she screens all the mail. She will never allow us to get close enough to hand him anything."

"I think we should hire a private investigator," said Jasmine in a matter of fact manner. She nodded her head sharply for emphasis. "He'll have to find Alex, catch him alone at some point, and hand him the transcripts. He can say they're from us and beg him to just read them. He'll give our contact information so Alex can get in touch with us once he's come to his senses."

"What if he refuses to read them?"

"We have to hope the detective is persuasive—and that Alex's curiosity gets the best of him. If not, at least we will know we have done all we can."

"Hmm…Sounds expensive."

"Don't worry about it. I'll get it."

"No, no. I'll split it with you."

"Alex is my responsibility."

"Is he?"

Jasmine shot Tracy a questioning look. "What's wrong? Are you upset with me? You sound a little annoyed."

"No. I'm not annoyed. Don't be silly. Why would I be annoyed? Alex was always your project. If he is Alex, which he probably isn't, he came here for you."

"Okay…if you're sure."

"Sure. I still insist on paying though."

That night, Tracy once again lay awake. She had spent the entire day with Jasmine including the conversation on the balcony and had not told her about seeing Carlos at the bar—dancing with Carlos at the bar. What was *wrong* with her? The minute she saw Carlos, she should have phoned Jasmine. There had been plenty of time for her to make it to the hotel and see him for herself. Had her own brain been so muddled that she didn't think of it, or did she subconsciously want that time with him all to herself?

On the other hand, wasn't she justified in keeping this secret from her friend? Wouldn't it hurt Jaz terribly if she knew how Carlos had danced with her—and everything else that she was trying not to think too much about. Never mind. It would all be a moot point soon. This private investigator idea would come to naught. Tracy shuddered when she thought of it. She was terrified that it would work and equally terrified that it wouldn't.

Chapter 33
Proof

The man approaching Carlos in Central Park looked like any other guy. Khakis, plaid shirt under corduroy jacket, sandy hair, tortoise shell glasses. He carried a brown leather messenger bag over his shoulder and held a manila envelope in his hand.

"Carlos Pereira?" he asked, thrusting the envelope into Carlos's hand.

"Y-yes?" Carlos's eyes darted frantically as he tried to decide whether to run and where.

"You've been served."

"Huh?"

"Just kidding. I just wanted to get your attention. John Rollins, private investigator." He took a business card from his pocket and handed it to Carlos. "Don't worry, man. You're not in any trouble. I just have a message for you from Jasmine Morrow."

Carlos looked down at the envelope as if it were a foreign

object that had fallen from the sky and mysteriously landed in his hands. "Is this it?"

"Yes."

"What is it?"

"I don't really know. My mission was to find you, hand you those documents and urge you to read them thoroughly. My client is hoping you will be convinced of something or other—I don't know what. If you find anything helpful in those papers, please contact Ms. Morrow. Her contact information is in the envelope."

"Is anyone called Tracy involved in this?"

"I don't know. Ms. Morrow is the one who hired me. That's all I know."

Carlos continued to stare silently at the envelope.

"Well?" said John Rollins. "May I tell Ms. Morrow that you will read the documents? If it means anything to you, coming from me, it seemed real important to her. Like life and death important."

"Life and death?" Carlos's eyes grew wide and his voice quavered.

John shrugged. "It's a figure of speech, man. Don't freak out."

"Oh," Carlos breathed. "Okay."

"Can I take that as a yes? You will read the material?"

"Uh…okay…I guess. Are you sure no one named Tracy was mentioned?"

"Yes, I'm sure. Maybe when you read the documents, everything will become clear. Look, you have my card. If you have any questions whatsoever, give me a call." He and Carlos shook hands and John Rollins was gone as quickly as he had come.

Carlos stood gazing at the envelope in his hands, wondering what it was and almost afraid to open it. He found a vacant park bench and sat down. Cautiously, he opened the envelope and pulled out a sheaf of papers secured with a metal clamp. The top sheet was a cover letter signed by Jasmine Morrow:

Hi, Carlos,

Attached are the transcripts of all the chats that Alex participated in. As you will see, they cover a six-month period—basically once a week during that time. We, Tracy and I, are not trying to be pushy or force you into something you don't want. We just want to make sure you have all information that may be pertinent to your search for who you are. We know that is your top priority—understandably so. We believe this material will be helpful and, we hope, convincing. Possibly something in these papers will jog your memory and bring everything back. Of course, we hope with all our hearts that our friendship will be revived. You have become very dear to us. But obviously we have no choice but to accept whatever conclusion you come to. We promise not to continue to bother you. My contact information is on the next page. I would appreciate your getting back to me once you have read the transcripts—whether your reaction is positive or negative. However, I will understand if you don't. Regardless of what happens in the future, we loved meeting you. In a strange way, it was truly thrilling—a fun adventure. Whether it has a sad or happy ending is yet to be discovered.

Best wishes no matter what,
Jasmine Morrow

Carlos weighed the stack of papers in his hands. Of course, he would read them. Who could resist? The one thing he was sure of was that Chandler should know nothing about this. He would not read them at home. He replaced the papers in the envelope, stood up and looked around. There was a diner across the street. He crossed over and went inside. A booth in the corner seemed relatively private. He sat down there and waited for the waitress to take his order. He didn't want any interruptions

Once his coffee and Danish were delivered, he carefully removed the packet of papers from the envelope and began to read

An hour and two coffees later, he sat slumped in his chair, feeling dazed and all at sea. It was true that certain phrases had seemed familiar, but was it from hearing Jasmine and Tracy talk about these things, or was he really remembering?

When all was said and done, only one item continued to gnaw at him—the posting of Tracy's photograph. The printout of the chat archives had not copied any of the photographs. Beneath Tracy's promise to post her picture, there was nothing but a blank space. If he closed his eyes very tightly and tried to conjure up what had once been there, he felt as if he almost could.

But try as he might, the image refused to resolve. And if it ever did, would he be remembering the Tracy he had met on Malaga Island or the Tracy of the chat room? It was all too confusing. With a sigh of frustration, he gathered up the papers and replaced them in the envelope. He knew for sure he had to read to them again, and, more important, find a good hiding place where Chandler would not discover them.

Chapter 34
Meeting of the Minds

Despite Chandler's constant admonitions never to open the door to anyone, Carlos peered through the peephole into the hallway. The face that looked back at him was surprisingly familiar. It belonged to Benjy Bryant.

Against all warnings and better judgment, Carlos opened the door. Benjy's jaw dropped. "You!" he cried. "You're that guy who was in my office that day. What the hell!"

"What are you doing here?" Carlos wanted to know.

"I think I'm the one entitled to ask the questions here. Are you going to let me in or what?"

"Sure." Carlos stepped aside and allowed Benjy to pass.

"What were you doing in my office that day? Checking up on me or something?"

"No. I mean not exactly." Carlos's cheeks colored, and he lowered his eyes. "It was an accident...mostly."

"Mostly? What does that mean?"

"If you'll just let me explain. Please have a seat. Can I get you a drink or anything?"

"No. Nothing." Benjy flopped down on the couch and crossed his arms over his chest. "Go on."

"It was like this." Carlos began pacing back and forth. "Tracy and I were there in Malaga…"

"Wait just a minute there," Benjy interrupted. "That woman with you was Tracy? Jasmine's friend Tracy? Oh, my God."

"If you'll just let me tell you what happened…"

"Knock yourself out," Benjy said with an exasperated sigh.

"So Tracy and I were killing time waiting to meet with Jasmine. Jasmine did tell you we met, didn't she?"

"Yes. Jasmine has told me everything. However, Tracy apparently never said anything to anyone about visiting my office that day," Benjy grumbled.

"Is that important right now? Can we get back to the point?"

"Sure. That would be great," Benjy agreed—with sarcasm.

"So…we were just walking around, and Tracy noticed the sign in front of your building with your name on it. What are the odds, huh?" Carlos let out a little chuckle before realizing the humor of the situation wasn't funny at all without Tracy there to share it. "Anyway, Tracy had always wondered what you were like, and we decided to go in and try to get a look at you. Uh…that sounds really bad, doesn't it?"

"Yeah," said Benjy, not in the least amused. "Why didn't Tracy just introduce herself?"

"I guess she thought it would be awkward."

"You mean because the guy with her happens to be the guy my girlfriend thinks she's madly in love with?"

Carlos blushed again. "Probably. And Jasmine probably wouldn't like the idea of us spying on you—so to speak."

"Well, I would hope not." Benjy stood up and began to match Carlos pace for pace. "Can I change my mind about that drink?"

"Sure. What would you like? Chandler has everything."

"Chandler! I forgot about her. She's not here, is she?" Benjy glanced toward the hallway that led to the bedrooms.

"No. She had a meeting. She'll be out for a while."

"Good. We don't need any additional complications. I'll take a scotch if you have it."

"That's sort of how we felt—Tracy and I—keeping it to ourselves about seeing you that day," said Carlos as he poured the scotch into a short glass. "No additional complications. That was a pretty complicated day already. If Jasmine explained it all to you—I mean about what a crazy day that was—maybe you can understand how we felt." He handed Benjy his drink and got himself a beer from the fridge.

"I guess I can," Benjy allowed reluctantly. He resumed his seat and sipped the whiskey appreciatively. It was a good one.

Carlos took a seat in the armchair. "May I ask how you found me?"

"Jasmine's P.I."

"Isn't that confidential?"

"Jaz gave her authorization for him to speak to me. She has nothing to hide from me."

"I see. Well, if it makes you feel any better, Tracy always

thought you were the one for Jasmine. She always told her that. And meeting you that day only reinforced her opinion."

A trace of a smile tugged at Beny's lips and his chest puffed out just a bit. "Is that so?"

"Yes. Absolutely."

Benjy's smile faded immediately. "For all the good it does." He chugged down the rest of his drink and held out his glass for a refill, which Carlos promptly supplied.

The two men sat in silence for an uncomfortable few minutes.

"Well?" said Carlos at last. "What did you want to talk to me about?"

"I want…I need to talk to you about Jaz. I guess I want to know what's the deal between you two?"

"Deal? There's no deal. Let me ask you a question."

"Shoot."

"Do you think she really believes I'm an alien from outer space?"

"Who knows? I think she thinks she's in love with whoever was posting in her stupid chat room."

"Well, it wasn't me. As far as the alien thing goes, we both know that's not possible. You're a doctor—a man of science. And so am I—though I have no idea how I became one. We both know her alien theory is impossible. And I swear to you I am not the guy from the chat room."

"I hear she and Tracy showed you transcripts. Nothing rang a bell?"

"Nothing really. Maybe one or two words or phrases but nothing I couldn't be remembering in some other context."

"They say you have amnesia. Is it possible you were in the chat room and have forgotten it?"

"It's possible I guess but I really don't think so."

Benjy studied Carlos for a moment. "You seem surprisingly normal."

"*Thank* you. No offense but if there are any crazies in the picture I'm afraid they are your girlfriend and Tracy. Likable lunatics—but lunatics just the same."

"Really," said Benjy dragging his hand down the side of his face.

"I guess I don't know what you want from me."

"Truth?"

"Yes. Please."

"I honestly came here thinking that if you had any feelings for Jaz, I'd try to encourage you to follow through—for her sake."

"Wow. That is pretty unselfish. You must love her a lot."

"I've loved her since birth—literally. Our parents were best friends even before we were born. I've never known a time when I didn't love Jaz."

"You know Jasmine doesn't really love me. She just has a crush because I look that that actor fellow. That's all it is."

"You think?"

"I'm sure of it. I think I agree with Tracy. Jasmine is making a mistake turning you down."

Benjy peered at Carlos over the rim of his whiskey glass. "Carlos, my man…I don't see any way on earth that we are going to make an argument out of this."

"Yeah?" Carlos said with a laugh.

"Yeah. I came here loaded for bear. But it looks like we are on the same page."

"So what now?"

"I have no idea. At least I don't have to worry about you as competition."

"That's one problem you can cross off your list."

"Yep. One down, a hundred and one to go."

"Will you tell Jasmine you came here?"

"Only if I want to be dead."

"There's too much secret keeping among this group, and I include myself in that."

"Maybe I will tell her after all—one day."

Chapter 35
Journey

There was an overwhelming sensation of fear. Blind terror. Second only to fear, was the sensation of movement—rolling, crushing, pulverizing speed. All his synapses were sparking wildly, threatening to short circuit. There was no pain yet, but pain seemed imminent.

The calculations had to be perfect or he would surely disintegrate. He couldn't think. How could thought break through all the fear and noise? Still, a few isolated words and phrases floated in the ether around him—Zeth, chocoholic, Dr. Who, You've Got Mail, call me Alex. What did it mean? He couldn't concentrate long enough to even consider what it might mean.

Then there were the flashes of memory. The girl. He had seen her before. The flashes were so brief he couldn't bring them into focus.

It seemed to go on forever—until suddenly it didn't. It all

stopped—instantaneously like a window slamming down on its sill. The motion, the words, the visions. They all stopped with a loud bumping sound and, for the first time, pain.

Carlos's eyes flew open. His hand went instinctively to his head where he had smashed it against the headboard. Rubbing the tender spot, he sat up in bed. His pajamas were soaked with perspiration. He could still feel the terror in the pit of his stomach, but as he looked about the familiar room, dimly lit by a variety of electronics and a sliver of moonlight between the drapes, the fear subsided.

"What the hell was that?" he murmured aloud though he was alone in the room. It must have been a dream, but it had seemed so real. Dazed as he was, he had to chuckle at the stupid cliché.

Still, it had not seemed like a dream. It had seemed like a memory. He squeezed his eyes shut tight and scrunched up his forehead with the effort to remember. Mostly he wanted to re-member that girl.

As he sat there trying to think, a stabbing pain slashed through his brain. For a second, he thought he'd gotten a headache from contorting his face like that. But, no, this was more than a head-ache. It was like a bomb going off in his head. He fell back against the headboard, hitting his head hard again. This time there was no pain. He was out cold.

Seconds later, though as far as he knew, it might have been hours, he opened his eyes. A parade of images was scrolling across his consciousness—images that he soon realized were memories. He had memories—all of them. In a flash of clarity, all was re-vealed. All was remembered. *All.*

He leapt out of bed and went to the door. He peered out, making sure Chandler was safely in her room for the night. Locking the door behind him just in case, he crept over to his bed and drew Jasmine's envelope from between the mattress and the box spring.

He climbed back into bed and turned on the bedside lamp. Quickly leafing through the papers, he found the page he wanted—Tracy's post of her photograph. There it was. The blank space. He stared at it as hard as he could, trying to conjure up the girl from the dream—or whatever it was—that he had just had.

He stared at the page for a long time and was about to give up when a pale, shapeless tinge of color seeped onto the white space. Gradually the image began to take shape like a photograph emerging in a darkroom.

When the process was complete, it was Tracy. He knew right then. He knew everything. He knew the dream had been a memory—a memory of his long trip to earth. He knew that he was not simply remembering the words from having read the transcripts. He remembered them from the first time they were "spoken" in the chat room by Jasmine and Tracy…and Alex. He *was* Alex.

He studied the image on the page, though he now realized the image was in his head, and the blank space was still blank. Short, choppy dark hair, a pixie-like face with wide blue eyes rimmed with long, black lashes, small turned-up nose sprinkled lightly with freckles. It was the Tracy he had met in the coffee shop, and it was the Tracy he had first seen in the chat room. It was Tracy. It had always been Tracy.

Chapter 36
Tracy and Alex

The sound of the ocean was thunderous—so unlike the gentle, lapping, of the surf at Malaga Island. Instead of calming Tracy, it made her heart pound harder in her chest as if trying to compete with the noisy sea. It was late, and she was alone.

She wished she'd worn long pants. The night air was chillier than she'd expected. She hunkered down into her sweatshirt and pulled the sleeves down over her hands. There was no music as there had been at Malaga, and if there had been, it would have been drowned out by the roar of the Pacific. But there were stars in the sky. Lots of them.

She envied Kelsey for being able to sleep so peacefully back in the hotel room. For Tracy, sleep never came easy these days. Her mind was always racing.

She had no idea how far she had come, but the cold was beginning to be too much. She turned around and headed back toward the hotel. The beach was deserted except for a tiny blip far off in the distance. She hunched her shoulders, bowed her head against the wind and trudged onward.

When she finally looked up again, the blip had grown larger. It was clearly a person coming nearer and nearer. In another second, she knew. She knew as well as she knew anything on this earth. How familiar the bearing, how black the hair, how slender the figure. How like her dream all those months ago.

She quickened her pace. He began to run full out until they were standing face to face. He smiled and winked and whispered her name before wrapping her in his arms. "It was you all along," he murmured, his lips against her hair.

"It was? I didn't know. I really didn't know."

He pulled back to look into her eyes. "Neither did I," he said.

He cupped her face in his hands and kissed her mouth just as in her dream.

****

They were safe and sound in their own room at the hotel. (Kelsey would understand.)

He kissed her again.

"That was good," she said. "You must have been practicing."

"Not at all." He raised his hand to swear an oath. "Just now on the beach was my first time—ever."

"Not Chandler?" she asked cautiously.

"I told you. There was never anything between us."

"That's our Alex," Tracy laughed. "Always the quick study

even when it comes to kissing."

"Hey…when did you decide I was Alex?"

"It's been a process. More important, when did *you* decide you were Alex?"

Alex thought a moment. "Can I tell you later? It's complicated."

There would be plenty of time to explain—about the transcripts and the photograph and the dream.

Tracy ran her hands down his shoulders and arms to his hands, which she grasped in her own. "You're not going to unzip this beautiful skin and be a lizard underneath, are you?"

Alex laughed. "I told you girls way back in the chat room that wasn't the case. No lizards. You watch too much TV." He put his arms around her and pulled her down onto the bed.

Morning sun washed the room in golden light. Tracy stretched out her body alongside Alex's. She studied his sleeping face for a moment before he seemed to feel her gaze and opened his eyes. "Everything okay?" he asked.

"Perfect," she sighed. "I have to admit I was a little worried."

"About what?"

"Frankly, I've worried about this ever since I began to suspect I'd fallen in love with you. I was afraid everything would not be in working order. After all, you are not actually a human being—at least you weren't. And until last night you'd never even tried the equipment out—so to speak. Sorry," she went on gamely despite her cheeks having colored deep red. "That was crude, wasn't it?"

"It's okay." Mischief glinted in his eyes. "Everything was satisfactory, wasn't it?"

"More than satisfactory. I don't know how you do it. And don't give me that old 'fast learner' line."

"Okay, I won't. But I don't know what else to tell you. Maybe it's just something that being in love brings out in you. Remember when you and Jaz schooled me on love and romance? I guess I took that all to heart. Love is the most important thing, isn't it?"

"Yes, I believe so."

"All I know is that if I had realized that such sensations as I felt last night existed, I would have tried to come to earth much sooner."

She sat up in bed. "I have questions, Alex. Lots and lots of questions."

"Understandably so. Shoot."

"I guess I'm just not sure how this whole thing works. For example, will you be able to reproduce? Not that that's a deal breaker. And you once said you were immortal. Are you going to stay young forever? Will I end up a shriveled old lady with a gorgeous thirty-year-old boyfriend?"

"I hope to be more than a boyfriend long before that."

Tracy blushed again and tried not to put too much stock in that comment.

"Look, I meticulously duplicated human cells and DNA so that this body should operate exactly as any other human body—only much more handsome," he said with the wink that was rapidly becoming his totally charming trademark. "If my calculations were accurate, my cells should age just like yours. There should be no problems." He pulled her into his arms. "But just to make sure, we should try out the equipment again."

"There's a lot more to talk about," she murmured against his lips.

"Later."

"Yes, later." She giggled and rolled over on top of him and pulled the covers over their heads. He began to laugh, too, and, next to making love, laughing together seemed the sweetest thing in the universe.

Tracy reached up and swiped his cheek with her fingertips. Alex followed suit and touched the corner of his eye.

"What's this? *Tears?*" he said incredulously, and he began to laugh again.

"What?" Tracy asked.

"They're my first. I always wanted them. I never expected they would be of joy, not sadness."

Chapter 37
Jasmine and Benjy

"B-b-benjy!"

"Jaz? Is that you? What's wrong with your voice? Are you all right?"

"Uh-huh."

"You don't sound all right. Are you crying?"

"Uh-huh."

"What is it?"

"Can you come over?"

"Come over?" Although Benjy had known Jasmine his entire life, he had rarely been invited into the inner sanctum. The only times he went there were when he had to pick her up for a specific occasion. Or when she needed him to move a piece of furniture or to kill a giant spider. Or when he sneaked in to nurse her through the flu. "I'll be right there," he said.

When he arrived at the condo barely ten minutes later, he

found Jasmine still in tears. He took her hand and led her to the sofa. Keeping her hand in his, he sat down next to her.

"Tell me, what's wrong, Jaz?"

She remained silent staring down at the floor.

"Come on. You asked me to come over. You must have something you want to say."

"Oh, Benjy! I'm such an idiot!"

"Why do I get the feeling this has something to do with Alex?"

"He doesn't love me, Benjy. Not the least little bit."

"You've got to be kidding," Benjy exclaimed, trying to keep any trace of relief from his tone. "You mean he traveled all that distance for someone he doesn't even want?"

"Uh…no."

"What's that supposed to mean?"

"It means he traveled all that way for Tracy. He loves Tracy! Can you freakin' believe it!"

"No! How do you know this?"

"He told me himself. He got his memory back after reading the transcripts and having some idiotic dream. And he realized he really is Alex."

"Uh, Jaz? You didn't think dreams were so idiotic when you were dreaming about him and acting goofy about it."

"That was different."

"How?"

"I don't know. It just was. Stop trying to confuse me."

"Okay, okay. Don't get upset. I mean any more upset than you already are." He grabbed a tissue from a box on the coffee table and handed it to her. "So he just calls you out of the blue and says he got his memory back and he loves Tracy?"

"That wasn't all. He wanted me to tell him how to find her. He wanted to go see her in California, and he never even knew her last name. But, of course, he knew *my* last name and address and everything!" Jasmine sobbed.

"So you gave him her phone number?"

"Oh, I did much worse than that. I gave him her address and even told him she's not there right now. She went to San Diego for the weekend with her friend Kelsey. I even told him the hotel where they're staying."

"Why?"

"He wanted to know where she is so he can go out there and surprise her in person. He asked me not to call her and tip her off. Surprise her! Can you freakin' believe it!" Jasmine blew noisily into the tissue Benjy was holding to her nose.

"I guess that sounds kinda romantic—for an emotionless alien. Who knew?"

"Hey, whose side are you on anyway?"

"Yours, of course. I've always been on your side from the day our moms put us in a playpen together."

"Pfft! You don't remember that."

"No, but I've heard the story often enough. I rolled over on you and you smashed your rattle into my head. It's been like that ever since," Benjy laughed.

"This isn't funny!"

"Of course, it's not," said Benjy promptly sobering up. "So… how does Tracy feel about all this? Does she feel the same as Alex does?"

"I think she probably does, but I'm not sure she knows it yet."

"Poor baby!" Benjy took a chance and pulled Jasmine into his arms. She cried softly on his shoulder and allowed herself to be comforted. But only for a moment before she disengaged roughly from his embrace, got to her feet and began to pace. "The thing is, Benjy, I should have seen it all coming. That's why I'm an idiot. It was all there. All the clues."

"What do you mean?"

"A lot of things I actually remember and others I see when I read over the chat transcripts."

She stopped her pacing and stood facing Benjy. "Like he was always sucking up to her when she was snarky with him—which was all the time. And it bothered him when she had that one lousy date with Mr. Garcia but it didn't bother him when I went out with you. And when he met her at the coffee shop, he immediately felt comfortable with her—drawn to her. I should have realized it at the time."

"Then what was it that made you think that you and he were the soul mates—that he was coming here for you? Was he conning you? Because if he was, I'll punch him in his movie star nose."

With a deep sigh, Jasmine sank down onto the couch next to him. "Noooo," she admitted reluctantly. "I really don't think so. I was the one who was always supportive of him. I think he was sort of being polite and just going along with the program."

"Well, he shouldn't have agreed to look like *your* idol, dammit. Now everything is fouled up. He should have looked like Tracy's idol."

"David Tennant."

"Who?"

"Exactly."

"Exactly what? I asked who."

"Right. Like I said—Dr. Who."

"Ah."

"Anyway, at the time, I don't think he thought it was that big a deal. And come to think of it, it was actually Tracy's idea for him to look like Ji Soo. She said it for my sake, but after that it became sort of a joint decision. I doubt he thought it really mattered. He didn't care who he looked like."

Benjy grabbed her hand and made her sit down next to him.

"It's just very upsetting," she said. "I thought that if and when Alex turned out to be real and got his memory back, I'd be so happy. Instead, it's all come crashing down around me."

****

When Benjy had gone, Jasmine made herself a cup of tea, put on a sweater and went out to the balcony. She sat down on a lounge chair and gazed out at the familiar scene—the busy boulevard, the tourists on their way to or from dinner, the view of the beach between the motels. This place that probably seemed so exotic to visitors was so normal to her. Thank goodness for normality. She wondered, now that Alex had his memory, whether this earth seemed normal to him or exotic, and what did he think of the place he left behind, that is, if he even remembered it. Perhaps she would never find out the answers from him. Perhaps she would hear them secondhand from Tracy. Alex would end up living in California and she would hardly ever see either him or Tracy. It was so unfair.

She was sitting back in her chair, sipping her tea and contemplating these matters when she had an earthshaking thought—so earthshaking that her teacup nearly slipped from her hands. "Benjy!" she breathed aloud. She jumped up, dashed inside to her phone and punched in his number.

"Jaz? What's happened now?"

"Nothing. I mean *everything.* Benjy! You believe!"

"Believe? Believe what?"

"You believe in Alex. You believe he's real."

"Yes."

"I knew it. It just hit me. You went through that whole conversation and hardly said anything snarky about Alex, nor questioned anything I said about him even before I told you Alex got his memory back. You called him 'Alex' and talked about him like he was any other guy. Right?"

"Right."

"Did you realize you were doing that?"

"Not consciously I guess."

"But what happened? You've always ridiculed the whole idea."

"I love *you,* Jaz. Always have, always will. This Alex thing is important to you, so it's important to me. You trusted me enough to tell me about him in the first place that night at the bar, and then tonight you needed someone to talk to, and it was me. How could I have even carried on that conversation if I denied its very premise? That would have been impossible. So I choose to believe. I do believe."

"How amazing."

"I'm sure that's the first time you've ever thought of the word amazing in connection with me," he laughed.

"I'm sorry. I've been so wrong—about so many things."

"It's okay. Don't be sorry."

"So…where do we go from here?"

"That's up to you. My position has been known lo these many years."

"Can I think about it?"

"Of course. Just don't take too long."

Once she had rung off with Benjy, Jasmine poured a fresh cup of tea and went back to the balcony. She couldn't help noticing that she felt a little better. She was certain that no one in her whole life had ever been willing to invest so much in her as Benjy had.

"Benjy", she whispered, "every time I look up, there he is."

****

"Already?" said Benjy immediately upon picking up Jasmine's call.

"Already what?"

"You said just yesterday that you wanted to think on our relationship. I can only assume that this call means you've already decided, and decided positively. If it were bad news, you would have procrastinated getting back to me."

"As usual, you are the poster boy for logic," Jasmine laughed. "You are exactly right. I have decided positively."

Benjy heaved a deep sigh as if he'd been holding his breath

since their last conversation.

"I've been doing a lot of thinking, Benjy."

"About me?"

"About you and about a lot of things. I feel so much more aware lately. When I walk on the beach, I really *hear* the waves washing up on the shore. I hear the karaoke coming from the big hotel. I feel the sand under my feet. That feeling I always get crossing the causeway? It seems to stay with me more and more. I'm aware of how much this place is a part of me and how you are a part of this place and, therefore, a part of me. In fact, you're so much a part of me that I couldn't see you. I think I had you so firmly in the friend zone—or, even ickier, the brother zone—that I couldn't see anything else." She paused to take a breath. "Bottom line—I love you and I want to be with you."

Benjy was ominously quiet.

"Well?" she said.

"I know I shouldn't be nit-picky, but I just want to be sure this isn't you settling because you couldn't have the one you really wanted. Or gratitude because I was supportive during this ordeal. I haven't waited thirty years only to be your rebound guy."

"No! It's so much more than that. It's sort of cosmic really."

"Alex was cosmic."

"*You* are cosmic."

****

The following evening, Jasmine entered the Sea Breeze Bistro and walked through the bar to the deck that looked out over the gulf. She spotted Benjy at once. He stood at the railing, facing the water, his back to her.

She paused a moment and studied him. It was as if she were seeing him for the first time. He was wearing a cream-colored linen jacket. Broad shoulders tapered down perfectly to a slim waist and hips. Why had she never noticed that before? He looked downright Gatsby-esque as he gazed out to the gulf. The only thing missing was the green light in the distance. He didn't need a green light. She was his green light.

She smiled as she joined him and slipped her arm through his.

"You're here," he said.

"Where else should I be? You told me to meet you here. Aren't we having dinner?"

"Sure. But I thought we could enjoy the sunset first."

Sunset was underway and a few other spectators were congregating on the deck to watch it. Great, rippling bands of pale pink and mauve and turquoise streaked the sky. In the middle of it all, the giant, fiery orange sun had started its slow descent to the horizon where it seemed to accelerate suddenly and plummet into the dark blue water.

"So beautiful," Jasmine sighed, snuggling closer to Benjy.

"All your talk last night about the water and the sand and everything we love about our little island reminded me that I haven't paused to watch the sunset much of late."

"Me either. Let's do a lot more of it in the future, okay, Buddy?"

Benjy grinned and, gently disentangling her arm from his,

reached into his pocket. "Speaking of the future…" He opened his palm to reveal a most unexpected little velvet box.

Jasmine let out a little gasp. "That surely isn't…"

"I'm afraid it is," Benjy replied, pulling the lid open. "Don't say no now. At worst, you have to say you'll think about it."

The diamond was huge and sparkly and surrounded by various other smaller but equally sparkly diamonds. And because it was, after all, Benjy, it was in exquisite taste.

Her eyes smiled up into his nervous ones. She took the ring from the box and slid it onto her finger. "I don't have to think." She threw her arms around his neck and put her lips to his ear. "Yes!"

"Really?"

"Yes." She pulled out of his embrace and regarded the ring on her finger. "However…"

"Please! No howevers."

"I was just going to say... *however,* this is a little weird. Why, we've never even slept together—that is, not counting all those times in the playpen or crib or baby blanket on the lawn."

"So? We're old school."

Jasmine eyed him skeptically. "Are you saying we have to wait till the wedding?"

Benjy laughed and pulled her back into his arms. "Not *that* old school. Shall we talk about it over dinner?" He held out his arm to her, but she paused to kiss him. It was their first real kiss ever, and it was lovely.

"I promise I'll always be by your side—whatever you need. I'll always love you as much as I do today—as much as I always have," Benjy whispered.

"And I promise I will never let you come to the same end as Gatsby."

"Huh?"

"Never mind," she giggled. "Let's go eat. I want to splurge and have lobster and maybe champagne…"

"And dessert?"

"Yes! Dessert. Something as full of calories as possible." Laughing more joyously than she had in a long time, she took his arm, and they headed toward the lobster and champagne.

Dessert turned out to be bananas Foster. Benjy leaned forward on his elbows as Jasmine scooped up her first bite. "There's something I need to tell you before you actually go through with marrying me. I don't want us to have any secrets."

Jasmine paused with her spoon halfway to her mouth. "That sounds ominous."

"It's nothing bad—really. It's just something I neglected to mention at the time."

Jasmine relaxed and swallowed the spoonful of dessert. "Mmm," she sighed. "Okay. What is it?"

"After you guys met with Alex, I went to New York and paid him a visit. I didn't tell you because…"

Jasmine began to laugh, cutting off his statement. "I already knew about that, silly."

"How? Alex knew at the time that I had decided not to tell you," Benjy huffed. "Although he didn't make any promises, I assumed he would honor my wishes."

Jasmine reached out and touched his hand. "Aww," she teased, "did mean old Alex betray your budding bromance?"

"Bromance?" Benjy sputtered. "What bromance? There's no bromance."

"I understood you two got along quite well. It was practically a mutual admiration society. Anyway, don't blame Alex. He told Tracy and she told me. After all, they are a couple now. They don't have secrets just like we don't. By the way, I know about him and Tracy stalking you at your office, too. I'm surprised you never told me that."

"I, unlike certain other people, was trying to be respectful of your friend Tracy and not get her into trouble with you."

"So does this mean the bromance is off?"

"I told you. There is no bromance."

"Aww, I'm a little disappointed."

"With them living 3,000 miles away, the bromance seems doomed anyway." Benjy sounded slightly disappointed himself.

"Oh, I don't know. Tracy and I have managed to maintain a friendship at that distance all these years. And who knows where their careers will lead them in the future. They could end up on the east coast someday."

Benjy eyed Jasmine narrowly. "You're not still carrying a torch for Alex, are you? You want them to move out this way?"

Jasmine thought carefully for a moment. She wanted to make sure she told the truth.

"I love them both, separately and as a couple. I love them as friends. I would love to have them nearby." She grabbed Benjy's hand and gave it a squeeze. "Do you remember what I said last night about how we are a part of each other?"

"Yes."

"Well, then. I love you like *that*."

****

Jasmine stood at the railing of Benjy's balcony—soon to be her balcony. They had decided she should move in now that they were engaged and marriage was not far off.

It was a clear Malaga Island afternoon. The gulls were wheeling and diving across the sky, and the occasional pelican glided serenely by. One lone sailboat sat on the horizon, its white sail shining in the sunlight.

The sun warmed Jasmine's skin, but it couldn't possibly feel any warmer than her heart, which was full of joy and peace and love. Real love. Not soap opera love, not kdrama love, not science fiction love, but real love.

She thought back to the evening right here on this balcony when Benjy had fed her the crab appetizers, followed by his own Asian-inspired stir-fry, fried rice and chocolate mousse pie from Jasmine's favorite bakery. Had that really been over a year ago? Their second date—or maybe third. It seemed like yesterday. So much had happened in between.

She felt like falling right through the floor when she remembered how mean she had been to Benjy back then and for years before that. But Benjy made it easy to open up to him about her feelings and she had dumped these very issues on him many times, compounding—in her mind—the problem. Benjy didn't see it that way. He just wanted her in his life. Period. That was the amazing thing about Benjy. Amazing, beautiful and real.

She didn't turn around when she heard the sliding door whoosh open. In a moment, she felt Benjy's arms come around her waist. He craned his neck to kiss her cheek and get a look at her face. "You're awfully pensive. What are you thinking about?"

"You, of course."

"I wonder if I will ever get used to hearing things like that come out of your mouth."

"You should learn to expect it. I owe you at least a million of them."

He pulled her closer and held her tightly against him. "You don't owe me a thing."

"Ah, but you do owe me something."

"What do you mean? Something other than my undying love and devotion?"

She turned in his arms and put her lips to his ear. "The recipe for the crab appetizers."

Benjy laughed. "On our wedding night. I'm not sharing until I have the piece of paper in my hands."

Jasmine smiled into his sea-blue eyes. "You drive a hard bargain, Buddy," she said, brushing her lips lightly on his.

"Not fair," he murmured just before his mouth covered hers entirely, and he clasped her so tightly to him that their bodies seemed one.

Chapter 38
Jasmine and Tracy

Jasmine's cell phone jingled insistently from the kitchen counter where she had left it. She dashed from the bedroom to reach it just in time. The word "Tracy" was lit up in green letters.

"Hey, Tracy," she said breathlessly.

"You picked up. That's a good sign."

"Did you think I wouldn't?"

"You have to admit the situation is a little awkward. I should have talked to you right away."

"What do you mean? We've talked."

"But only briefly, and we didn't get into all the details about me and Alex."

"I don't feel awkward about that. After all, I'm the one who told Alex where to find you."

"I know, and I appreciate that. You didn't have to do that."

"Did he find you all right? Details please"

"Yeah. On the beach. He called the room, and Kelsey told him where I was."

"On the beach? Was it just like in our… I mean your dream?"

"Pretty much."

"Was it achingly romantic?"

"Are you being sarcastic?"

"No! I hope it was. You deserve that, Tracy."

"It was."

"Good."

"Has something happened that's made you so calm about this whole thing? Not that you wouldn't have been anyway," Tracy quickly added.

"I don't know. I might not have been. I'm not sure. But fortunately we will never have to find out because of the incredible thing that's happened—quite apart from the incredible thing that happened to you and Alex."

"Really? Tell me."

"Hold on to your chair now. Benjy and I are engaged. Yikes!"

"Oh, my God, Jaz! That's wonderful. What ever happened?"

"It's a little hard to explain…but I had some kind of epiphany, and all of a sudden everything became clear."

"Clear that you'd loved Benjy all along?"

"Noooo…not quite that. It just suddenly became clear that whenever he comes on the scene, things seem to get magically better. Besides, I finally realized what a part of me he is."

"But weren't those things always true?"

"Maybe but until recently I never let him get close enough that he could make things better. As for being a part of me…well, maybe I didn't like myself all that much and that rubbed off on the part that was him."

"Uh…would you mind repeating that?" Tracy laughed.

"I don't think I could if I tried," Jasmine replied beginning to laugh too. "It doesn't matter. I know what I meant."

"That's the important thing.

"You know, there is nothing wrong with obsessing over Brianna or Ji Soo…or…or…"

"Dr. Who?"

"Yeah."

"Where did that come from, and who said there was anything wrong with it?"

"Nobody I guess. It's just important to keep things in perspective, isn't it?"

"Why are you bringing this up now?"

"No reason. It's just that I've been doing a lot of thinking lately, and no matter how much we love those other things, they don't compare to feeling the sand under your feet or hearing the waves washing up on the shore."

"Or obsessing over a real person like Benjy or Alex."

"We're not obsessing. That's the beautiful part of it. But it's kind of ironic—you holding Alex up as the embodiment of reality after being the skeptic for so long."

"Embodiment," Tracy laughed. "That's the perfect word I suppose. There are still moments when I think I dreamed the whole thing and that I'm still dreaming. If it is a dream, I don't want to wake up."

"Don't worry. You won't have to."

"Promise?"

"Promise."

"In any case, I'm really happy for you, both of you. Tell Benjy I said congratulations."

"And I'm happy for you."

"You mean that?"

"Absolutely. One day, years from now, we'll look back on all this and know that everything happened just as it was meant to. I can see us now, the four of us, sitting on some veranda, sipping margaritas—you and I in sheer, floaty dresses, the guys in white linen shirts, the breeze ruffling our hair—and we'll reminisce about how we all met and how perfect it was aside from a few complications and tears along the way. And we'll say how lucky we are and what amazing lives we've led. Nobody can say it hasn't been amazing, can they?"

"Pardon me, but that sounded an awful lot like a dream."

"You just wait and see. It'll happen."

Chapter 39
Chandler

Chandler peeked into Carlos's empty room. She missed him. The apartment was lonely without him.

Back in the living room, she stood helplessly in the middle of the floor and looked out through the French doors to the balcony, half expecting to see Carlos reading a book in his customary spot. For a moment, she fancied she actually saw him—so many mornings she had arisen to find him there, sitting in the lounge chair, book in hand.

She thought about how he loved books...and video games... and chess. Anything that involved quick intelligence, calculation, analysis. Chess. She had beaten him exactly once—their very first game. It had taken just that one match to learn the game from scratch and to master it completely. She never won again.

With a sigh, she opened the terrace door and stepped outside. Wearily, for she felt as if she'd been through a hurricane and barely survived, she sank into Carlos's chair. She felt exhausted from thinking about him. Had it really been only two days ago that he had sadly, kindly and yet somehow ruthlessly told her. It seemed longer ago than that. Still, she felt sure she would never forget a single word he spoke that day.

He sat her down in the armchair and knelt at her feet. And then he uttered the words that every person in love dreads: "We have to talk." Sometimes it astonished her, if it was true that he was not a native speaker, that he knew the nuances and subtexts of the language so well.

He proceeded to tell her that he had fallen in love with that very ordinary person called Tracy, whom he had met only a couple of times and only recently at that. He told Chandler how grateful he was for the way she had taken care of him when he had no one else in the world. He hoped to be able to repay her one day. He apologized for not loving her back the way she loved him. He hoped they could remain friends. Those beastly words! Almost as bad as "we have to talk."

Her response was the one detail she couldn't remember. She could hear only the echo of his words in her head. All she knew was that she had somehow released him without histrionics, which was surprising coming from her. He'd had a determination in his eyes that had convinced her any resistance would be futile. She did recall, at the very end, asking if he'd gotten any part of his memory back and whether that had anything to do with this sudden change of heart. He'd answered no.

Now, sitting on the balcony and thinking over all that had happened, she made a decision. She knew what she wanted to do.

She stood up, threw back her shoulders, held her head high and went inside. With resolve, she picked up her phone and selected the number.

"Chandler, honey! What a nice surprise," her father said upon hearing her voice.

"Daddy, I need a favor."

"Of course, you do." Justin Davies's words may have been sarcastic but his tone was jovial, indulgent.

"Don't you know somebody in the State Department?"

"Uh...*yeah*. The Secretary of State."

"Oh, yeah. The head honcho, huh?"

"Sure. We were at Yale together."

"Daddy, do you think you could pull some strings and get someone a green card?"

"That sounds doable."

"Really? Great!"

"Is this about that young man who was living with you?"

"We weren't living together in the usual sense. He was just staying with me for a while."

"Really? I only met him a couple of times, but I got the impression you were sweet on him."

"Sweet on him? What an archaic term."

"Well, weren't you?"

"Okay, yes, I was, but that's over."

"In fact, didn't your mother tell me he ran off with another woman?"

"Ran off? Not exactly. But, yes, he is with someone else now."

"I assume he's the one you want the green card for. You want to help him even though he left you for someone else? I've never known you to be so altruistic."

"Carlos is a very special person. There's something about him that makes you want to help him. And, frankly, the girl he likes seems pretty nice, too—though I hate to admit it."

"I'm sure she's no Chandler Davies," said Justin protectively.

"That's a given."

"That's my girl. I'm proud of you, honey. This is very mature of you."

"Thanks, Daddy. So will you help me?"

"I'll try. May I ask why this guy can't go through normal channels?"

"It's complicated. Very complicated."

"Was it for him, by any chance, that you needed to borrow the company plane and refused to answer any questions about it? The pilot said he flew some Asian guy to San Diego. There better not be anything illegal going on. Did he need a private plane because he has no papers?"

"Yes, it was for him, and, no, it's nothing illegal. And thanks for not making me answer questions about it."

"I have questions now."

"Let's have lunch tomorrow and I'll explain all the details. Okay?"

"Absolutely. You know I never say no to spending time with my best girl."

"Meet you at the little cafe by your office, one o'clock tomorrow?

"Sure thing. See you there, hon."

Chandler took a deep breath and laid down her phone. Done! She was pleased with herself, and that fact served to temper her sadness and regret over Carlos, whom she had genuinely loved more than any other man she had ever known.

She stuck her perfect chin out bravely and started out to make a pot of tea. No sooner had she set the kettle on the stove than the phone rang. She checked caller ID. It was her agent, Stu Hirsch.

She picked up the phone. "Stu!" she said incredulously. "I thought you'd dropped off the face of the earth."

"Don't get smart with me, young lady," Stu teased. "If you don't behave, I won't tell you the news."

"News? Good news?"

"Very good. Listen up. You have an audition Wednesday at three. It's for the lead in a sitcom pilot. It's going to be a rom-com type of thing. They've already cast the male lead and they want you to read with him."

"Really? Who is it?"

"Name's Mark Sutton. Never heard of him. They specifically said they're looking for two unknowns for the roles. They're very high on this guy. In fact, they're very high on this project. I know it's only a pilot, but I have a good feeling about it. As for you, they love your look and were very impressed with your reel."

"I wonder if they realize I'm pushing forty."

"You're thirty-eight."

"And a half."

"Anyway, it's an older woman/younger man story."

"Ah! A *noona* story. I love those."

"A what?"

"It's a Korean drama term. You wouldn't understand."

"Whatever. All I care about is that you go in there and knock 'em dead. You need the business, and, frankly, so do I. You're not my only client who's in a dry spell."

"Dry spell?" Chandler laughed. "More like the Sahara Desert."

"Exactly. I'll messenger you the script and text you the details. Break a leg, kid."

On Wednesday afternoon at precisely three o'clock, Chandler walked into a conference room at the offices of the producer of the new sitcom tentatively titled, *This, That and the Other*. Mark Sutton was already seated at the table, the script lying open in front of him. He looked even more gorgeous than the Google images Chandler had already studied thoroughly.

He held out his hand to her. "Chandler?" he said. "Mark Sutton. Looks like we're reading together today." She shook his hand and took a seat across the table. She reached into her bag and pulled out her copy of the script.

"Nervous? I am," he said with a clearly nervous laugh.

Chandler smiled sympathetically. "Mark, I have been on so many auditions in my life that they really don't faze me anymore. I don't want to be a downer but it's just a pilot, and even if I do get hired, it's a long shot that it gets picked up. No need for you to be nervous at this point. You've already got the job—for the pilot anyway."

Mark reached across the table and grabbed her hand. His eyes had that desperate-actor look. "I really, really need this gig. Not just the pilot, the whole series. I hope we get it."

His shockingly blue eyes, despite the desperate look—or perhaps because of it—were sweet and vulnerable. Chandler squeezed his hand, which was still holding hers. "I'm sorry I was negative before. It gets to be a habit. We *are* going to get this job—both of us. I just feel it."

Mark withdrew his hand carefully—maybe reluctantly—and grinned.

Chapter 40
One Last Chat

Alex   Hi, Jaz. Tracy tells me we've been summoned
                to the chat room.

Tracy   Hi, Jaz.

Jaz   Alex! You can now post as Alex. No more
                Copy/Paste?

Tracy   Yeah. It's weird. Before he was actually on, you
                know, *earth,* the chat room wouldn't let me
                register him. In some strange way, the
                copy/paste feature was the "doorway" to our
                internet.

Jaz   You mean like a wormhole or something?
                And if so, why wouldn't he just go through the

wormhole and get here instantly?

Alex   There wasn't a wormhole—at least as far as I know.

Tracy   The internet works in mysterious ways.

Alex   Was there something special you wanted to say to us, Jaz? I know you and Tracy have continued to chat as usual, but why did you want all three of us together? And on a Tuesday!

Jaz   Not quite as usual. We used to chat every Friday like clockwork, but lately it's been kind of sporadic.

Tracy   We've been busy. All of us.

Jaz   As to why all of us and why now, do you guys realize what today is? It's the anniversary of when Alex first appeared in the chat room. I thought it would be nice for us to commemorate the occasion together. After all, that night was the catalyst that changed all our lives profoundly. No?

Tracy   Absolutely.

Alex	It seems like a million years ago. So much has happened.
Jaz	Of course it does—to you. A million lightyears. LOL
Tracy	Haha. You're so funny.
Jaz	Alex, have you heard from Chandler? I hear she has a show that's been picked up by ABC.
Alex	We text now and then. Yes, the pilot she shot did get picked up. She's very excited.
Jaz	There's a lot of buzz about the show. And I read somewhere that she's dating her co-star.
Alex	Also true.
Jaz	Good for her!
Jaz	Alex, I've been wanting to talk to you. We only had that brief phone call. I want all the details.
Alex	What details?
Jaz	I understand you got all your memory back. Tracy told me that, but she didn't give me details. I want to hear about your journey here and what happened when you got here and

how you adjusted to earth.

Alex   That's a long story. We'll talk about it next time
              we meet in person.

Jaz   Well, heaven knows when that will be. I want
              to know now. I think I deserve that. If not for
              me, you would not be here and would not
              have fallen in love with Tracy.

Alex   Good point. Okay, I will tell you a little. The
              journey was harrowing. The speed was
              overwhelming. But my main concern was
              whether my calculations had been correct.
              My human body had to materialize at the
              exact moment I arrived on earth. If it formed
              any earlier, it would have disintegrated at
              once. As it happened, it came out just right.

Jaz   Of course, you did miss your geographic
              target by 1,000 miles. LOL

Alex   A tiny discrepancy out of the millions of miles
              I traveled. Better to make the error on the
              target than on that whole disintegration thing.

Jaz   LOL Touche.

Jaz   So…then what?

Alex	Well, you've heard about how I landed in front of Bloomingdale's and met Chandler. As for adjusting to earth, every sensation was new and shocking since I didn't have senses before. Every taste, every sound, every feeling. I learned almost immediately to mask my reactions. Chandler, because she thought I was an undocumented alien from another country and still does by the way, told me never to draw attention to myself. So although I was bombarded with shocking sensations, I never allowed my expression to reflect what I was feeling—except for those first few occasions before I realized what was happening.
Jaz	Wow. That must have been overwhelming. One thing, among many, that always amazes me is how perfectly you speak the language, including slang expressions, subtleties, implications. And then the body language— so like Ji Soo.
Alex	Why are you surprised? Didn't I have slang and idiom pretty well mastered here in the chat room? As for Ji Soo, you told me to study his videos and movies. I just did as you said.

Jaz	It seems like you retained everything you learned off the internet from back in our chat room days—that is, the big, wide internet—not our little chat room. Anything about us and about the place you came from was erased by the amnesia.
Tracy	I suppose, generally speaking, you could say anything of a personal nature (if you can even call the emotionless entities where he came from personal), was erased and any knowledge from the internet was retained.
Jaz	It's a good thing we were there to give him some guidance through the web. Otherwise his head might be filled with nothing but porn and cat videos.
Tracy	LOL
Alex	LMAO
Jaz	Speaking of Ji Soo, it would be so cool if you actually met him face to face. I wonder what he would think.
Tracy	Oh, dear God! Let's not tempt fate. This whole situation is weird enough.

Alex	I agree with Tracy.
Jaz	I see you got the memo. The wife—or wife to be—is always right. Words to live by.
Alex	I intend to. LOL Anyway, that's really about all there is to tell. You know most of the rest. And we will get together soon. We can talk more then. Okay?
Jaz	Sure. I'll settle for that. What are your plans now? I haven't chatted with Tracy for a couple of weeks.
Tracy	Now that he has his green card, he can go to school and get a degree. He should be able to go through UCLA in no time since he already knows everything they have to teach. He just needs the diploma for credibility out in the world. Once he has his degree under his belt, I hope he goes to work solving global warming. I'm sure he can do it.
Jaz	Alex?
Alex	Totally on board. You know this has been a concern of mine all along.
Jaz	Tracy, what will you do without him while he's

over at UCLA?

Tracy	I've already told Mom she will have to move to L.A. or allow one of my brothers to look after her.
Jaz	That's major. How did she take it? And has she met Alex?
Tracy	Yes and she adores him. Is there a woman alive who can resist Alex? LOL
Jaz	Only me. Now that I have Benjy.
Tracy	You *always* had Benjy.
Jaz	I did, didn't I?
Tracy	We're so happy for you.
Alex	Absolutely!
Jaz	Well, I don't want to keep you guys. I know you're busy.
Tracy	We can do it again sometime. I mean all three of us.
Jaz	Hey, we could invite Chandler to join us. And her new bf too. And Benjy.

Tracy	Do you really think a big TV star is going to want to visit our little chat room?
Jaz	He's not a big star yet. The show hasn't even aired yet.
Alex	Uh, ladies. Let's keep in mind that nobody can find out the truth about me. The three of us and, for some reason, Benjy are the only people in the world who know. As far as Chandler knows, and anyone else, my amnesia has not been cured. We have to keep it that way
Jaz	You don't have to worry about Benjy. He's a straight arrow to a fault. And he's the most disciplined person I know.
Alex	I wasn't worried about Benjy.
Jaz	Anyway, I was sort of kidding about having Chandler and her bf here. OTOH you never know what can happen in this world, do you?

****

Tracy closed the laptop and smiled serenely at Alex.

"What are you thinking?" he asked.

"I was just thinking about what you said about how you and

I and Jaz and Benjy are the only people in the world who know the whole truth about you. I was thinking about how we all came clean eventually about the various secrets we were keeping from each other, though none of them was really important."

"But?"

"But I will never, ever tell them about how we met and danced that night at the beach bar, and I don't want you to either."

"I wasn't planning to. But why exactly?"

"Because that is ours and ours alone. It feels so special—almost sacred really—that no one else should be allowed to intrude into it. Does that make sense?"

Alex put his arm around her and pulled her close. "Perfectly."

"I can still smell your cologne and feel your breath on my skin. I can feel your arm around me and remember how natural it felt to lay my head on your shoulder. I can still hear the melody in my head, though I never knew what it was."

"'Where or When.'"

"Was it? How did you know that?"

"I don't know. Something I picked up in my studies at some point. You know how my brain retains everything," he laughed.

"Why didn't you tell me?"

"I didn't know that you didn't know."

"Ah, anyway, that was the very moment that we fell in love, wasn't it? Even though I couldn't recognize it at the time. If I had, I would have never let you go."

"Yes," he said.

A Very Long Epilogue
Or What Ever Happened To...

Jenna and Brian

Jenna and Brian Morrow lay in their puffy, white king-size bed. It was late and they had had a long day. They were in the middle of a messy, expensive renovation of their kitchen. Living in the mess was beginning to wear on them, and they had spent the morning arguing with the contractor about cost overruns, completion date and real or perceived errors. At the start of the project weeks ago, Jenna had suggested simply leaving. A nice long vacation in the Keys sounded good—or even a move to a local hotel. Brian had not agreed. They couldn't possibly stay away as long as the renovation would take, and besides he wanted to be on the premises where he could "oversee" things.

Jenna sighed and nestled into the crook of her husband's arm. Brian resisted the urge to recoil in shock. In the best of times,

Jenna could not be described as affectionate, and the stress of the current situation had made things even worse.

"Jenna?" said Brian, wondering if this was some kind of mistake.

"Yes?" she murmured, snuggling even closer to him.

"Is everything okay?"

"Of course. Why shouldn't it be?"

"Oh, nothing. I'm just surprised that after the day we've had you're so...shall we say...relaxed? What's going on in that head of yours?"

"I was just thinking how lucky we are."

Brian raised up slightly to look her in the face with astonishment. "That's so unlike you. You haven't been drinking, have you?"

"No!"

"Drugs?"

Jenna gave his arm a playful slap. "Now you're just being silly."

"I know."

"Despite my image, which I am well aware of, I do have a heart."

Brian put both his arms around her and pulled her closer. "I know that too. You hide it pretty well most of the time."

"Sorry."

"It's okay. I agree we are lucky, but did you have anything in particular in mind?"

"Lucky to have a kitchen to renovate, lucky to have good jobs and enough money, lucky to live in this town that we love, lucky to have stayed married for thirty-five years despite my...my...

quirks?"

"That's a nice word for it," Brian laughed.

"But most of all lucky to have our beautiful daughter."

Brian's gentle laugh changed to a definite guffaw. "The way you two have pushed each other's buttons over the years, I never thought I'd hear you say those words."

"Nonsense. You know I love Jasmine."

"Of course, you love her, but you haven't always appreciated her. You have to admit that."

"Okay."

"Let me guess. Could this sudden attitude adjustment have anything to do with the fact that our daughter has finally consented to marry your hand-picked, mom-approved candidate?"

"It didn't hurt."

"But why today all of a sudden? Did something happen?"

"Not that I can think of. Unless…"

"Unless what?"

"Unless it was our talk on the phone this morning."

"I didn't know you talked today."

"It was while you were arguing with Bob about the countertops."

"Oh, yeah," Brian groaned. "That guy really burns my butt. I told him at least a dozen times we wanted the quartz, not the granite. So what shows up on our doorstep? The granite."

Jenna sighed loudly.

"Sorry. Go on. What did Jasmine say?"

"It wasn't any one particular thing. It was more the way we were with each other. Sort of easy. You know? For the first time in a long time—ever maybe."

"Because of Benjy? When he was right under her nose the whole time?"

"I guess."

"She seemed really unhappy the past year or so. Did you ever find out what that was about? I've tried and tried and got nowhere."

"I don't know. Maybe there was a guy involved. You know she would never confide in me, and I'm certainly not going to ask now—not now that she's okay. It seems like whatever it was—or whoever—somehow led her to Benjy." Jenna squeezed Brian's arm. "And now I get to start planning a wedding!"

Brian laughed and held her close. "You have finally found your calling in life."

"And once we get this kitchen done, I'm going to start being a lot nicer to you."

Though it wasn't visible in the dark, Brian's eyes teared up. "You don't have to be any certain way with me. Just be with me."

He pulled the covers up over her shoulders and closed his eyes.

Libby and Malcolm

Not long after Chandler finally let go of Carlos, her friends, Libby and Malcolm Arden, found themselves in the middle of a divorce. This came as a surprise to everyone, including themselves. No one saw it coming. Although the two of them had always been regarded as a bit of a mismatch—Libby, precise and stylish, Malcolm, rumpled and relaxed—their marriage had appeared solid. They were both gorgeous—if that had anything to do with it.

Libby came from a well-to-do family like Chandler's. They had first forged their friendship at the fancy private school they both attended. Libby met Malcolm at Northwestern where he was a scholarship student.

For the past several years, Libby had worked as a stockbroker. She was good at it, and it was a lucrative career. Malcolm taught history at Columbia, where he was in a continual struggle to attain tenure.

Libby and Malcolm had no children. They had both pretended, to the world and to each other, that this was no big deal. Somehow each had got it in their head that making it a big deal would upset the other.

After the first few years of marriage, they had stopped birth control and had assumed nature would take its course. When nothing happened, their stance was that if it was meant to be, it would be. Gradually, as they approached their forties, that stance changed to "we didn't really want kids anyway." This was a lie. In their hearts, they both had really wanted a family. They didn't admit this to anyone—not even each other.

Because of this position, which they had fallen into without really planning to, they naturally did not pursue fertility treatments or any other procedures which medical science had to offer.

Whether all of this figured prominently in the demise of their marriage, no one could say for sure. Was it the failure to communicate on such an essential aspect of the relationship? Or was it more simply the absence of the children they had dreamed separately of having? Perhaps a combination of both. Neither of them was particularly introspective, nor did they like to confront their deepest fears. At least, besides being unusually handsome, they had that in common.

On a sunny spring afternoon, Libby and Malcom had made a date to meet for lunch. The purpose of the meeting was to discuss some final decisions about the property settlement. The divorce had remained amicable. They had just grown apart. That was their official story.

Lunch was at an outdoor café, a regular haunt of theirs. Malcolm was already seated, sipping an espresso, when Libby rushed in. She looked frazzled and excited at the same time, her color heightened, her usually perfect bob slightly mussed. As she sat down opposite Malcolm, he noticed her blouse was buttoned wrong. This could only mean that the universe was out of alignment.

"Here," he said. He reached across the table, unbuttoned and rebuttoned the three offending buttons. "There." He eased back into his chair. "Are you okay? You don't seem like yourself today."

"I just came from the doctor."

"Ah. Thus, the hastily buttoned shirt. Makes sense. Your annual check-up. I had a sudden fear that you rushed here directly from a tryst with a secret lover." He let out a nervous laugh.

"That is so far off that it's not even funny. I'm pregnant, Mal."

Malcolm choked on a mouthful of espresso. "What!" He began to laugh. "For a minute there, I thought you said pregnant."

"I did, you idiot."

Malcolm's face went ashen, and his saucer clattered as he attempted to settle his cup in it. "You're serious, aren't you? You're really serious."

"Would I joke about a thing like this?"

"I guess not. But how? When? It can't be mine, can it? No offense."

"Remember Julie's birthday party when we both got wasted on tequila?"

"Oh yeah." The color returned to Malcolm's cheeks in a big way. "I kind of forgot… N-n-not that it wasn't great," he stammered. "It *was*."

"You don't remember if it was great or not, and neither do I. We were both too out of it. And for your information, there hasn't been anyone else since we separated."

"Me either." Malcolm raised his hand in the Boy Scout pledge.

Libby's eyes flickered with something resembling relief. "Anyway, that's beside the point."

At that moment, Malcolm returned to his senses, and his customary considerate nature kicked in. He jumped up, went to Libby's side and squatted beside her chair. "Are you all right? I mean is everything okay health-wise? Are you feeling sick or anything?"

"No. I'm fine. And get up. People are staring."

Abashed, Malcolm returned to his seat.

"Well?" said Libby. "I guess I need to know how you feel about this."

"I'm just trying to wrap my head around it. All those years we never tried but we never *not* tried either. And now that we're, well, older…"

"*And* getting divorced."

"Yeah, that too." Despite his unenthusiastic words, Malcolm's lips looked as if they were fighting a smile, a circumstance not lost on Libby. Her communication with her husband may not have been great, but at least she could tell when he was about to smile.

"What do we do?" she asked.

"What do you mean what do we do? You're not thinking of not having the baby, are you?"

"No! Of course, not. I didn't mean that." She paused, waiting for him to say something, but he was silent.

"You never really answered my question," she went on at last. "How do you feel about this?"

"Honestly? I'm happy. I always wanted kids."

"You did? You never actually said. I thought you were sort of neutral on it."

"At first, I was. But then later, when it wasn't happening, I realized I really did want it."

"Why didn't you say anything, Mal? There were things we could have tried."

"Why didn't you say anything? I thought you didn't want children. You always said if it happens fine, if not that's fine too. I just wanted to support your position—since, after all, you were the one who would have to actually, you know, have the baby."

"I guess human beings always want what they can't have."

Malcolm eyed her closely. "Does that by any chance mean that you wanted a family too, deep down inside?"

"Maybe." Libby had been tearing her napkin into tiny pieces. Now she tossed them onto the table like confetti. "Look, there's no use rehashing all that. We're having a baby which we both apparently want. We should be happy."

"I am happy. I told you that."

"Could you get me a lemonade or something? I guess coffee is out for the duration."

Malcolm called the waiter over and ordered the lemonade and sandwiches for lunch.

"It seems like our communication has been lacking," Libby observed.

Malcolm laughed. "Tell me something I don't know. Remember, I tried to get you to go with me for some counseling before opting for divorce. You were having none of it."

Libby pulled some papers from her bag. "This is what we were supposed to discuss today."

"The settlement? Do we add custody and child support to the discussion…or what?" Malcolm cringed a little as he spoke.

Libby sighed and took a sip of the lemonade which had just been delivered. She regarded her husband soberly for a moment. Then she picked up the papers, folded them and put them back in her bag. "You're in charge of finding a good counselor, okay?"

Despite being chided earlier for the same behavior, Malcolm

sprang from his seat and ran around to embrace Libby. "I will find us the best damn counselor in all of Manhattan," he declared, and he bravely kissed her right on the mouth.

Jonathan and Claire

On opening night of Jonathan Raditz's play, Chandler Davies had pronounced it "good." Carlos Pereira had agreed and, going forward, so had everyone else—the audiences, the critics, and Richard Anselm. Mr. Anselm was a Hollywood producer who was in the house one evening about six months into the run of the play. A few days later, he offered to purchase the rights for a possible film project. Since Jonathan had never expected to make any real money off his creation, he jumped at the chance. The thought of seeing his work on the big screen was more than he had ever dreamed of.

Months went by, and Jonathan rarely thought about the potential movie project. These things take time, he thought, and often never come to fruition. No need to worry.

And then one Friday afternoon, he received a package by messenger. The return address was that of Richard Anselm. Jonathan's heart beat a little faster in his chest as he ripped open the manila envelope. Inside was a script—an apparently complete screenplay. There was a cover letter, but he couldn't take time to read it. His eyes wide with anticipation, he dropped onto the sofa, opened the script and began to read.

Halfway through the first scene, he checked the cover page to make sure he had the right document. Even then, it was hard to tell. The title had been changed. Beneath the new title, he read, "Screenplay by J. Andrew Winfield."

The feeling of euphoria was replaced by a sense of dread as he returned to the script. By the time he finished the last scene, his breath was coming in short, agitated pants and an anxious sweat had formed on his brow and upper lip. He turned the last page, closed the script and tossed it onto the coffee table.

His brain was racing. What had happened? Angela was no longer the female protagonist. Gina was. Gina, who had been the comic relief, was now the main character. His play about the lonely desperation of life amid the anonymous crowds of New York City had become a romantic comedy. Gina's one-liners were highlighted and expanded upon. Most of Jonathan's favorite lines—dark and poetic, incisive and philosophical commentary on the human condition—lines that he had labored over, written and rewritten, prodded and poked toward some semblance of perfection—were missing.

He got up and poured himself a scotch before returning to the sofa and picking up the cover letter. With fear and loathing, he read the letter.

Richard Anselm was sending Jonathan the completed screenplay as a courtesy. They were lucky to have gotten Andy Winfield to write it. After all, he had just come from writing five seasons of television's hottest sit-com. Not only that—and this was top secret—it looked like they had a good chance of signing Emma Stone to play Gina. With Emma already on the project (they hoped), they had every expectation of snagging a top star as their leading man. Mr. Anselm was sure Jonathan would be pleased with the screenplay and looked forward to seeing him in the future.

Jonathan laid the letter on the table and drained his glass. He was still sitting there staring into space when Claire came home from work. She came up behind him and put her arms around his neck.

"What are you doing, just sitting here?" she laughed.

He nodded in the direction of the coffee table.

"What's all that?" she asked.

"See for yourself."

She came around and sat down next to him. "Looks like a script. Is it for me?"

"Definitely not. Check it out."

Claire picked up the script and skimmed though it—enough to get the gist of it. "What the hell!" she cried. "They've changed it all around. Gina is now the main character? They've turned it into a rom-com?"

"And took out all my best lines. Read the letter."

She read the letter and threw it down on the table. "I'm so sorry, honey." She laid her head on his shoulder. "I know this isn't what you expected."

"I'm such a dope. Why did I sign all the rights away? I didn't even go through an agent or an attorney. And I'm supposed to be such a whiz at business. What a crock."

"You did that because you just wanted your play made into a film. You knew it was highly unlikely you would get another offer so you just went for it. There's nothing wrong with that."

"I never even told you half of my pipe dreams. I actually fantasized that they would ask me to write the screenplay and that they would want you to play the lead and they would even have Tommy star opposite you like in the play. He was such a rock, such a loyal friend through all the ups and downs of getting the production off the ground. And on top of that, he was good—really good."

"Aw, hon. Those really were pipe dreams. Even if they had kept the play intact, none of that was going to happen."

"I know." Jonathan sighed and pulled Claire closer.

"These things happen," said Claire after a while. "Sometimes the second lead becomes the leading lady. Sometimes in real life, the sidekick becomes the heroine of her own story."

Jonathan turned to face Claire. "When did you become a philosopher?"

"Contrary to popular belief, I am not just a pretty face."

"I knew there was a reason I fell in love with you." Jonathan sighed and laid his head back on the sofa.

"You're still bummed though."

"A little."

Claire ran her fingers through his hair the way he liked. "Look at it this way, honey. Your play is going to be a major motion picture starring none other than Emma Stone! And they did at least keep your basic plot line, and they did use some of your dialog—if not your favorite lines. To be honest, the odds were against a movie getting made at all. This might be better than nothing. And someday we'll see the words 'adapted from the stage play by Jonathan Raditz' in ginormous letters on the movie screen. *And…*"

"There's more?"

"And maybe if you ask Mr. Anselm, he'd be willing to put one or two of your pithiest lines back in. It can't hurt to ask."

"Do you think he would?" Jonathan asked, noticeably perking up.

"It's worth a shot.'"

"Yeah. It's worth a shot."

"Meanwhile, you've got your work in progress—your new play. Next time you'll know better."

"Like you said, this was a rare occurrence. There probably won't be a next time."

"But maybe there will."

Jonathan kissed her. "You're wonderful. Next time I won't sell the rights unless they cast you as the lead."

"You're silly."

"I know. I think we ought to get married."

Mr. Garcia

"Maria, Elena! I'm home," Julio Garcia called out.

Ten-year-old Elena, the expressive one, came running from her bedroom. "Daddy!" she squealed, throwing her arms around his waist. "Did you bring me something?"

Julio laughed. "You are too old to be expecting a treat every single day. *But...*" He reached into his pocket, pulled something out and held it in his closed fist.

"Open!" Elena commanded.

He opened his hand to reveal a keychain with a little fuzzy kitten attached.

Elena grabbed it. "Oh! It's so cute! I love kitties."

"I know that, *mi hija.*"

"Can we get a real kitten?"

"Don't press your luck, little one."

"You spoil her too much." Maria, the somber one, was now standing in the doorway to the hall, leaning against the jamb with her arms crossed.

"And hello to you, too," said Julio with a grin. He went into his pocket again. "Just because you are now fifteen, it doesn't mean you are too old for presents." He held out another keychain, this one with a miniature teddy bear.

Maria accepted the gift with the slightest of smiles. "Thank you, Papa."

"Do you like it?" Julio asked hopefully.

Maria looked up from under her long, dark lashes and finally allowed a genuine smile to form on her lips. "It's adorable, Papa. Thank you."

"Come here, *mi hija.*" Julio opened his arms and enclosed both of his daughters in one of his famous bear hugs.

"I made dinner, Papa," said Maria, wriggling out of his arms.

"I smell that. It smells delicious."

"It's chicken quesadillas. Your favorite."

"Thank you, honey. That was so sweet of you."

"I helped!" Elena cried.

"She did—a little," Maria admitted.

"My two girls. I'm so proud of both of you." Julio washed his hands at the kitchen sink, got a beer from the refrigerator and took his seat at the head of the table. Maria served the food and joined the family at the table. She watched her father as he bit into his quesadilla. He crinkled his brow and thought a moment. "The verdict is…" he intoned solemnly. "Perfect!"

"Really?" Maria scrutinized her father's expression for signs of fatherly indulgence.

"For sure." Julio took another bite and a swig of beer. "Definitely the best quesadilla I have ever tasted."

"Better than at Antonio's Grill?" Maria asked dubiously.

"Absolutely," Julio smiled. His smile faded, and he was quiet then, eating his dinner and taking an occasional sip of beer.

Maria studied his face. It had not escaped her notice that in between smiles, his expression seemed more melancholy than it used to—more like the serious look he always accused her of.

"Is anything wrong, Papa?" she asked at last.

"Oh, no," Julio protested, snapping out of whatever thoughts he'd been having. "Of course, not."

"I was just wondering…" Maria paused and gazed down at her plate.

"What, honey?"

"I was wondering what ever happened to that Tracy lady from your work? She was the only lady you dated since Mommy…left." She hesitated painfully over the word "left."

The color rose to Julio's cheeks. "Why are you bringing that up now? That was months ago."

"I know, but it seems like ever since then you've been a little down."

Julio smiled kindly. "Don't worry about me, honey. I'm fine. It was a little disappointing, but, you know, we just didn't hit it off. These things don't always work out. Anyway, we only went out that one time. It was no big deal."

"But you were always happy when you talked about her— even long before that date. Is she still there—at the hospital?"

"She is. But I hear she's moving to L.A. And I hear she met someone. So I'm very happy for her. She's a nice person. You should be happy for her, too."

"I don't see how she couldn't have liked you, Daddy," Elena piped up. "You're the best, most handsomest man in the whole world."

"Maybe I should have bought her a kitten." Julio smiled and his eyes misted.

In a most un-sober fashion, Maria leaped up and ran to her father. She put her arms around his neck and hugged him tightly. "You'll meet someone else, Papa. I know you will."

When Julio gazed into the hopeful eyes of his daughter, he could not doubt that she was right.

Lydia Malone

In Columbus, Ohio, Alice Carson's phone was ringing. She picked up right away.

"Hey, Liddie. How are you?"

"I'm good. And you?" replied Lydia Malone.

"Doing well. Everything's good out in sunny California?"

"Yeah. I just felt like talking to my little sister. It's been a while."

"Too long. I've been thinking about you though. Does Tracy still have her amazing new boyfriend?"

"Oh, yes. She's very happy. He's getting his green card soon. Then they'll really be able to get on with their lives. He plans to go to school in L.A."

"That's great. I can't wait to meet him."

"I'm sure you will soon."

"Hmm…does that mean I'll be hearing wedding bells soon?"

"Nothing's been decided, but I think it will be sooner rather than later."

"Yay! That's so exciting. So are they moving to L.A.?

"Apparently."

"Um…why don't you sound more upset? You sound positively serene."

"I am."

"So…will you move in with Sam or Danny…or, heaven forbid, Ethan…no offense."

"None taken," Lydia laughed. "We all know Ethan is bit of a loose cannon. Did you know he voted for Trump?"

"Horrors!" Alice gasped.

"I know."

"What ever will you do without Tracy?"

"I'm going to stay right here in this house that I love."

"You mean *by yourself?*"

"All by myself. And get this. I've gotten myself a job! I start on Monday."

"Oh. My. God. You haven't worked outside the home since before Erin was born. And with seven kids who could blame you? What's the job?"

"Nothing major, of course, with my experience or lack there-of. Just cashiering at the convenience store down the road. At least the location is good."

"Goodness. I couldn't be more surprised if you said you had taken up sky-diving."

"It's almost as scary as sky-diving after being out of the work force all these years."

"Not just being out of the work force but living almost like a hermit since Paul died. Sorry. I don't mean to be rude, but it's true."

"Don't apologize. You're right."

"To tell you the truth, I'm kind of surprised you didn't decide to move to L.A. with Tracy. She's the only one who has really taken care of you."

"They offered. She and Alex. They even offered to let me live with them."

"Yikes!"

"Yeah, I know."

"Okay, Sis, I have to know. What has brought about this borderline miraculous change in attitude?"

"I don't know," said Lydia thoughtfully. "I guess having Alex in our lives made me realize I couldn't keep holding my daughter back. It was easy…or, I should say, I could remain in denial as long as she didn't really have options on the table. But once she met this terrific guy, I realized I had to let her go."

"Terrific guy," Alice repeated. "And yet…that whole amnesia thing is weird, isn't it? How do you know he's not a serial killer or something?"

"Alice, when you see his sweet face and gentle eyes, you will know that is not possible."

"I can't wait. If there's no wedding soon, I just may have to fly out there for a visit."

"I would love that. You're welcome anytime. You know that."

"I know." Alice's voice began to quiver a little. "Sis, I can't tell you how happy I am for you and for Tracy. I know losing Paul really knocked you for a loop. You deserve some happiness. And even with Tracy out in L.A., you still have family nearby. They may not be as attentive as Tracy was, but I'm sure they'll step up when needed. Hey, this may be good for them in a way, too."

"Maybe," said Lydia, sounding none too sure. "Anyway, it's not as if L.A. is on the other side of the world."

"Hon, I don't want to cut you off, but I have to get going. I have a hair appointment in twenty minutes."

"Okay. Just one more minute. I have something else to tell you."

"Really? There's more?"

"I have a date."

There was a silence before Alice said, "Excuse me while I pick myself up off the floor. A date? Are you sure this is Lydia?"

"It's really me," Lydia giggled. Giggling was an entirely new thing, too.

"With whom?"

"Remember the Watsons who lived down the street from me? Well, he…Henry, that is…and Jane got divorced a couple of years ago. To be honest, he's asked me before and I always said no. You know how I was."

"Do I ever."

"So this time…I hope you're sitting down…I asked him!"

"No!"

"Yes! I ran into him at the grocery store last week, and I just asked if his offer was still operative."

"What ever came over you?"

"I don't know. I guess I thought everything else is changing, might as well go for broke. Honestly, I don't know where I got the courage."

"We're not getting any younger, you know."

"Exactly."

"Well, I am going to have to get out there for a visit as soon as possible. I have to see this guy and pass judgment."

"It's one date, Alice. Who knows if there'll be more?"

"Who knows? Who knew Tracy would meet a gorgeous immigrant with amnesia? Who knew she would move away and you would decide to live alone? Who knew you would get a job for the first time in forty years? Who knows anything, my dear?"

Lydia laughed. "Run off to your appointment, Sis. All questions will be answered in time."

Geneva Bailey

Not every story has a happy ending. Witness Geneva Bailey.

Two weeks before her scheduled and eagerly awaited retirement, she suffered a cerebral hemorrhage and died. Never married and living alone, she fell to the floor at her home, and nobody knew it until she failed to show up for work the next day.

The mood at the bank was somber once the news hit and sank in. Aside from the president, Geneva was the longest serving employee. No one could imagine the place without her. Although she was set to retire soon, she would still have been around town. They would have kept in touch. But this was real. Reality had made its appearance in a most cruel way.

The women walked around in a daze, their eyes misted with tears. The men were more stoic, trying to comfort their coworkers, but they were quieter than usual. Even the dreaded Grigsby was noticeably dismayed.

At break time, Jasmine sat in the lunchroom with Karen and Missy. Every once in a while, a tear slid down her cheek and a choked sob escaped her control.

"It's so strange without Geneva, isn't it? How could this happen?" she asked, her voice quavering.

"She wasn't exactly young," Karen offered unhelpfully.

"But she wasn't old!" Jasmine protested.

"Of course, she wasn't," said Missy soothingly.

"And we were half done with planning her retirement party, too," Karen pouted.

"She was so looking forward to retirement," Jasmine went on, choosing to ignore Karen's comment. "I never knew anyone as excited about retirement in my life. She had so many plans—trips and cruises with her lady friends, volunteering at the art association, working on her crafts. So many plans. It's just so unfair."

"Life is unfair," said Karen. "And so is death, I suppose."

"I suppose." Jasmine stood up and threw her donut into the trash. She couldn't swallow a bite.

A few days after the funeral, Jasmine received a call from Geneva's niece Regina—just about the only relative Geneva had who lived anywhere near Malaga Island. After confirming that Jasmine was indeed Geneva's closest friend at the bank, Regina asked if she would be so kind as to go through Geneva's desk and box up any personal items. She would pick them up the following day if that was all right.

Directly after the phone call, Jasmine hesitantly entered Geneva's cubicle. Setting foot inside felt strange, but there was no use putting it off. Some empty boxes sat next to Geneva's desk. She had already been preparing for her departure.

Jasmine picked up one of the cartons and began loading in the items from desktop and the little shelf above it. Family photographs, a paperweight commemorating her thirtieth anniversary at the bank, a couple of the romance novels she liked to read at lunchtime, a philodendron in a ceramic pot shaped like a kitten, her personal fountain pen—a college graduation gift which she used occasionally out of nostalgia. Most of the rest was company property—stapler, scissors, business-related books and manuals.

When she had finished the desktop, Jasmine opened the center drawer. There wasn't much there—ballpoint pens, paperclips, rubber bands, a nail file. Jasmine hesitated about the nail file but finally decided to put it into the carton. In the very middle of the drawer there was a pad of sticky notes. No need to pack that. She was just about to close the drawer when she thought twice about the number printed boldly on the top sheet of the notepad. She hadn't thought anything about it when she first saw it. The number was "22." That was curious.

Why was that one numeral written on the pad with no accompanying information? It couldn't be an address or a phone number or anything of the sort. She lifted the top sheet.

The next sheet was printed in the same hand, same ink, with the number "21." Flipping through the pad, Jasmine saw that the numbers continued in descending order down to "0." It took her a moment to realize the significance. Even so, just to be sure, she picked up a calendar and calculated from the last day Geneva was at the office to her planned retirement date. Of course, they corresponded exactly.

Each day, Geneva had come into this cubicle and torn off one sheet—counting down the days.

Jasmine's emotions were in a jumble. In a way, she felt as if she had intruded on Geneva's most private hopes and dreams. And somehow it seemed as if Geneva was speaking to her from beyond the grave. But mostly she felt terribly sad and full of regret.

She paused with the notepad in her hand. Should it go into the box for Regina or into the wastebasket? It took only a moment to make the decision. She tucked it into the pocket of her sweater. It was hers. It was the last thing she had of Geneva. It was Geneva's last message to her.

John Rollins

John Rollins was searching for the Bronstein file. His desk was a mess. He had learned over the years that keeping a messy desk was the only way he could ever find anything. So far, he'd had no luck finding the file, but he did come across a manila folder labeled "Morrow, Jasmine." His brow crinkled as he recalled the case.

The folder still in hand, he sat down in his chair. Funny, he had never gotten any feedback from the client. It had been a rather odd case, and he wondered what had happened to Ms. Morrow and the subject, Carlos Pereira. He had been a pleasant-looking guy—seemed nice enough, but skittish. He vaguely recalled Ms. Morrow's boyfriend later asking for Pereira's address. Aside from that, he hadn't heard a word from any of them.

John's only task had been to locate the subject and hand him an envelope. That envelope had contained the same material that he now held in his hands. As was his custom, he had made a copy before successfully handing the original off to the young man. To this day, John had no idea what was in that folder. Ms. Morrow had stressed its confidentiality, appealing to his honor as a licensed private investigator. The material was not to be shared with anyone other than Mr. Pereira. On the other hand, she had never expressly forbidden John to read the contents of the envelope. He turned the file over in his hands. Surely, it couldn't hurt to read it now.

He opened the file and began to read. It began with a cover

letter:

> *Hi, Carlos,*
>
> *Attached are the transcripts of all the chats that Alex participated in. As you will see, they cover a six-month period—basically once a week during that time. We, Tracy and I, are not trying to be pushy or force you into something you don't want. We just want to make sure you have all information that may be pertinent to your search for who you are. We know that is your top priority—understandably so. We believe this material will be helpful and, we hope, convincing. Possibly something in these papers will jog your memory and bring everything back. Of course, we hope with all our hearts that our friendship will be revived. You have become very dear to us. But obviously we have no choice but to accept whatever conclusion you come to. We promise not to continue to bother you. My contact information is on the next page. I would appreciate your getting back to me once you have read the transcripts—whether your reaction is positive or negative. However, I will understand if you don't. Regardless of what happens in the future, we loved meeting you. In a strange way, it was truly thrilling—a fun adventure. Whether it has a sad or happy ending is yet to be discovered.*
>
> *Best wishes no matter what,*
>
> *Jasmine Morrow*

The letter was both innocuous and intriguing. It sounded as if Mr. Pereira suffered from amnesia. What were these women trying to convince him of? And who was Alex?

John leafed through the rest of the papers. All appeared to

be transcripts of a chat room conversation. He began at the beginning but nearly quit halfway through the first page. It seemed like fairly mundane online small talk between two women, but something made him persevere until a third party broke into the conversation with some undecipherable nonsense. Now he was fully engaged.

He read straight through without moving, not even to refresh his coffee which had gone stone cold.

"Wow," he breathed when he had finished. He tossed the folder onto the jumbled desk and leaned back in his chair. What a weird deal that was. Did those women truly believe this Alex was an extra-terrestrial? He gathered that Alex and Carlos were one and the same. How the hell did that happen? And did he really have amnesia?

He almost felt like he should do something. What government agency covered extra-terrestrials he wondered. NASA? Should he call them? Was it okay for lunatics like Jasmine and Tracy to be walking around freely? More important, was there any chance this guy really was an alien?

He slapped himself on the forehead. "What the hell am I thinking?" he said aloud. That alien thing was impossible. On the other hand, after all, lunatics were a dime a dozen just outside his window on Lexington Avenue. Most of them were harmless.

He thought the case would make a good movie. But he was not a writer. He wished all of them well—Jasmine (she had seemed nice), Alex/Carlos (a likable fellow) and Tracy (whom he had not met but seemed like an upstanding and halfway sane person). He pulled out the contents of the folder and began to feed them into the paper shredder.

He poured a fresh cup of coffee and stood staring at his phone. He wished it would ring. He could really use a new case.

Acknowledgements

My thanks to Ruth for her encouragement and feedback. And to Brennan and Nick for technical support and for their beautiful cover design.

About the Author

Kathryn Welch studied fiction writing at the University of Illinois at Urbana-Champaign. She resides in Springfield, Illinois, with her dog Misha and cat Coco. This is her second novel.

Made in the USA
Monee, IL
26 October 2022